D1118106

The Fox with the White Scarf

A novel by

Joseph A. Psarto

AuthorHouse™
1663 Liberty Drive, Suite 200
Bloomington, IN 47403
www.authorhouse.com
Phone: 1-800-839-8640

First published by AuthorHouse 9/28/2007

ISBN: 978-1-4343-3219-6 (sc)

Library of Congress Control Number: 2007906451

Printed in the United States of America
Bloomington, Indiana

This book is printed on acid-free paper.

- Imprint -
Fox Publishing
----

for Sunae

The Temple (tanka)

wooden temple floor
stone-born Buddha gazing down
silent monks soft drums
cobwebs trembling quivering
the beginning and the end

--- the author

One

1597

The Fox and the Bird

This cuckoo bird was different than his brothers and sisters and cousins. The other cuckoos liked talking to each other from across the valleys - but not getting too close to each other or talking too much, preferring their dialogs to be from mountain top to mountain top and in short, clipped sentences. But this bird, this cuckoo, was more interested in flying very high in the sky all by himself, and not talking. All the way up to the heavens. Of course, he talked to his fellows from time to time, but he was more interested in soaring higher than any of the other birds. As for the humans, the cuckoo birds knew their voices were especially pleasing to these creatures who could not fly. The birds talked to the humans now and again, but from even greater distances. It was said that the humans loved cuckoo talk.

But Saja wasn't interested in talking. He only wanted to fly as high as possible.

This was the day. The sky was higher and a deeper blue than usual. The few clouds were miles away, far up in the heavens, rippled, like sour milk. Saja noticed the breezes were uneven, coming and going in sudden bursts blowing up from the ground and then suddenly down again. If he took advantage of them he hoped to climb higher than ever before. The sun had just brought another day into existence and now was the time. Early morning was always best for flying. This could be the grandest flight of his life. Perhaps he could even get high enough to see both the East Sea and the West Sea at the same time.

The adventurous little bird took off from his mountain home and, sure enough, a brisk, upward gust gave him a quick boost upward. A nice start. He climbed higher and higher. The sounds of the valley and the mountain slowly faded and were replaced by the quiet, almost silent, hum of the wind and the tinkle and sprinkle of bright sunshine dropping quickly past him on its journey from heaven to earth. He heard the wind calling his name. "Saja, Saja." A thrill entered his small heart and momentarily the beauty above and below made him dizzy. But the feeling passed and he righted himself and resumed his upward journey.

The higher Saja climbed the stronger the wind became, and it never changed its direction. It moved west to east, west to east, west to east, and became stronger and stronger and stronger, not exactly horizontally, but at a slight upward slant. Saja was soaring higher and higher and higher.

He was frightened. He had no control of his flight. The wind had taken over and was forcing him to travel not only faster and faster to the east, but also higher and higher into the heavens. He stopped flapping his wings and tried to angle them in a way that would let him glide back down to the earth, a maneuver he had used many times. But nothing happened for the wind was too strong. It was forcing Saja upward and eastward. The sun got brighter but with a strange coldness. He was closer to the sun but it didn't matter. It was colder. The earth grew smaller and smaller and the sound of the wind louder and louder. The clouds now were below him and the ground disappeared into their whiteness creating a fresh beauty. But also danger.

Time closed. Creation returned to a purer frame of reference. Saja stopped thinking about what was happening to him. Mystery and beauty have such an effect. He just let the wind carry him along to wherever it might go and to whatever might happen. He wondered if there was a purpose to this journey or not. He seemed to be sleeping but not sleeping. He had never felt like this before. It was as if he was watching himself from a distance and that the danger was not his danger. He felt something - or someone - was watching along with him and that what was happening was inevitable, that he could do nothing about it one way or the other. He relaxed his body and mind.

Hours later the clouds opened up under him. No land below. It was the East Sea. A choppy wind streaked its gray surface with white lines. Saja had seen the sea before but not like this. Not without a shore line to limit its size, nothing but water in all directions. More time passed and a hazy, brown and green line appeared to the east. It rushed toward him and Saja realized that land was coming his way. Was the world really round after all? Had he been pushed all the way around and back to Korea? Or was this a new world? He felt like an explorer.

The wind carried Saja over this new or old land - whatever it was - and the sea disappeared into the west. The wind changed ever so slightly and Saja felt himself dropping, just a little bit, down toward the land. He feebly tried flapping his wings in an attempt to gain control of his flight. But nothing happened for the wind was firmly in control. It moved him slightly to the southeast, but ever so slightly. Saja looked down at the land. It looked like Korea, but in a certain way it was softer. The mountains were rounder if it is possible to describe mountains that way. The forests seemed thicker and more mysterious, but it might have been his loneliness. He promised that if he ever got back home he would talk more to his fellow cuckoo birds, and even to the humans. Loneliness has a way of fathering new-found intentions.

The wind made a drastic change sending Saja down at a steeper angle. The ground rose quickly and roared at him, daring him to land safely. Saja bumped into the top of a tree and sharp glittering lights exploded in his head.

It was that magical time between day and day's end. Light danced in the forest trying to decide whether to stay or go. Daytime animals and nighttime animals met for a few moments and compared stories. Some insects sang songs of love and other insects slept. Saja woke up. Again, he sensed someone or something was watching him. He felt a wave of fear, the same as when the wind had taken control of his flight. A lack of self-control. Where was he? When he turned around he saw three cuckoo birds gawking at him. They looked like him but were slightly larger.

"Hello, my friends, where am I? What am I doing here? Do you have any food? I am starving." The three birds continued looking at him. They turned to each other and mumbled in a foreign squawk. Saja didn't understand a word they said. So he pointed one wing to his mouth and the other to his stomach. One of the birds took flight after a few more squawks. The two remaining birds kept their eyes glued on Saja as though wanting to tell him to remain where he sat. He did. After a while he tried talking to them again but their only response was something that sounded like a "cooo" and another "cooo". Or was it a "squawk" and another "squawk." But again in a foreign language. Saja was confused, and his head was still pounding from whatever it was he had hit when tumbling down to the earth. He couldn't understand a thing these strange birds were saying. They looked like him, but that didn't make any difference. What should he do next? Saja closed his eyes and went to sleep.

When Saja awoke the three cuckoo birds were sitting where they had sat before, but they were not alone. And what Saja saw sent terror into his heart, for to the right of the birds sat a fox. But what a fox he was! His pelt was clean and groomed as if he lived in a house like the humans. The fox's eyes, now staring directly into Saja's eyes, resembled deep, pure pools of water from a mountain spring. But the biggest wonder of all was that the fox wore a white scarf, and it was immaculate. Where the scarf had folds it undulated like a brilliant white alpine flower, and where it lay flat it sparkled with that most perfect whiteness that contains, if you look hard enough, all of the colors of the universe. The fox spoke and Saja was astonished to realize he could understand the fox's language.

"Saja, please forgive us for the nasty ending to your trip to Japan and for the nasty bump on your head. But we have never done this before and we really didn't know how to handle your landing. I hope you feel better by now." The soothing tone of the fox's voice calmed Saja.

"Perhaps you have some questions you want to ask me before I deal with the purpose of your trip here?"

"Japan? What is Japan?"

"Japan is where you are now. It is a land that lies over the sea, to the east of Korea. That is where you are from. The humans call your country Korea. Its ancient name is Chosun.

Saja frowned. "Why can't these birds talk to me? They appear to be cuckoo birds, just like me. And how can you talk to me? You're not even a bird!"

The fox smiled. If he thought the tone of Saja's voice was the least bit impertinent he gave no indication of his feelings. He smoothed one end of his white scarf, although it didn't appear to need smoothing, and said, "These cuckoo birds cannot talk to you because they speak a different language than you do. They are Japanese cuckoo birds."

The fox paused for a moment, just as humans do before they say something most important. Or, at least the way humans should pause, but sometimes do not. "You and I can talk to each other because we are special. I am special here in Japan and you are special in Korea. That is, you will be soon. You see, you will be used in a special way from time to time to talk to the humans concerning certain matters. That is, if they let you do so."

"Who wants me to talk to the humans?" Saja asked.

"Why can't this person talk for himself?"

The fox, once again, paused, as though to add a verbal italic to his words. "You will be able to figure out for yourself who you are talking for when the time comes. But this I can tell you, we only talk to children. And I don't mean by time or age. We only talk to humans with the innocent hearts and souls of children. We ask them to do or think about certain things. But we can only ask. The humans are free and can do what they want. We suggest. We guide. We help them because we love them."

Then the fox emphasized his point, repeating himself. "These humans, the ones we are asked to help, yes, they are free, they can do whatever they want. Sometimes in spite of us they do the wrong things. You will discover this quickly enough.

"But we add some spice, we stir the pot. Sure, they are free but they still have to deal with our soup. At least they can smell it even if they decide not to eat it. The soup is there, in front of them."

The talk of soup reminded Saja that he was hungry. The fox read his mind. He waved a paw at the Japanese cuckoo who had previously flown away. The bird produced a packet of worms, bugs, and flower petals and placed it in front of Saja. It looked and smelled delicious. Saja enjoyed his banquet and even remembered his manners. He offered some to the three birds and the fox. All four of them declined, but they watched as Saja feasted, vicariously enjoying his pleasure. The darkness of the forest finally overwhelmed their meeting ground. The fox told Saja to sleep on the very spot where they were talking, that he was perfectly safe, and in the morning he would return to continue their conversation.

Saja had a full belly. He felt relaxed and secure. The fox's voice had been so gentle. A soft piece of moss mysteriously appeared near his head, a clean and fresh pillow, and he was sound asleep in a moment. Saja's dreams took him back to Korea and it was so beautiful that it made him cry with happiness in his sleep. The mountains and valleys and the morning mists and the winding rivers were singing to him. Even the work of the humans - the sculptured rice paddies climbing up the mountain sides and the soft, yet bumpy, thatches on the house tops - were love poems. The sighing and moaning of lovers filled the air. Saja had one of those grand sleeps that last a very long time, a sleep that is deep and clear and soft and silent. A sleep that dreaming improves but does not shake or churn.

The new morning broke crisp and clear. Saja was curious as he rubbed the sleep from his eyes and looked around. Japan! Even the name sounded funny to him. But another feeling soon came on. It was as though this were the very first morning in the kingdom of time and that he, Saja the Korean cuckoo, was watching a genesis, that everything was beginning for the first time, new and fresh. He looked about him and there, to his left, sat the fox with the white scarf. The fox was alone, no Japanese cuckoo birds this time. A new parcel of food lay at Saja's feet. It contained the same tasty morsels as the night before. Quite fresh, too. Some of the fat worms were wiggling around. Breakfast al fresco. Saja ate and enjoyed every morsel. When he was finished the fox stepped nearer to Saja and sat down. Saja, in spite of himself, laughed a small, delicate laugh. The fox needed no explanation. A fox and a bird settling down for a conversation. Sort of funny, an incongruent event. The fox also laughed.

"Where are the birds? Don't they like foreigners?"

"Oh, they are good birds. Just because they don't speak your language doesn't mean a thing. In fact, they themselves insisted on helping me. It was their idea. They thought you might need food after your trip on the wind. They figured you would eat the same food as they did, and not fox food." The fox then cleared his voice and pawed at the earth, a habit Saja would notice many times in the years to come.

"First of all let me explain, we can understand each other's speech because, as I said last night, we have the same mission in this world, although mine is an old one and yours hasn't started yet. I mentioned some of this last night, but please let me repeat it because it is important. From now on you will give messages, or let's call them suggestions, to humans from time to time. You will be told when to do this and what to say when the time is ripe."

"But who will tell me what to do and say?" Saja was impatient.

"I am not here to tell you everything. It will come to you in time. Just listen closely." The fox was slightly impatient and Saja understood that he was to listen and not talk.

The fox continued. "Korea is now ready to receive the same kind of assistance we give here in Japan. It is the proper time for you to start your mission. In fact, there is a circumstance developing now that will soon need attention." The fox was pleased to have used such a good word. *Circumstance*!

"This is why you were brought to me, to Japan, so I

might talk to you, teach you, and get you started. You are assigned to do our work in Korea. We want you, so to speak, to stir up some soup. This problem I mention cannot be solved here in Japan. It must be solved in Korea. Until now there has been no one there to do such a job. So we are sending you back as one of us. That is, of course, if you agree. You must agree."

The fox again pawed at the soft, mossy ground. He had been talking perhaps too quickly and wanted to slow down. After a pause he continued. "I will explain the mission to you soon and, little by little, you will understand what you are to do, and who you are doing it for. Now is not the time for you to be impatient. That is a problem of the humans, not us. They are impatient and always want to know everything all at once. But I will say this to you. There is one thing about your new position that you may grow to dislike. Oh, at first you might like it, but your mind may change later. It is that you will live a long, long time. Much longer than is normal for a cuckoo bird. Some of your missions will appear to be the same thing over and over and over again. You may get tired of that. Our message is always the same. It's so simple the humans should have figured it out for themselves a long, long time ago. In fact, they did know it once, but that was, as I have said, a long time ago. Most of them have forgotten it. Those who still remember it do not need our soup. But we feed it to them anyway. Call it a reward if you must give it a name and say that we visit them to tell them they are right. And for some humans we may even help them express it in a way so other humans can understand. They call it poetry in their language."

"What is this secret that has been forgotten?" Once

again, Saja let his impatience come to the tip of his beak.

"It's not much of a puzzle at all! It is that love might be the answer to their problems. And love and free will are closely connected. Without free will there can be no such thing as love."

The fox was ready for business. He continued. "And now for the present situation. There is a good man here in Japan. Like a child, he is a simple man, innocent, unassuming. He has very little guile, almost none at all. Although a grand and skillful warrior, he is a peaceful man, a man wearing a mask, a man who admires the beauty of nature and also the beauty of words. In plain speech - he is a poet. But Japan, a country you didn't even know existed until yesterday, is a very dark place these days, a country of warriors and violence. There are poets here but most of them write of battles and soldiers and honor and loyalty. The poets who do write about love and beauty and men with women together, yes, they write their poems and store them in books. Books for a Japan of the future to read and caress.

"The man we are concerned with lives here in Japan, today. As I said, he has the skills of a warrior, but also a poet. Because of his warrior skills, his shogun will not let him alone. He must serve the shogun as a fighting man, an officer in Japan's navy. He is a samurai. His case was sent to me. Now here's my plan -

"There is no hope for this man here in Japan. I have been told to send him to Korea to live out his life. I have been told Korea is a very beautiful country and that the people there, although they are rougher than the Japanese, although their language is harsher than Japanese, and although their social customs are less polished than Japanese customs, I have been told they are very special humans. They know how to love each other. But they love to fight too, and their battles can be quite exciting. Especially between men and women. It reminds me of poetry.

"They have an attachment and tenderness for poets and artists. They especially love their language. I suppose it's where their love for poets is created.

"Sending this man to Korea is the easy part. You will soon see how we arrange that to happen. But once he gets there you will learn the reason you were blown on the wind to meet with me. Once he gets there, if and when he needs some of our soup, you will be there to help him. You will be the one to do that. I'll come to you from time to time to help out, but not too often. You are the one for our poet. Of course, that is, if you agree to become one of us."

So much information, and strange information at that, in such a short period of time. Saja felt overwhelmed. But he did have a question that bothered him.

"But why me? Why have I been picked for such an important mission?"

The fox laughed, not at Saja but at himself. He remembered the same question being on his lips many, many years ago.

"Saja, when your mother placed the egg containing you into another mother bird's nest, as is the custom of cuckoo birds all over the world, she picked the eagle's nest for your infant home. Now the eagle is the most royal of all birds and its nest is the highest of all birds. It was, perhaps, a sign of things to come because no cuckoo mother had ever placed her baby's egg in an eagle aerie before. But that is not why we picked you.

"Do you remember what happened next? You were quite young and maybe time has erased the memory from your mind. So let me tell you. The instinct of your race is to fight for survival in the new nest that your real mother places you in. Baby cuckoo birds develop much faster than other baby birds. And when this happens they try to assure their survival by pushing their adopted siblings out of the nest when the mother and father are away looking for food. This is the way they get enough food for a healthy survival. But you were different. In a way, you defied your own nature. And what you did was very noble, perhaps we might even say poetic. You loved your adopted brothers and sisters in the eagle nest so much that you didn't kill them. You actually helped them survive. You will never know how many smiles you created in this universe on faces that not only saw your actions but also knew your intentions."

The fox stopped for a moment as though he wanted Saja to think hard about what he had just said. Then he continued. "And, of course, there is your love of flying so high. Ever higher, ever higher. That, too, was noticed. Any bird can try going up and up. But you did it because it permitted you to see the beauty of creation on a grander scale. Again, your true intentions were known on smiling faces. You should know that your daddy loved to soar high, also. He flew very high, just like you. But Korea was not ready for one of us in his lifetime. Now it is."

The two of them, fox and bird, had been talking for hours. As time passed it brought changes to the look and feel of the woods. The morning mists had left the forest floor and a new magic took over. Sun beams mixed with fresh, sweet breezes and, as the light was bent by trees and bushes, phantoms were created and sat in a circle around the two of them. And the fox nodded to these spirits once in a while as he spoke. And the phantoms nodded back at him.

"There is one last thing you must know Saja." The fox leaned closer. "You must always remember - you, too, just like the humans, are free. Think, always think before you act. Yes, think before you act!"

Saja had a question. "Who are you? What is your name?" His question echoed through the Japanese forest and returned. It sounded altered, different, wiser than he felt.

The fox looked pleased, his fox face reflecting delight. He was looking at a brother although he was a fox and Saja was a bird. He didn't answer immediately, but looked proudly up to the forest canopy and then back down to Saja, moving his head in a dramatic sweeping gesture. What a mysterious animal.

"I am the fox with the white scarf."

Two

The Sea Battle

The murky sea between Korea and Japan was busy. Boats filled with Japanese soldiers came to Korea and then returned empty to pick up yet another human cargo. The Emperor of Japan had grand ideas. He wanted to expand his empire into mainland Asia, and that meant first Korea, and on to the grand prize, China. The landing point was on the east coast and, so far, the Korean capital at Pyongyang knew nothing of their presence. Once their main army was assembled the Japanese would march to the west, seize the capital and other important Korean cities. Of course, in this sixteenth century by the calendar of a far away European civilization, this meant any town of one thousand or more.

But they also planned an attack from the west. An armada of warships would sail around the bottom of the Korean peninsula, up the west coast, and capture the natural harbor of the village of Inchon. This maneuver would split the Korean forces. There were rumors of a Korean navy, but no one knew for sure about that. A visiting Korean trader from Seoul had talked of an Admiral

Yi and his "turtle ships." But the Japanese were faster than turtles. The rumor didn't scare them or change their plans.

Captain Iwata looked across the waters of the Yellow Sea. His ship was one of twelve sleek cruisers sailing around the bottom of the Korean peninsula and up the western shoreline. They would be followed in seven days by the main Japanese Imperial Fleet. The invasion of the west coast of Korea would quickly follow. In the meantime the cruisers were to find out if there was such a thing as a Korean navy and destroy it if they met. The sailors and officers joked about the situation. They expected victory everywhere they fought and didn't want anything less than that in these waters. Soon Korea would be just another province of Japan, and they would have an excellent new labor source. Plus a path to China. These Korean savages with their garlic food and their good humor and their dependency on the Chinese for peace and commerce would soon be taught an expensive lesson, and lose their freedom in the process. Then on to China, and Japan would control Asia as it was destined to do.

The officers and men were happy and hoped they would soon find some Korean ships to fight. That is, all except Captain Iwata. He looked at the Korean coast laying off his starboard side. The mountains came almost down to the beach. From time to time small villages were tucked on a small strip of land between the mountains and the shoreline and he could see smoke curling up from a thatched roof house. Iwata thought of the family living there, perhaps a happy family with no idea that Japanese warships were sailing up their coast about three miles out to sea. Iwata forgot the war as he looked inland and a poem began tracing itself onto his brain. The family, the house, the smoke, and the mountain rising up behind the house, and the swelling of the sea that stretched away from the land. He even noticed a strange looking bird that flew so low over the ship. He saw the bird's eyes opened wide and gaping at him. The bird spoke and said, "Cooo, cooo." Iwata wondered what the little cuckoo bird was doing away from its mountain home and flying over the water.

The bird circled the warship several times and then flew back toward the land. Iwata followed its flight until it disappeared into the brown and green maze of the largest mountain along the coast. How wonderful it must be to be so free. Iwata wished he had wings and could fly away from the military adventure his cruiser was heading toward. He was not afraid of battle if there had to be one. But he craved the freedom of time, yes that is what he wanted. Time.

Iwata's thoughts snapped back to the present. One of his men was shouting and pointing to the west. There was something out there about three miles away. The choppy seas made the object appear and disappear in a musical rhythm. Then two or three objects popped up from the sea where only one had been before, and they were heading toward the Japanese ships. The alarm went out and sailors and officers were running here and there. The poetic mood left Iwata and he felt the excitement of the sounds and thoughts of battle. His training and education as samurai were part of his nature.

Was this the mysterious Korean navy they had heard about? The sailors hoped so. That would mean a fast end to this matter. They would quickly defeat these stupid garlic eaters and then their Japanese army would do the rest of the job. Korea would be theirs, with China next. China would be the real battle. Korea was just a diversion.

All Japanese eyes were on the approaching objects. The sea continued bobbing up and down, up and down. But as the mysterious floating objects got closer the moving sea could hide them no longer. They were ships, and there were three of them. Only three, and small ships at that. A few of the sailors laughed. This job would be too easy. No fun. Twelve against three. Each of the three approaching ship flew the banner of Korea from its highest mast, a red and black circle of yin and yang. Several of Iwata's men joked that they could already smell garlic. Their mood was festive. Iwata thought of war and death, and then the laughter of his men, and a sadness seeped into his soul.

What is wrong here? Is this the way it is meant to be? Are we animals? Samurai must mean more than war. Its code of honor and morality, our dear Bushido, should lead to things other than our death or that of others.

As the three Korean ships got closer they took on a strange shape. They looked like turtles, yes, turtles. Front and back legs stuck out on the sides of each ship and turtle heads jutted from their fronts, turtle eyes open and glaring and turtle mouths scowling. The Japanese laughed and conveniently forgot their own twelve ships were designed to look like serpents. But what the Japanese officers and sailors did not see was that underneath the veneered wooden sides of each turtle ship was an iron sheet that wrapped a mantle of protection around each vessel. The Korean Turtle Ships were the world's first ironclad navy.

The three turtles sailed directly toward the Japanese

cruisers and when they were about a half mile away one of them veered to the right and another to left. They circled into the Japanese flanks. The middle turtle headed straight for Captain Iwata's ship which was at the front of the armada. It approach quickly and as it neared the range of the Japanese guns, it came on even faster.

"What a brave lot of garlic eating fools. Let's have some turtle soup." Iwata's first mate said with total disdain. The Japanese sailors were in a humorous mood and saw no great danger from the approaching enemy ships. After all, they outgunned them twelve to three and, besides, they were Japanese fighting men led by samurai. But Captain Iwata's feelings were mixed. He sensed something important was about to happen, something historical. He had no explanation for such thoughts. Perhaps it was the village nearby and the villagers' lack of concern or even knowledge of what was taking place so close to them. They seemed separated from war's reality, yes, that was it. It was indeed a strange emotion Iwata had for them. He seemed to be watching and not participating.

The Japanese ships opened fire on the command of Senior Captain Yamamoto, who was the leader of the entire armada. Twelve ships shooting at three. The battle should be quickly over and the armada able to continue its trip up the west coast. But what happened next altered history. Asia would never be the same. China, without even knowing it, was handed a gift of four hundred years free of Japanese occupation.

The Korean attackers dove right into the Japanese fleet. They were fearless. And for a good reason. The Japanese cannon balls bounced off their armor and landed harmlessly into the sea. Some of the Japanese seaman had been fighting naval battles for many years, but they had never seen anything like this. The three Korean ships darted quickly in and out, in and out, their guns blazing at close range, and because they were smaller and faster than their opponents, and were armor plated, the contest went their way in spite of the uneven numbers.

It was all over in a matter of minutes, this first battle in the history of the world between wooden ships and speedy, ironclad opponents. One by one the Japanese invaders were destroyed. The three Korean ships remained untouched. The turtle ships searched for Japanese survivors who now were swimming about in a frothy sea filled with the debris of the Japanese armada. The Koreans swept through the now quiet waters killing any swimming enemy they found. If they expected to defeat the main Japanese fleet when it arrived there must be no survivors to report what happened. When they were convinced no one was left alive, they sailed away to the north. The secret of their ironclad turtle ships was safe.

The cuckoo bird circled the sea that was now calm and quiet as death. Even the white caps had disappeared as though they, too, mourned the dead Japanese sailors. Saja thought the humans strange creatures. They killed each other and food or sex was not involved. Then he saw what he was looking for. A large piece of wood that had been a part of the deck of one of the raiders bobbed up and down in the sea directly below him. Coming out of the sea was a human hand holding onto its edge. Hiding underneath was Captain Iwata. He was the only Japanese sailor - officer or crew - still alive. But now he was hurt and confused. Blood seeped out of his left shoulder where a piece of hard Korean metal had cut into the bone. He had no idea which way his sorry raft was floating or if any Korean ships were still in the area.

Saja flew down to the surface of the water and landed on Iwata's hand. He scratched with both claws. What was going on? Iwata peered out from under the wood, but Saja was gone by then. And so was the Korean navy. Land lay to the east, and not very far away. The sea had turned deep gray as the sun ducked below the horizon. Iwata saw that he was about two miles from shore. If the moon came out and provided a beacon for him, he should be able to make landfall. But his shoulder ached and blood was seeping from his body. He had to reach shore as soon as possible and tend his wound. He moved his raft around, extended his feet behind it, kicking, and crept slowly toward the Korean coast.

A full moon helped. Every time a cloud covered it Iwata thought he heard a squawk and a cooo, cooo and then, each time, the moon pushed the cloud away, sending light down on him once again. Later Iwata remembered this battle in the night sky between moon and cloud. In the early morning hours he reached the beach. Darkness finally came on as the moon and everything else simply switched off. Time passed. Then he felt a blanket being thrown over him. No dreams, no thoughts, nothing. And then a change. Random thoughts returned and flashes of light buzzed in and out of his mind.

He heard human voices and, for a moment, it seemed he was lifted up, and then set down. Water and food were forced into his mouth and his wounded shoulder treated. The pain stopped. A dream? Iwata didn't know and didn't care. He sank into nothingness and it was very comfortable there. He stopped thinking.

The voice was singing in a strange language. It was soft and clear and beautiful. Yes, that was it. So pleasant. Iwata opened his eyes. He was in a small dirt-floored courtyard, cleanly swept, and he lay on a quilt of some kind. His first impression was that he was quite comfortable, he was fine, and the singing voice pleased him. It was definitely a female voice.

Iwata spoke and, after a pause, laughter came from the singing voice, but not a laughter of disdain or ridicule. It was the kind of laughter that makes you want to chuckle along with it, even though you have no idea what the laughing is all about. But when the laughing stopped, and the voice answered, he knew what had brought on the laughing. For the voice answered him with sounds meaningless to him. It was Korean, the language of the garlic eaters. Iwata had spoken in Japanese and he now realized that he had sounded just as strange to the listener, the one who had laughed. He tried to sit up but a pain shot through his shoulder stopping him. The voice walked around to the front of his quilt bed and Iwata thought he saw an angel peering down.

Dolsun was indeed as beautiful as her voice.

If this was a garlic eater Iwata was ready to praise such a vegetable. The lady moved about with the grace of a swan, aware of every moving body part and yet having decided to use each as sparingly as possible, skating across a diamond, and still reaching her destination as required. Fast and slow. A haiku, yes, a haiku, that's is how she walked. Iwata could not help comparing her to the classical Japanese poetic form that very carefully rationed the use of syllables, just as she rationed her movements, clashing two disparate word pictures to arrive at a third.

The laughter, and then the walk, created the beauty. A perfect haiku.

Soft sounding beauty
Noble lady walking by
Shifting grace to grace

They started talking at the same time and then, just as before, laughed, this time in unison. That is how Iwata met Dolsun, the daughter of a mudang, the village witch doctor.

He looked around the courtyard surrounding a thatched roof house. There were large ceramic pots in one corner and small bales of hay stacked in another. The house itself was made of mud bricks. A stone wall circled it all creating the courtyard. A wooden gate was the only entrance. Iwata noted everything, especially the entrance, which he knew was also an exit. His military training had taught him well. Exits are important. But after this quick survey his eyes returned to the lady with the singing voice and regal motion. She was, indeed, beautiful. Her olive skin and dark hair and eyes were similar to Japanese women, but there the likeness stopped. She was taller and her slim figure presented an enigma for it was both strong and delicate at the same time. Her face had sharper cheekbones than common among the Japanese, more like a northern Chinese lady Iwata once saw on the streets of Edo. And her clothes. Iwata would always remember her clothes. This first image of a Korean woman stamped itself into Iwata's memory, the samurai giving way to the poet. The dress consisted of two parts, top and bottom. The top reached from her neck, like a short vest, to the bottom of her breasts. But it was pulled tight against her body and hid her breasts as though they were not there. But a man knew they were there! The bottom part of the dress started under this vest and flowed like an hourglass down to the ground where snow white muslin booties acted as stockings. Her shoes were sandals made of woven straw. The dress appeared to be silk and had different strips of color running horizontally across her body. There were greens and blues and reds and whites, and yet the complete effect was subdued. How was that possible with so many contrasting colors? Iwata felt dizzy.

Dolsun's jet black hair was neatly tied into a pigtail hanging to her waist. It was flung artfully over one shoulder and down the front of her body. Iwata wondered how magnificent it would look and smell if unraveled and freshly washed. His fingers ached for the touch of it.

He found out later that Dolsun had found him on the beach the morning after his ship had been destroyed. The villagers had carried him to her mother's courtyard where she had attended him. She dressed his wound and forced him to take nourishment. When he woke up two days later he felt well enough and within several hours was on his feet.

Iwata stayed at the house of the mudang. He quickly learned the language of the Koreans, mostly from Dolsun and from the mudang herself. In return, he taught the villagers how to make a certain type of plow, very common in Japan, and it made their work in the rice paddies easier. He also taught them about Japanese poetry, but making subtle changes to accommodate their harsher sounding language.

No word came concerning the Japanese invasion up north or of any further naval battles. Iwata didn't know that when the main Japanese fleet, having no idea what happened to his scouting armada, sailed around the west coast of Korea they, too, were totally destroyed by the ironclad turtle ships, and that the Japanese army up north retreated back to Japan in disgrace. The war was over. The danger to Korea and China had passed, at least for the time being. The next two years went by quickly. Iwata realized, slowly at first, but finally with certitude, that his life had started anew and he was a different person, reborn. He no longer felt Japanese, yet he still felt samurai, but in a different way.

So here I am in Korea, and what a country it is. I have been here but a short while and I am in love with this place. I love its people and its rivers and its villages and its mountains, especially its mountains. But most of all, I am in love with the people nearest to me. My Bushido code confuses me.

From time to time, Iwata noticed a cuckoo bird flying nearby, a strange thing for cuckoos lived in the mountains and seldom came near villages. The bird seemed more like a phantom than a bird and Iwata had the strangest feeling it was watching him.

Iwata climbed the mountains that were everywhere across the land. Sometimes he would be gone for days at a time. Dolsun packed him rice and kimchi to eat, but he could do without prepared food if necessary. The plants and herbs and nuts and berries were enough for him. Occasionally he would even catch a small animal and enjoy roasted meat. The first time he did this Iwata heard a squabble coming from the sky and it took him a while to realize a cuckoo was flying in circles above him and making loud scolding noises. It made Iwata sorry for killing the animal.

The Korean mountains were different than those of Japan. The Japanese peaks were rounder and softer, and the Korean mountains harsher, with sharp angles and deep gorges and rock summits that gave them a mystical, lonely beauty. Icy waterfalls could be heard before they were seen, popping into sight without giving any advance notice other than their roar, a roar that could easily be mistaken for the wind. As for the wind, when it crossed an arete phantoms sang sad songs and scrubbed Iwata's thoughts of impurity, and he became magically washed of unnecessary things. The mountains were alive. A thousand voices talked to him. But, mysteriously, he heard them all as though they spoke one at a time. At night the mountain had insect sounds Iwata had never heard before.

Early every morning, several hours before the sun arose, temple bells, perhaps several mountains and several miles away, joined the wind and played a symphony. The bells competed with the breeze (sometimes a gale) to see who could create the most elegant sound. But neither added a complication to the music for both were clear and pure and simple and when mixed together became even more clear and pure and simple. A paradox. And then in the evening the bells and the wind played an encore as unseen monks across the valley said their prayers and went to sleep.

Three

A Secret Place

There was a special place on the mountain. It was off the trail, falling away to the left, about halfway up to the summit, a small plateau down from the ridge line and then down from the trail. It could not be seen from the normal climbing route. Iwata had found it when his scarf blew off and he left the trail climbing down to get it. It was a secret place surrounded by trees. The trees gave it a second protection even though the twist and drop in the trail would have been enough.

Iwata went there often. He sank into the isolation of the place and used its loneliness to clear his thoughts of everything but the things he wanted. It always worked for there was magic there. Even the mountain wind had a different voice, as if placed into another dimension. Far off, other mountains, clouds, other villages, even his village on the other side of the ridge, became distorted and colors and shapes blended into a bigger picture, a picture that was the entire world and yet was nothing but the secret place.

Bushido showed its face. It crept over rounded mountains and down to a coast, then across a sea, and then climbed up the rugged mountains of another land. Iwata could not get away from it. He was samurai, and Bushido was everywhere he was. It flew to his secret place and landed inside Iwata's mind, into his soul. A paradox! For it already was inside him but came back again and again and strengthened itself. He welcomed it because it was a part of him. But it also confused him. What was he to do? Why not be samurai here in Korea? The code was universal, was it not? Why was it drawing him back to Japan? The voices of the secret place told him differently, that Bushido was Korea now. But there was more - Dolsun. He had given her his loyalty. The mudang was aware of it. She could feel the emotions of others, especially love and hate. She had grown fond of Iwata and felt as though he was her son, the son she had never had by natural birth. But Dolsun was her blood and she was not yet ready to give her up.

Since his arrival Iwata had lived with the mudang and Dolsun. They gave him their back room and furnished it with a sleeping mat, blankets and a small table where he could sit on a pillow on the floor, read and write, and drink his tea. They ate their meals together in the mudang's room or on the wooden porch that curved around three sides of the house. But after a few months, and after Iwata had become proficient in the language of Korea, he built himself a small two room house nearby. The mudang and Dolsun continued to cook for him, and he paid them by working in their rice paddy and doing other things around their home. Besides his work in the rice paddies Iwata was a good toolmaker and this made him a valuable member of the village. He built a small kiln and used it to melt iron scrap and make a plow or a hoe or an ax.

And the children. They loved Iwata because he told them stories of battles and ships and even threw in some monsters here and there. For the older boys there was not much interest in stories. They wanted to learn the martial arts, and that's what Iwata taught them. But he stopped at the killing. He would not teach them how to kill.

One day as Iwata was pounding away at a hot slab of iron, fashioning it into an ax. Dolsun appeared with a cool cup of goat's milk for him. Iwata bowed and accepted the milk. As he looked at the snowy white liquid he felt Dolsun's eyes resting on him. He gazed back and saw it. Her eyes twinkled with light.

"I think your mother is casting a spell on me. I drink this milk and your eyes sparkle."

Dolsun's cheeks glowed red and she felt a rush of heat on her forehead. A strange feeling indeed. She turned and walked swiftly back to the mudang's house without saying a word.

Iwata spent as much time as he could at the mudang's house. He always ate his meals slowly and told his stories slowly. Then when he left to go to his own lonely bed his thoughts brought the house with him. But it wasn't the house that possessed him. It was Dolsun. When he looked at a flower he saw her. She lived in the clouds. Mountain brooks sang of her. The cuckoos called her name, especially one bird who followed him when he climbed on the mountain. And every night the cicadas played violin concertos in her name. Up the mountain, up to Iwata's secret place, she traveled. When he climbed to his retreat she was there waiting for him, and when he fell asleep on the mountain he was always in her arms. Then he would awake alone, and the night was deeper and darker without her. But if he thought hard enough she would come back to him. The mudang's spell worked very well. But, of course, there was no mudang's spell. A real spell had been set, there was no doubt about that, but it had been cast by Dolsun.

The mudang and several of the grandmothers of the village watched this play being acted out with great interest, a play performed millions and millions of times since the world was born. A cuckoo bird named Saja also watched.

This time it was no dream. This time it was real. This time he was not alone. Iwata climbed steadily up the trail. He was heading for his secret place. He had told Dolsun about his mystical haven where time splintered and stopped. He asked her to go there with him, and she knew it was time to listen to him. She had no choice. She had to go with him.

They arrived at the secret place as the sun dropped deep into the western sky. Only a few moments of daylight remained. But neither of them thought about that. There was silence while Dolsun carefully arranged their food on a ground cloth - a simple meal of rice and kimchi and eggs. She bowed and motioned Iwata to eat. He looked down to the ground and said nothing. Dolsun reached across the food and touched his cheek lightly with her finger tips. Iwata softly wound his thumb and finger around her wrist and pulled her hand to his lips. He kissed each finger with a long, soft kiss. He felt her body grow weak. The weakness traveled through her fingers and down her arm and into her bosom. No words were spoken. Finally the two looked into each other's eyes and Iwata's eyes sparkled along with hers, no goat's milk spell needed. Iwata wrapped his arms around Dolsun and placed his lips on hers.

The dance began.

The magic of the secret place was not needed. Time stopped for a different reason, for a more powerful reason. The magic of the dance was the reason. Just as the magic of the place caused the mountains and the clouds to blend together and become one, this magic dance transformed Iwata and Dolsun into one being. The sun disappeared into the west and the moon and stars gave as best they could. But it was dark. No matter. The dance produced rainbows of colors and a sun made of different material danced and spun out of their bodies and in the sky.

Over and over. Again and again. The sparkle and lights returned - departed - returned. A shy mountain god snuck a look and quickly turned his eyes aside, feeling like an intruder stumbling onto a private scene not meant for him. And animals listening to the sighs and the moans smiled their animal smiles. Insects of the night sang their own siren arias faster and faster, attempting bewitchments of their own.

And in the morning the food sat untouched on the simple white cloth.

Two things were created at the secret place during that enchanted night on the mountain. One metaphorical, one real. A new love, a repeating love. But the other was not metaphorical at all. It moved. Movement is life. It was very small but it was growing. And living.

The mudang sat alone in the dim evening. When Dolsun didn't return she grew sad and realized things were changing as she knew they would some day. But she was still sad. And then she was happy. Again, mothers and fathers, sad and happy at the same time, for a daughter is a most difficult thing to let go. The mudang looked at the food sitting uneaten on the round table in front of her. Then without touching a morsel she arose, left the house and walked the village paths as the moon and the stars spoke to her, trying to give her solace. A cuckoo bird landed on her shoulder. It startled her. The bird looked directly into her eyes. She heard his apology for invading a human village. At least that's what the mudang thought he said. Then he explained that he seldom left the mountain unless the reason was important. But he didn't tell her his reason. She thanked him and he flew off, his message half spoken. But the mudang understood.

Moon and stars and a night-bird. The mudang continued along the path and looked up the mountain, toward the summit.

Four

The Wedding

Iwata had taken Dolsun as his wife at the secret place with the finality of a sacrament. As for the mudang, the timeless and universal - past, present, future - feelings and planning common to every daughter's mother began. A wedding at the Buddhist temple on the mountain. Not to legitimize the marriage, but to celebrate it. The abbot was happy about this turn of events even though he never thought for a moment that the mudang or Dolsun were ready to accept his faith, and he knew nothing at all about Iwata's beliefs. He felt the Buddha wouldn't mind. Another wedding at the temple, be they believers or pagans, would be just fine.

The mudang invited the entire village. When the great day arrived people walked up the mountain path that led to the temple. The winding trail reached a point where it broke into two paths. The path to the right led to the temple. The one to the left led around the other side of the mountain and past the secret place, although few knew it was there. But, of course, Dolsun and Iwata knew. When they reached the adjoining paths Iwata whispered into

Dolsun's ear. It would be more fun to climb to the left and leave the villagers to themselves. Dolsun gave him a playful slap on his cheek. She would admit to him later that evening she, too, had felt the tug of the secret place on her body. But for now they had a wedding to attend.

Birds looked down on the humans winding their way up the side of the mountain. The villagers appeared to them as thin strings, long and white, undulating up a brown and green cloth. Crisp, clean clothes, starched wedding guest clothes, sparkled in the cool mountain air. Bright sunshine reinforced the whiteness, giving it a strong look.

Iwata walked along with Dolsun's hand entwined in his. His mind traveled back through the time since his wounded body had washed up on the shore of this land. Dolsun found him and saved his life. It would have been an easy decision for her to have left him there on the beach to bleed to death. A stranger, and a fierce foreign warrior. She must have felt a danger. The safest thing would have been to walk away from him. But she didn't. She helped him. A young girl saving the life of a samurai warrior. And now here they were - together - walking up the mountain to marry.

His early memories of her returned. She was young, but already had many of the charms all women desire. Her skin was an almond silk. He remembered her walk, a charming and graceful rationing of motion that magically increased movement while accenting stillness, the soft perspiration glistening on her forehead below her ebony hair and bare arms in the summer heat. He remembered the smell of her hair and skin, a musky fragrance that was there both in summer and winter, and that no perfumery of Japan or Korea could ever equal. Even here on the mountain, with the air blowing as clean and fresh as anywhere in the world, Iwata could smell the fragrance of musk, the scent of woman, as Dolsun pressed close to him. Perhaps he had loved her from the beginning with a special man-woman love. But not the way he loved her now.

He remembered the very first time he looked at Dolsun and saw a woman. It was like a hard smack in the face, a physical force hitting his body and soul. At that moment he felt their relationship turn. He remembered exactly when it happened. One evening Dolsun was preparing the meal and as Iwata watched she cut her finger while chopping a daikon. As her red blood flowed over the vegetable Iwata felt a sharp pain in his own finger. The mudang saw him flinch and knew her only daughter, her little girl, was now a woman. Iwata felt the pain move from his finger into the very marrow of his bones. He looked deep into Dolsun's eyes and knew she too felt it, his aching mingling with her own. That is how the two of them changed their feelings from friendship to love. Soon afterwards they climbed up to the secret place and completed their attachment.

Now they were walking up the mountain to the temple to celebrate that love with their village friends and, best of all, with the mudang.

Dolsun also had thoughts of the past as she walked up the mountain. She thought of that day along the ocean's edge. Was she a girl or a woman at the time? She couldn't remember. There was a battle on the ocean. She heard the guns boom across the waves and then heard them once again as their echoes slapped the face of the mountain full force and created even louder noises. That evening she wandered down to the water's edge to look out at the sea, not knowing what she would find there. The fighting was over. But there on the beach was a man covered with blood. She remembered the brightness of red on his strange multicolored uniform, a strange uniform indeed, with a black band wrapped tightly around his slim waist, and two long swords, one secured at each side. She remembered running home as quickly as she could and her mother's response. The mudang had acted quickly, never considering any alternative but helping the stranger. She and her daughter carried the man to their village home.

The man didn't die. The next two years Dolsun watched him closely, saw his patience, and then his impatience. She saw his perfection and then his imperfection. He dealt with the boys of the village teaching them the martial arts of a samurai but stopping short and not teaching them how to kill. And when they became unhappy he showed his impatience and almost stopped teaching them anything.

He was impatient with Dolsun when she couldn't quite understand his description of samurai and Bushido. Sometimes his fastidiousness, his exactness, made her angry. It was as though he tried to scrub away existence's flaws and when he failed to do so became angry at the world. She saw him struggle with a new language, finally accepting it but not without a fight. It took him time to realize the language wasn't going to change to suit him, but that he must fit himself into it, he must think in it. Many times Dolsun laughed at his funny pronunciations, his strange accents. But the Korean language slowly became his friend, his helper. Little by little she accepted him as he was, flaws and all, and was strong enough to make him accept her along with her own flaws.

And now they were in love, true love, a love strong and exciting. Strange how these very same flaws now became something to laugh at, a sort of poetry of errors that mixed together and became human.

The mudang arrived at the temple earlier that morning. She was concerned that arrangements be made perfectly and didn't completely trust the abbot to do everything properly. He was only a man, and not even a father. What did he know! Her only daughter was being wed and care must be taken. This was a most important day for Dolsun, and also for herself. Her memories called out to her missing husband and she pined to hear him answer her. She knew how excited he would be if he were here with her now. She knew he would approve of Iwata even though he was a foreigner. But what a foreigner! Iwata the warrior. Iwata the poet. Iwata the man. Iwata the samurai. And now, Iwata her son.

She pushed back darker thoughts. Her prescience pulled at her happiness, tugging at its edges. She felt a sadness awaiting to be born, a sadness that would not go away. She resolved not to let Dolsun or Iwata know of these dark feelings. For that is the way of a mudang. They know dark things, things better not known by others, things others would know soon enough. The mudang had grown to love Iwata as a son, and this love made her melancholy. She thought she could brush the sadness off her shoulders if she tried hard enough. She could only wait and hope. Perhaps her feelings were wrong.

At the temple gate the abbot and the mudang stood waiting for Iwata and Dolsun. But the couple were still further down the trail. Preparations had been made in spite of the mudang's interference with the temple workers. They simply tolerated her as they did all pesky mothers and went about their work. Right on schedule the roast beef was being prepared on small metal grills. The guests were arriving. Of course, the monks were not supposed to be meat eaters, but no matter, even they knew a Korean wedding without plenty of pulkogi - fire beef - was no wedding at all, and if they wanted to eat some animal flesh in spite of their credo, no one cared, not even the abbot. There was plenty of rice wine, and the abbot himself planned to consume his share of this golden nectar born out of the village paddies. It conveniently slipped his mind that monks were not supposed to drink wine.

As Iwata and Dolsun arrived at the temple gate a quiet clapping of hands became louder and louder, but it stopped growing before losing its softness. The monks and the villagers were greeting the couple with their hands. The soft sound echoed across the valley and returned, as though the mountain itself was saying "happy wedding day." The sun sparkled down and the buttermilk clouds winked. Then the mountain air purified itself and became a lens that brought other mountains closer to the gathering party.

The whole world was happy for Iwata and Dolsun and all creation invited itself to the wedding feast. The mountains, the sky, the wind, the animals.

The fun had started the day before the wedding, and Iwata's bleary eyes were a witness to the fact. An age-old Korean custom had prompted the men of the village, Iwata's friends, to tie him to a tree, poke and hit him with sticks, attempting to make him change his mind about marrying Dolsun. They didn't want to lose a drinking partner at the village taproom. But it was all in fun. When Iwata refused their suggestions (as they all knew he would) they left him tied to the tree for several hours while they went to the house of the mudang and made a terrible noise yelling and clapping their hands and singing rather suggestive songs. And, of course, she knew how to satisfy them for all Korean daughters' mothers knew this ritual and what was expected of them. She was happy to play her part. A grand feast was waiting for the rowdies inside the courtyard. The grandeur of the food was challenged by the glory of the rice wine, several different kinds, and that may have been the bigger attraction for the singing, bawdy mob.

In the meantime, Iwata remained tied to the tree. He could hear the noise of the party, but until someone took pity on him and untied his ropes he was not part of the madness. Eventually he was freed and when he joined the activity the party took on a newer, stronger life. Everyone was expected to make a toast and, while some spoke of heartfelt happiness for the bride and groom, others said things that made even the mudang blush as she eavesdropped from inside the house, not having been invited to her own party. The party lasted well into the evening. Finally the mudang forgot about tradition. She bellowed and protested so loudly that the men gave up. The party was over. But, as the guests walked away the remaining food and drink left with them, being carried to another locations where the party would resume. Later that night they continued eating, drinking and singing as they walked along the village paths until each of them tumbled into his own home and went to sleep. Iwata was relieved when it was finally finished, although he didn't let his impatience show. He wanted to get what sleep he could before walking up to the temple in the morning for his wedding and yet another party.

The temple property was a wonderful place for a wedding. Built three centuries earlier by Korean monks who had been educated in China, it was located about halfway up the mountain. The main temple building dominated the middle of the compound. Steep wooden steps led up to its doors. Inside, a large, golden Buddha sat on his haunches on a platform behind the main altar. Along the side walls a hundred small alcoves had been built each containing a small white Buddha. First-time visitors were overwhelmed as they entered the temple. They, more likely than not, immediately bowed all the way to the floor, their foreheads touching the creaky, wooden slats. Flowers, food and money were placed on the altar as an offering to the Buddha, and burning incense sticks were stuck into small vases filled with sand.

The rest of the compound consisted of several smaller chapels, each with a large Buddha of its own, living quarters for the abbot and his monks, and other work buildings. The monks were farmers, carpenters, masons, cooks (vegetables and fruits and rice only, no meat, that is, except for weddings), and some of them, the better educated ones, were confessors and advisors to the village people. Others wrote books. Others translated older Indian and Chinese works into Korean. But each monk, regardless of rank or job, led an intensely contemplative prayer life and their daily routines were carefully structured. They arose at three in the morning and went to bed around seven or eight in the evening.

The monks were supposed to live as equals even though the abbot was in charge. But one feature of the temple belied equality. At the rear of the temple compound, where they could not be seen by worshipers or other visitors, were six small huts lined up in a perfectly straight row. The six huts had no windows, but the door of each had a small cutout shaped like a crescent moon. Unseen under each hut a deep pit had been dug for these six huts were the monks' toilets. The first one on the right, slightly bigger than the others, was used only by the abbot, and the one on the far left, slightly smaller than the others, was used only by the newest and youngest monks and workers from the village. The four in the middle were divided by the importance of the monks' duties, the scholars using the hut next to the abbot's, and next came the cooks' hut. Even here at the temple, where the material world was scorned and detachment from existence became a way of life, a hierarchy was created that controlled the most common of bodily functions.

Every morning at three o'clock bells were bonged and chants chanted as the monks arose from their sleep. The symphony was repeated at noon when they prayed, and in the evening when they went to bed. The staccato sounds of wooden sticks beating on a prayer drum were heard throughout the day and night as individual monks contemplated eternity and sought separation from the world by concentrating on the noises. The ratta-tat-tat of the sticks resembled a woodpecker at work on a mountain tree or a village woman pounding her dry laundry with wooden pegs to iron out wrinkles. The screeching of a rusty prayer wheel sometimes competed with the drums and the woodpeckers for attention.

But today was different for it was a wedding day.

All the guests had finally arrived. The bride and groom were ready. It was time for the abbot to begin the ceremony. Iwata and Dolsun approached the foot of the steps to the main temple where the abbot was waiting for them. He was dressed in his finest gray frock, which was no different than the one he wore every day, day in and day out. Except this one was spotlessly clean and had been starched to a stiffness that had a liturgical aire to it. He made the couple hold hands and then placed his own large and callused hands around theirs. He spoke loud and clear, but in a language known only to several of the other monks. His words were a chant consisting of but two notes, one very high and the other very low. As his singsong continued the wind stopped. The birds listened in silence. Some of the villagers even stopped breathing. Many of the older women, believers in the Buddha, nodded their heads in approval even though they didn't understand the words.

Another monk appeared from within the temple doors carrying a golden censer filled with smoking incense. He handed it to the abbot with a slow, ceremonial flair. The abbot waved the shiny, fuming container at Dolsun, and then at Iwata, all the while continuing his arcane chant. The smoke wafted out of the censure and clung to Dolsun's dress, then mysteriously made a right turn and attached itself to Iwata. Apparently, this was a good sign.

Bong! Bong! Bong!

Another monk was striking a huge bell attached to a wooden frame off to the left and slightly up hill from the main temple. His clapper was a log hanging vertically and swinging back and forth. Each blunt, hallow tone had no echo and died instantly after a brief moment of existence, like a loud thud falling off a cliff, never to be heard from again. But as soon as its sound disappeared another one arrived. Finally the twelfth and final whack ended it. The big bell had done a fine job.

Now the abbot finally spoke in the Korean language. He instructed Iwata and Dolsun to go, one at a time, into the temple and ask the Buddha for a happy marriage and many healthy children. After that they must go into the temple together and repeat their requests once more. This time as husband and wife.

Dolsun went first. As she walked into the temple the big, golden Buddha looked down on her. She looked up at him and apologized for lack of belief. Instead of bowing to the Buddha Dolsun turned toward the front doors of the temple, now closed behind her separating her from the crowd outside. The Buddha glared disdainfully down at her back. She bowed toward the spot where she knew Iwata was standing.

"Dear husband, I give you all my love and take you for my very own. I give you myself for your very own." Then, remembering the abbot's instructions, she added, "And please, please, many happy, healthy children."

Iwata was next. He entered the temple and closed the doors behind him. Again, unbelief. Iwata turned toward the east. Toward Japan. He bowed and said, "I am a samurai, and I pledge my sacred honor to take Dolsun as my wife, my very and only wife. I give her my love and my life." He bowed low, toward Japan. Then he turned and bowed toward where he knew Dolsun was waiting for him.

And then together. The happy couple walked up the steps and entered the temple. They were alone as the doors shut once more. Again, the big, golden Buddha sat there and glared at them. Iwata ran his hand through Dolsun's hair and traced a finger down her brow, past her nose, and onto her lips. He bent her back and kissed her long and intimately. Then he looked up at the Buddha and said, "Well, my friend, just in case you are really there, thank you for giving me this greatest treasure of all."

Dolsun laughed and said, "Yes, thank you Buddha, just in case."

Husband and wife, the mudang, the abbot, the other monks, and all of the villagers now had a feast. Small children ran about, making for even more excitement and happiness. Everyone sat on the grass around low tables. Each table was loaded with dishes and each dish contained a different item. There was no duplication on any table. It was a food lover's paradise. There was an abundance of beef, pork and many kinds of fish. There were cucumbers, bean curd, bean sprouts, roots, soups, other things defying description, and many kinds of kimchi. There were pots and pots of fluffy, white, steamy rice. The feast was a work of art, as colorful as it was delicious. The contrasting hues looked like a watercolor landscape, impressionist, and the tastes were from heaven.

The rice wine was excellent. It was served both hot and cold in order to meet every whim. And the singing started. Toast after toast was made and at the end of each salute to the bride and groom someone had to sing. Iwata was especially in demand, but Dolsun and the mudang also had to perform. Daughter and mother. Even the abbot was called upon. This time he used more than two notes.

As the evening came to a close a final round of wine was served. Then chilled, round pears, thinly sliced, were brought from the springhouse. "Good for your digestion," said the abbot.

The last two people to leave the temple grounds were Dolsun and Iwata. They gave the villagers a good head start. When the new husband and wife reached the point in the trail that broke into two paths they were quite alone. They turned away from the village.

The full moon was waiting for them. The night sky, deep blue and speckled with moon dust and stars, was waiting for them The secret place was waiting for them.

Five

The Mudang

Captain Iwata attended the mudang's every word. She was a remarkable woman and it didn't take him long to realize that she could teach him more about his new country than anyone else. He wasn't sure if she believed in her charms, spells and chants or if she really talked to the spirits and phantoms of the mountain. Or if, in fact, they existed. But he was sure she knew how to make these things, be they real or not, work for her and her clients. She had a personal charm and beauty, an older beauty, of course, but still with erotica enough to turn a head or two. She was a very formidable power in the village, a natural leader.

The mudang was a widow and when Iwata's conversations with her got close to that part of her she skillfully, quickly, moved away from it. Dolsun treated the matter of her father the same way. And so Iwata, ever the samurai gentleman, moved away with them, to other areas, other subjects.

Dolsun was a true daughter of the mudang. She, like her mother, was a leader. Her physical beauty and graceful movements copied the mudang. But she added youth, buds, greenery, expectations of more to come. They were both quick to laugh, quick to anger, but also quick to comfort. Indeed, Dolsun's decision to help Iwata when his almost lifeless body plopped onto the beach was never questioned by her mother. That Iwata would stay in their home, at least until his health returned to normal, was also a shared decision made without discussion. Both mother and daughter captured the samurai's heart, each in her own manner. The mudang was Korea, all of it, all together in one lady, the humor, hard work, childlike love for life, beauty and grace, excitement, mystery.

As for Dolsun, she was all of this and more. Captain Iwata was confused. She made him feel wanting, happy, miserable. Iwata had never been in love before and it was a confusing situation he found himself in. Of course, the physical side of it was ever present. He listened to her breathing and it made him ache to touch her. He saw her walking along a path and wanted to run to her and take her in his arms. For Dolsun was beautiful, charming, exciting and Iwata was a healthy young man. Their marriage magnified his passion. Every night became a new adventure. As though for the first time.

He could see that Dolsun was truly the daughter of a mudang as she cast her spell over him time and again.

The silk ribbons were cut neatly and carefully, all the same length. They were red, blue, yellow and white. But most were green, which is the color of reproduction. The green ribbons could talk to the mountain spirit of fertility as they flapped and fluttered in the air. They could ask the spirit to make a wife pregnant if the mudang gave them to the one wanting a baby and she carried the ribbons up the mountain and tied them onto the branches of the baby tree. But the other colors were important, too. They represented additional things worth wanting. What good is a pregnancy without health and happiness? As long as you are on a mountain hanging green ribbons, there is no good reason not to pay homage to the other spirits as well. And so the other colors also sang in the wind.

The mudang had lived in the village for many years and while some of the farmers, but not many, laughed at her and her magical activities, there were others, especially the older ones and their wives, perhaps wives who fancied themselves sort of amateur mudangs, who would never make a major decision without her advice or, in many cases, her consent. They asked her to cast spells conjuring up assistance from the spirit world. She told fortunes if they had the right fee. And the right attitude.

Her snipping and cutting finished, the mudang carefully placed the ribbons, with the green ones on top, into a very neat pile. She then folded the pile three times and chanted some words in an ancient Korean dialect that no one in the village understood. The meaning of the words was lost on her audience of three. Two older ladies and a young woman twenty-one years old. A mother, a mother-in-law, and a wife of two years who had not yet gotten pregnant. This was the "green ribbon ceremony," a sure way - but with the necessary help of a healthy husband - to produce a baby.

The sun had not yet risen and the cool morning piled mystery upon mystery. The mudang, a master dramatist, knew early mornings were more effective for her work, that the pale stillness magnified the moaning wind and added mystery to her craft. She opened her ancient leather bag - it appeared to be as old as the words she had just muttered - and produced a pinch of powder made of finely ground rice. She flung the powder over the ribbons with some of it missing its mark and falling onto the clothing of the three women. By design. Then she swooned and fell to the floor. Her three guests had no idea what to do. So they did nothing. They waited.

"Ah, yes. I have had a vision." She rolled her eyes and shook her body, moaning deeply. "I saw a baby, a healthy baby, and wrapped around his head was a green ribbon, but also a blue one." At the word "his" the three ladies snapped to attention. She continued, "Blue means good health." The mudang's eyes moved toward the ladies. "And the green ribbon around the baby's head tells me that you will have a son." Then, looking at the two older women, she added, "and a grandson."

When the three guests had departed, she swept up the white powder that had landed on the floor and abruptly threw it into the kitchen fire. No words, magical or ancient, accompanied her action.

Of course everything has a soul, not just people. Animals and rocks and the wind and the rain, also flowers and rice and trees and mountains, especially mountains. If you knew what each soul-phantom-spirit guarded or influenced or helped or, woe be it, harmed, and if you knew how they could be made to do what you wanted, or avoid what you did not, well, this made you a very powerful person. The mudang was such a person. She knew the language of spells and incantations. She knew the magic of colors. She knew the wisdom of old trees and the mischief of smaller plants, and the enchantments of bitter herbs. She knew spirits and phantoms and how to make them talk to her. Some said that she knew Satan himself! The evil one, the Maagwee! But most of all, she knew people.

The marriage had been the biggest in years in the village. But that was a year ago. And then another year ago. Still no baby, no little person for a grandmother to take into her arms and hug to her bosom and know that her son's name would live on. No one for a grandfather to take for walks through the village and then up the path to the edge of the mountain and look for the wild rabbits and wait for the cuckoo's song to come down from the heights.

Poor Sunja. Her husband loved her, there was no doubt about that. But without a child, without fresh fruit, there was danger. Sunja's mother and father worried, too. The chungmae had promised children and a marriage broker was supposed to know about things like that. But now, after two years of trying and trying, there was still no baby. And that is what had brought the three women to the mudang's house.

The leader of the Buddhist temple on the mountain behind the village told the young couple to be patient. But patience was wearing thin. Finally, a suggestion was made by Mother-in-law, first cloaked as a joke and then changing to a plea intended to push and jab. A seed planted in the mind of the listener.

"The mudang might help. Doesn't she deal in this sort of thing? Isn't there a special spirit in charge of this business of baby-making? What can it hurt? The monks may say that we aren't supposed to do such things, but we are Korean first and after that, perhaps Buddhist. We Korean people have always had our mudangs. The Buddha gives us his saints and their prayers. The Mudang does the same thing with her spirits and phantoms. What's wrong with that? She's even closer to whatever or whomever she calls on, even closer than the monks are to their statues and bells. What can it hurt?"

Mother-in-law was very persuasive.

With the mudang's swooning still in her thoughts and before the white dust had been completely purged from her clothing, before she could change her mind, Sunja climbed her way up the mountain to the spot where the mudang told her the baby tree grew. The path twisted and turned, now facing eastward into the direction of the rising sun. She saw the tree. It had produced leaves several days earlier. They were small and bud-like and had not yet unfurled, looking like green snow resting on almost barren branches. The mudang said this was the best time of the year to call upon the tree's magical powers, for the tree was itself being wrapped in the pains and happiness of birth.

Sunja approached the tree piously, the ghostly early morning defeating her unbelief. She placed the green ribbons high on the tree. The mudang had stressed the importance of this and the danger of doing otherwise. The others she fastened lower, the blues and the reds and the yellows.

Sunja was alone. The mudang said that too was important. "You must go to the tree alone!" To not confuse the tree, or to keep an old grandmother from getting pregnant by accident? What a silly question! The magic was wearing off. Sunja wondered if this walk up the mountain made sense at all, let alone posed a danger to an old woman who happened to catch a stray bit of magic from the spell.

But her mother had advised her. "Believe or not, that's your own business. Just keep quiet and go up to the tree. Do what the mudang says. Mother-in-law needs no extra incentive to stir up her nasty nature. We'll do what she wants and buy you some peace. Go up to the tree with your magic ribbons. And then let your husband do his job."

A Korean mother-in-law! Sunja wondered how it was to be a son-in-law instead of a daughter-in-law. The one so loved and the other so poorly treated, in one case overlooking all the stains of a husband, and in the other picking and picking at the smallest matters concerning a wife. Men joked about the situation, but it was not funny to young women preparing for marriage. Nothing was good enough for these shrews. Nothing! There was an expression men used to describe a man who always fussed and worried. "Shee omah." Mother-in-law! Applied to a man it became an insult.

Her pilgrimage completed, Sunja sat under the tree to rest. The sun had just appeared and the birds were singing their morning arias, the mountain air was still cool but now in the morning's sun was not giving her much of a chill. Sunja prayed for a son. Then she looked up at the tree and laughed. What nonsense!

The light dimmed and the mountain regained its lost chill. Sunja was frightened. She hurried down the mountain path and returned to the village.

The mudang and abbot Keeyong were friendly and respected each other's beliefs. But the question of the baby tree was a matter they could never agree on. The deep meaning of marriage and the procreation of the human race was not a subject of superstition for the abbot. He was the leader of the temple and had a duty to carefully guard the Buddha's true teaching. He drew the line. No baby tree!

Only a few hours after Sunja returned from her early morning visit to the mountain abbot Keeyong heard about it. It so happened that a good temple worshiper, the widow Kim, had also been on the mountain before sunrise. She was doing a special penance. Or was she looking for a wild herb that she made into a very delicious soup? The widow Kim told a different story depending on who was listening. She had seen Sunja climbing up the trail and had watched from a safe distance as Sunja approached the tree and took the colored ribbons out of her bag and tied them to the tree's branches in a pattern that placed the green ribbons highest. The abbot listened to the widow Kim and his anger grew. Sunja and her husband were Buddhist. They never should do such a pagan thing involving such an important aspect of their marriage. Mother-in-law's feelings should not be a consideration! Why, only last week the mudang and the abbot had had a pleasant and humorous conversation at the edge of the village where he had gone to bless the farmers who were planting the rice seedlings into special paddies. Later, the rice plants would be transplanted into the regular paddies and he would bless them again. And now, a few days later, the mudang had performed the one divination the abbot had let her know he would not tolerate.

It was noon by the time the abbot reached the baby tree. He was covered with sweat. The morning had grown quite warm and he had climbed up the trail faster than his normal pace, his anger racing ahead of his climbing.

He ripped the ribbons from the tree and didn't pay any special attention to their colors. For him, the greens and the reds and the blues were all the same. Meaningless! He tucked them into the same pocket holding his hankie. If he needed to blow his nose he might even use one of them. He headed back down the mountain and to the house of the mudang. She was taking her midday nap when the abbot arrived. The wind increased in small gusts as he neared the gate and two small dust eddies appeared on the ground between the gate and the house. They touched and kissed each other and joined, becoming a single, larger eddy, a miniature tornado, that stopped moving forward but continued spinning. This new thing, this changeling, whatever it was, bowed slightly toward the abbot as though challenging him to enter the house. Spirits and phantoms of Asia were greeting a simple monk as he approached a mudang's house. Then the wind stopped, the strange tornado died, and the monk was back in a little village, ready to shout and yell at his friend, for she had overstepped the boundaries of their coexistence.

"Mudang! Mudang! Come out here. I want to talk to you."

She emerged from the house rubbing sleep from her eyes. She saw an angry abbot Keeyong standing in her yard, between the gate and the house. A couple of broken kimchi pots were laying on the ground close to his feet and the mudang tried to remember if the chards had been there earlier. Were they a signal of his anger or just broken pottery like that found throughout the village? No, these pieces of red clay were covered with dust. They had been there quite some time. A good sign, or, at least, not a bad one. No magic pottery here.

The abbot yanked the ribbons from his pocket and threw them onto the ground in front of her. "Here are your stupid charms, these inanimate and senseless ribbons that are as ignorant as you are." The words had no sooner left his mouth than he felt sorry. He was being too harsh with her. Ribbons such as these were as old as Asia, and even though what he said was true perhaps there was a better way to say it. She looked older and sadder than moments earlier. Perhaps she had misread the chards.

They heard singing farmers working in the rice fields at the edges of the village. The songs added warmth to the day. The mudang went back into the house and a moment later returned with a small table, two cups of tea and some sugar cakes. She said, "Now let's calm down and discuss this like friends. After all, we both want the same thing. Poor Sunja's happiness is at stake. Do you agree?"

The abbot agreed to a truce, unstated, by sitting down on the narrow wooden porch circling the house. The tea looked and smelled delicious. The cakes were sweet and the tea hot. She took a deep breath, and looked at the monk.

"My friend, do you know anything about me? Do you know who I am or where I come from? Do you know how I became a mudang?" She spoke in an accent the abbot had never heard her use before. It was from the north, and much harsher than the rounded southern sounds of the village people. The monk nodded his willingness to listen, so the she began her story.

I was born up north, near the city of Pyongyang, you

know, the city that is now the capital. But in those days bandits were everywhere. They controlled much of the countryside. My father was a well-to-do landowner. The lawlessness of the times devastated him. He was a good man and when he resisted the bandits they assassinated him. They said he was the leader of the movement to bring the legitimate government of the King back to the area. But Father was never interested in politics. Grandfather and Grandmother grabbed our small family - myself and Older Brother and Mother - and we walked many miles, hundreds of miles, all the way to this village. I have lived here ever since. I married here. And here I raised my daughter, my dear Dolsun. In time I even changed my accent. I became a true daughter of this province.

When we first got here we were destitute, but these good country people helped us. Mother and Grandfather worked in the rice paddies while Grandmother stayed home and made our family life as normal as possible. We worked hard and, finally, owned our own paddies and built our own house.

When the time came for me to marry, a chungmae found me a husband in the next village who was also from the north. My husband had come south for the same reasons we had. Love came quickly, just as the chungmae promised. My dear husband was a dealer in roots and herbs and spent much of his time on the mountains where he searched for his medicines. No children came to us. Sometimes I went with him on his trips to the mountains and I became quite good at finding our magical materials. I learned what kind of soil yields ginseng and where to look for the bitter herb that cures woman problems. I learned from the mountain itself. The mountain talked to me, the rocks and the trees, and the very earth itself. I had a dream and a phantom came to me and told me how to help people who needed help, how to call good spirits and how to expel bad spirits. I know you don't believe me. But that is what happened.

So I became a mudang. But first I made a trip to a small island off the southern coast, where I studied with an old woman who knew everything about spirits and phantoms, and where they live and how to call them. She knew more than anyone else in the world about such matters. She played drums in our classic Korean style, but not quite with the same results as at the King's court. The drums of this old hag called up ghosts and goblins that can help humans. But bad spirits had a way of fooling her from time to time.

The life of a mudang is a dangerous life.

My husband and I finally had a baby, a daughter. You know her today as Dolsun. She is beautiful and intelligent. My dear husband seemed to know that he would leave me early in our life together and so he left me a wonderful child. Dolsun is better and stronger than any son could be. She is my daughter in body and also in spirit. She is strong and tender at the same time. Soft and harsh at the same time.

When my husband got sick I was not confident enough in my skills to do anything to help him. He died in a few days and on the night of his death the old lady, the old mudang, came to me in a vision and said that I was a very stupid mudang because I had not used the powers she taught me, not even for my own husband.

But now I use my powers. Yes, now I am a full time mudang.

But even if there are no spirits, no phantoms, no good, no evil, what I do works. I help people. I don't know how it works, but it does. Perhaps I help them help themselves. Isn't it the same as what you do? Don't you pray to your Buddha and ask him for help? Maybe we both send our prayers to the same God - you through your Buddha and me through my spirits and phantoms of the mountain.

The abbot had listened to her story very carefully. That night as he lay on his mat he thought about it. She was a remarkable person and even if her theology was wrong, at least she believed in something and she gave comfort to her clients. He just wished she would keep her ribbons and charms away from the good Buddhists of the village. Finally he went to sleep. But the mudang remained. Dreams - starting and stopping, churning and stirring - mixed into his mind. None made sense. They were unconnected feelings and scenes blending and changing as quickly as they arrived.

Finally, a deeper sleep brought on a different kind of dream. He was on the mountain, somewhere above the baby tree and was climbing higher and higher. It was darker than black charcoal. At the end of the path there was another tree and tied to its branches were silk ribbons. The moon came out from behind a cloud. In the moonlight he saw that every ribbon was blue, no other colors. He knew they were meant for him.

The abbot woke up. He was covered with sweat even though the night was cool. He had no idea what the dream meant. Or if it meant anything at all.

Some of the ladies and men of the village arrived at the temple earlier the next morning. They found the abbot lying on the floor directly in front of the main altar, the only sign of life being his labored breathing. They carried him down to the village.

The old women tended him. He did not regain consciousness for three days and even then he was too weak to eat solid food. A fever was eating him alive. The old women despaired for his life.

A gentle rain began to fall. The mudang reached the baby tree but never stopped. She had another destination. There was another special tree higher up the mountain, another two miles to go. The rain stopped but it had done its job. The air was now thick with mystery and strange noises came from above and below. The spirits and phantoms, specters and shades, ghosts and haunters - good and bad - sang and groaned as the moon sent magical dust instead of light, a dust that clung to her. The enchantment of the mountain was almost too much for her to bear. She stopped and rested against a large rock. The spirits came and danced around her faster and faster.

Why help a monk? Let him die along with his damn old-crone religion"

The message was not in Korean. It was whistled into the mudang's very soul by ten phantoms, all shrieking at the same time.

"But he is my friend."

She climbed until she reached the second tree. It was the Tree of Health. There were five blue ribbons inside the pouch tied around her waist. Blue, the color of health. She tied the ribbons to the tree as high as she could reach and sang a magical song in her strange mudang language. One name came out in human speech, "Keeyong." Then she bowed three times to the tree and left.

Many of the village people came to see the abbot on his sickbed. They brought his favorite foods. He thanked them, but as soon as they left, his nurses took the spicy gifts away and brought him the bland food that his sickness demanded. Slowly his health returned.

The abbot became restless. He wanted to return to his temple. His last night in the village he was tucked into bed by the old woman attending him. He was more than half asleep when he had a feeling that someone was watching him. He looked up and saw no one. Then a familiar call came from outside his window. It sounded like a cuckoo bird. But cuckoos never came down to the village. In fact, they were seldom seen even on the lower parts of the mountain. Then he heard the call again.

He struggled out of his covers and over to the window. And there he saw it. Indeed it was a cuckoo bird. The bird looked directly into the abbot's eyes and bobbed its head up and down in several short jerks. As the bird nodded, the monk saw a piece of material hanging from its mouth. It was a blue ribbon. The cuckoo bird dropped the blue ribbon onto the window ledge, looked once more at the monk, and said,

Oh, what a fearsome place this universe is become.
Perhaps there is only one way to survive its pains.
Become a child. Deal with phantoms and ghosts and
spirits and things of the night. But fear them not!
A child sees things that wise men say do not exist.
But a child is not afraid to love and hate.
Monk - keep your religion.
But love the Children!

The cuckoo bird turned and leaped back into the dark

pool of the night.

Several hours later there was a knock at his door and before the monk could say a word a lady entered the room.

It was the mudang. She was dressed in a blue gown that was, other than its solitary color, as Korean as it could possibly be. The tight upper part of the dress pulled her breasts tightly into her body, giving her chest a flat appearance that excited men. For they knew the flatness was only pretend. The bottom half blossomed out all the way to the floor like the lower part of an hourglass. Her white muslin booties sharply contrasted with the blue. This simple, beautiful design showed the majesty of Korean women in all their nobility.

Stillness is motion. Silence is strength.

The quiet of the room was accented by the muffled human voices and other small sounds from the village.

"Well, this is a pleasant surprise. I am fortunate. As you know, I am going home to my temple tomorrow, and your visit makes my last night here a happy one."

Keeyong closed his eyes and the night swiftly conquered him. He fell into a deep sleep. No dreams. No thoughts.

When he awoke the mudang was gone.

Six

Tangun

A large bonfire was burning a short distance outside the village near the early slope of the mountain. Embers, like rockets, shot up and attacked the highland above, but dying before reaching their target. No one noticed. The tip of the sun had already touched the edge of the earth and was streaking the sky with a special redness that comes once a day, and sometimes not at all. The village people were eating and drinking, singing and dancing. The festivity had started just a few hours earlier and was now at the stage that the mudang called the noisy time. That's the way she described it to Iwata. Simple words. And indeed it was becoming louder and noisier with the sounds of singing, drum beats and wooden flutes. The music was being made not by the best of musicians, but by those village men who had the most rice wine in their bellies. Everyone sang, both the sober and the intoxicated. Sparks shot into the air as hungry feasters poked sticks into the flames as they roasted skewered chunks of meat and vegetables. Pots of rice placed among the red coals boiled and steamed and were attended by several grandmothers. Everyone laughed and jiggled their bodies to the music. Even those standing still. The musicians swayed and jerked more than the others. Every once in a while a man or woman shooed the crowd aside and danced alone. When this happened claps and yells of encouragement arose from the others, the solo dancer now jerking wildly to the beat of the music, exciting the spectators more and more, and finally, they could not keep still any longer. They all joined in. End of solo. The mingling, dancing bodies looked rubbery, relaxing and then each new beat of the music snapping them to attention. Over and over, back and forth.

The village was celebrating the rice harvest. A very good rice harvest. Now the winter could come with small harm. There would be plenty of rice for everyone. Several pigs and a cow had been slaughtered for the party and there was plenty more meat on the hoof for the winter.

Iwata sat next to the mudang and watched the revelry. The happiness was contagious. Once he even danced by himself as the people roared their approval. He mimicked the rubbery snappings with an exaggeration that brought tears of laughter from some of the old grandmothers and grandfathers.

Two farmers came straggling down the mountain toward the gathering. They moved slowly, dragging a large sack, a heavy load, each grasping an end. As they approached the bonfire squeals of delight came from some of the men. "Did you get one? Is it still fresh?"

"Yes, we got one! Just over an hour ago."

Several farmers ran toward the two men and opened their sack by ripping it apart. Its grisly contents brought murmurings of delight from both men and women. It was a wild boar, a dangerous looking animal, even when dead, who was known to kill a human from time to time. A very ferocious animal indeed! But it was indeed dead, and there was a knife handle sticking out of its chest. His squinting eyes were open and he glared a death grin at the people as though daring them to approach.

One of the two hunters shouted to the crowd, his face glowing with heroic shine. "Bring a sharp knife and some cups. Now we can be assured of some new baby sons for our village." He took the knife that was offered to him and neatly slit the throat of the boar after propping the animal into a good position for what happened next. The village men, at least those who were married and healthy enough to father a child, lined up in a twisting, somewhat unstable row that led to a fountain of blood that was now flowing from the boar's throat. Cup after cup was filled, drained, filled again, and quickly passed down the line. Not one drop of blood was wasted. The men drank frothy red toasts as the women squealed.

Iwata looked on in astonishment but did not join the drinkers. He asked her, "What's going on? Why are they so excited? Why drink the blood of this ugly animal?"

She laughed a deep, roaring laugh and almost rolled on the ground. "My dear samurai, my gentleman, is this behavior too rough for you? Why don't you drink the red nectar? You might like it, and it may help you have a son, a strong and handsome son. Perhaps even another samurai."

"Oh, so that's it. Yes, give me some, too." But Iwata made no move toward the boar, hoping no one had heard him.

"Well, being a mudang, I am probably the only woman here who can get you a cup of this magic blood." She spoke very loudly. Loud enough for the men in the line to hear her words. They motioned her to the head of the line and one of them handed her a cup. Filling it to the brim with the bubbling red nectar the mudang walked over to Iwata and offered it to him. Iwata mumbled something to himself in Japanese that no one understood and drank the cup all the way to its dregs. Then he wiped his sleeve across his lips, but not before a small crooked line of creamy redness formed a mustache on his upper lip.

"Ah, wonderful. I already feel the strength of the boar soaking through my body. Ah, give me more."

The people laughed with him. The Japanese samurai was one of them.

"No! One cup is all you get. If you drink another you might need more than one wife." The mudang pretended to scold Iwata. Dolsun blushed.

Later, sitting on the ground while eating and drinking, Iwata spoke. "These people are remarkable. Such a simple life they have here in the village. They are so happy and content. And yet at other times I have seen them get very angry over a trifle. They enjoyed fighting as much as they did anything else. Sometimes when they play games it is like a war. Then at other times they are tender and kind, such as they were to me when I first came here. And today I find out they drink the warm blood of the ugliest animal of all because they think it will help them produce sons."

The mudang looked at Iwata and laughed. "Yaaa, yaaa! This is what we are. We can change our moods in an instant. But it is because we are Korean. It is in our blood. It comes from Tangun."

Iwata glanced at Dolsun who had said very little since the arrival of the two hunters and the boar. Then his eyes shot back to the her. "Tangun? What is Tangun?"

"No, not what. Who!"

"You must tell me what you are talking about. Who is Tangun and how has this Tangun, is it a man or a woman, rubbed his or her extremes into you Koreans? From harsh to soft, from love to hate, from hot to cold. You Korean women! You either love your man to death or nag him to death. Even your food. You love rice, the blandest of all foods and at the same time crave your kimchi which is always hot and sour, and always very stinky. Your perfume is garlic! And yet you love the mountain's wildflowers." Iwata waited for her answer as though anticipating an opponent's sword thrust.

She shot back, "And you! You never eat our rice and kimchi, do you? You never touch our garlic, do you? You are lucky to live here with us. For the sweet Japanese food would have eventually turned your brain soft. And as for our women! All the world's women should be like us. Then men would know what a woman is all about, what a woman is meant to be. But I think you are beginning to realize what I am saying."

She glanced from Iwata to Dolsun. Her daughter turned her eyes away and raised her hand up to her face, a face as red as the flames of the bonfire.

"Now I will tell you the story of Tangun."

Before the world had any people in it, at a time when the animals had the earth all to themselves and the beauty of Korea had only itself to sing to, a strange thing happened. It was almost six thousand years ago and the universe was ruled, as even now, by Hanunim. One day as Hanunim was walking around the earth and watching the animals play and enjoy themselves he heard a male tiger and a female bear saying their prayers. They wanted to become human.

(At this point in the story Iwata wondered how the animals could know about humans since none existed at the time. However, being a poet and a storyteller himself he didn't break the flow of the narrative. The rice wine had made him quite friendly and happy. A question about a story is uncalled for so early in its telling. After another cup of the hot rice wine he forgot his question anyway!)

Back to the story. Hanunim decided to answer the prayers of the two animals. He gave them both twenty pieces of garlic and a log of wormwood. They must eat only this foul diet and live in a cave with no light at all for one hundred days. So the pair went into the cave and ate their special food. But the tiger gave up in two weeks claiming the darkness and the garlic were fine but he couldn't eat bitter wormwood. The lady bear, apparently the more determined of the two, made it through the one hundred days. When she walked out of the cave she was human. Her first wish was to have a human baby. So she did what all the animals did in those day when they wanted to become pregnant. She prayed for a child beneath a sandalwood tree.

(Once again, Iwata had a notion about the tale. He looked at Dolsun and was joyful that humans didn't depend on sandalwood trees for their babies today. He liked the modern human method better.)

Back to the story. A child was born to the lady bear who was now a human. A son. She named him Tangun.

He was born on October 3rd, almost six thousand years ago. Tangun ruled Korea for the next 1,211 years. The Koreans, all of us, are his descendants.

The story was finished. The mudang looked proudly at Iwata. "So you see, that is why we are so, well, all the things you said. And that is why we love garlic."

More rice wine. More singing. Much more dancing. The mudang and Captain Iwata, the samurai from Japan who was becoming a true native of this harsh and beautiful land of Korea, had a grand time together. They were alike in many ways. Perhaps they were both poets. Dolsun sat quietly and watched them. She didn't say much. She just watched and listened to her mother and her husband. She was happy and it was enough.

And when the evening was over the three of them went home and took their happiness with them.

Seven

Bushido

The warrior knights of Japan had a code controlling their behavior. These grand fighting men, known as samurai, were tied to a code of virtue that bound them to rectitude, endurance, frugality, courage, politeness, veracity and, especially, loyalty to their shogun and country and to each other. In addition to these virtues their training was physical to an extreme degree. They were strong, lean and tough. They were the best archers and sword fighters in the world, and they knew how to kill. They knew ways of killing most people didn't even know existed. They could kill with a touch or they could kill with sword or arrow or dagger.

But killing did not bring honor. It was only through Bushido, the way of the warrior, that a samurai could maintain his honor and virtue. The highest virtue of all was the loyalty that had to be given to the sovereign. Samurai pledged complete loyalty to their shogun. He was their leader. If this code of honor was broken there was but one penalty, death. Either by assassin or by the samurai's own hand.

The title "shogun" officially means a general who fights barbarians. There were many shogunates, large and small, and many shoguns, some important, some not, even some not too noble. But from time to time a grand and powerful shogun would arise above the others and, by military power and force of personality, become the ruler of all Japan. The Emperor was a god, and the people needed a god, but the shogun ruled the land.

Shogun Toyotomi Hideyoshi had summoned three of his knights to his palace. Hideyoshi was shogun of all of Japan, the military dictator. (Even the emperor-god listened to him behind his closed palace doors if not publicly.) The three warriors entered Hideyoshi's presence and immediately dropped to their knees, their heads pressing the floor. They did not stand until a chamberlain clapped his hands sharply three times. The three samurai were fully armed, with swords strapped to their sides and daggers tucked into their belts. Even in the presence of their sovereign a samurai would not disarm himself. He thought his weapons, especially his swords, part of his body.

"Everyone out! I will speak to my three samurai alone." In an instant the room emptied except for the four of them. Shogun Hideyoshi studied their uniforms with pride for they were made of the multicolored material of his samurai. And each man had a black sash wrapped tightly around his waist.

The black sash made them special, the shogun's private samurai. Special assignments, special protectors. A very elite group.

"Come near to me, my knights. I want to speak of Bushido. As you know a samurai warrior can never lose because no foe can remove him from his Bushido, and that is more important than his life. If we lose Bushido the world will end as we know it." Hideyoshi paused as the large room echoed his words. The three knights made no sound, no movement. Their very breath stopped for fear of making a disparate vibration on top of the echoes of their sovereign's words, for that would dishonor them.

"Several years ago a fleet of our ships sailed to Korea and our glorious warriors brought us honor by nobly offering their blood for Japan." The shogun made no mention of defeat. Just the offering of blood.

He continued. "Until recently we were led to believe that all had perished following the code of Bushido, that there were no survivors. But now I have some new information. A traveler, a Japanese on business in Korea, tells of a Japanese man who is living in one of the villages there. The man had a noble bearing and might have been a military man, perhaps a naval man."

Again, Hideyoshi paused. He found it very difficult to say what he had to say next. He hoped he was wrong. He looked out the window into the courtyard where groups of samurai were training, some using their weapons and others only their hands. The slapping of steel against steel and flesh against flesh was heard from across the training field. These noble young men were the life blood of Japan and Hideyoshi loved every one of them. He loved them more than his own life or his own family. A wife may give you sons but these warriors were his brothers and his children in a more powerful way than that. He loved his men even more than his love for the Emperor, but he would never say that. Only his love for Japan itself was greater. Trying to calm his emotion Hideyoshi walked to an inner door and ordered tea be brought into the room for his samurai.

"If there is a samurai living in Korea he must be there against his will. If he is there of his own accord he must be brought back to Japan to answer to the code of Bushido or, better yet, he must be killed either by his own hand or by the hand of another samurai. Our Bushido demands no less than this!"

The room grew deadly silent as the meaning of what the shogun said became clear to the three warriors. They were to become agents of the Bushido. A high honor indeed. The shogun then provided them with other details. The man was their age and so, if he was a samurai, his training was complete, deadly. He would know how to fight and how to kill. A physical description of the man seemed to fit a certain Captain Iwata who had served in the naval forces as a cruiser commander. Until now he had been presumed killed in battle. But nothing was certain. If it was Iwata it meant he had survived the defeat of the scouting group that had preceded the main Japanese armada. The Korean "turtle ships" had destroyed both scouts and armada. But Hideyoshi was careful not to speak of any defeat having taken place.

"I hope the man, if he is samurai, is being detained against his will."

The door at the far end of the room opened and a lady entered carrying a tray with a teapot and four cups. The men were surprised to see it was Kasuko, the shogun's wife, and not one of the palace servants. She approached the men, her eyes modestly looking down toward the floor, and proceeded to serve the tea. With the simple task completed Kasuko stepped back but did not leave the room. She sat on her haunches in a corner, a safe distance from the men.

"Gentlemen, as you can see, my wife Kasuko herself has honored you by serving you your tea. This is indeed a rare happening." The shogun looked at his wife. She kept her eyes on the floor. But her husband felt her hidden smile.

The men finished their tea and the shogun quickly dismissed them without finishing the discussion. They were instructed to return the following morning. Then, looking at his wife he said, "Now you can tell me what that was all about. Why is my wife acting like a common retainer? Come on. I know you. What's on your mind that you dare to interrupt an important matter of state and serve tea?"

Now that they were alone Kasuko finally looked directly at her husband. It was an unspoken secret that samurai, all the way up to the shogun himself, did indeed love their wives and listened to them more than official Japanese convention told the world was the case. Great changes in career or family matters were always discussed between husband and wife. The wife's position was powerful indeed. It was only in the world of killing and battles that wives were not permitted. For samurai had a wonderful ability to put their wives into separate compartments that did not mix with blood and war. But now they were alone and Hideyoshi was not reluctant to show her his affection, his love, and to listen to anything she had to say.

"My Lord Shogun, my husband. Yes, I do have something to say to you." She decided to use her husband's formal title even though they were alone. Hideyoshi knew this meant she did indeed have something important to ask him.

"Speak up, my love." He attempted to disarm her formality with his informality.

"Maggo the hunchback has come to me with a story that needs to be brought to your attention and I cannot defer any longer talking to you about it. I think it might involve this meeting of yours I have just disrupted. I apologize for that, my sweet husband." She bowed. The battle of wits, tone of voice, formality, informality, baiting, listening, that is common all over the world between husbands and wives was being performed in the shogun's palace. An ancient ritual, no doubt about that.

Kasuko continued. "The whole palace is talking about the traveler's story that Captain Iwata may be alive and living in Korea. Everyone is wondering what you will do about it. Some say perhaps Iwata is acting as a spy for you, and will return soon with valuable information about Korea and their defenses. Others are saying Iwata has chosen to live his life out in that foreign country and, therefore, he must be destroyed, for a samurai defeated in battle must perform seppuku."

Seppuku, ritual suicide by disembowelment.

Hideyoshi waved his hand to silence her. For a moment he paused and then he asked, "And what do you say?"

Kasuko looked out the window for a moment and then swept her eyes back to her husband. She was indeed beautiful and she hoped Hideyoshi noticed her beauty, nature's trick given to all women and used by them as a weapon when necessary. Hideyoshi looked at her eyes, her skin, her hair, her slim body, her bosom. He decided to give up, surrender. He would listen very carefully to what she had to say. After all, a samurai is a gentleman who loves beauty, virtue and loyalty. And that includes loyalty to family, and Kasuko was his family, his wife. She also was his closest friend.

"Maggo the hunchback is one of the smartest men in this palace. I know how some of your warriors despise him because of his hump, and that they only tolerate him because they are stupid enough to think a hunchback brings good luck in battle. They even mock him with the name they give him. Maggo. But you, my dear husband, know that Maggo is more than a good luck token. He is a poet. That is why you let him live here with us. His words tell of the beauty of Japan and he honors your Bushido. He talks to animals and mountains and shows us beauty that otherwise we would not know existed."

"What is your point, woman? The point! The point! Remember, I am the shogun and a busy shogun at that." Two can play at the husband-wife game. The shogun was reminding his wife that a game was fine as long as she understood the husband was always one step ahead, and in charge.

"Maggo had a dream, and then I had the same dream. Now how can this be? The same dream comes to two different people? But it happened, and I am frightened.

"A fox wearing a white scarf appeared to me as I sat in a shaded and pleasant forest clearing. He spoke to me in our Japanese tongue. He said Captain Iwata was a better samurai than any of the others, but that his gift was to be a poet, to create beauty with words and thoughts that were even better than samurai virtues. The fox told me Iwata did not need battle to make him a great samurai and that I should tell the shogun that true Bushido permits Captain Iwata to live and not die. And someday, somehow, Japan will be very proud to claim such a son, such a samurai. The fox said battles and blood and fighting skills are not everything that being samurai entails."

Kasuko arose to her feet, bowed to her husband, and slowly left the room without turning her face away from the shogun. But unlike the three samurai her eyes never left his. Hideyoshi sat in silence for a long time. Left unsaid was that he had known Captain Iwata when he was in training at the palace to be a samurai. Iwata was a natural warrior and was far ahead of his fellows in all of the martial arts. But there had been more to the man. Much more. He was intelligent and sensitive and quick to feel the moods and fears and concerns of others. Hideyoshi had noticed this from his observations of the man and from talking with his commanders. Hideyoshi knew Iwata was a special warrior, and more, he knew he was a poet.

The shogun sent for Maggo. The little hunchback entered the room and immediately got on his knees with his head bouncing against the floor. The shogun clapped his hands, the signal for the man to stand up and prepare to answer the shogun's questions. But not all the way up. A little bend at the knees showed the proper relationship between ruler and ruled. Hideyoshi was a wise man. He looked at the hunchback and felt several emotions. First of all he thought about the vagaries of birth. One man born to be a shogun. Another born to be an object of scorn, a hunchback. There was no doubt in Hideyoshi's mind that Maggo was brilliant. His writings were beautiful and gave words to ideas and impressions of nature itself. He was a master of haiku and tanka, Japanese poetic forms that rationed words and created striking and contrasting views of reality. Yet the man himself was ugly. The shogun wanted his wife to appear, as before, and serve tea to Maggo, but, of course, that was impossible. That would be a weakness. A samurai is one thing and a hunchback is another.

Maggo told the shogun about his dream. A fox with a white scarf had come to him also and had said the very same words the shogun's wife had heard in her dream. The shogun was undecided. His three samurai would not return until tomorrow. He had time until then to decide for himself what a samurai really was meant to be, a soldier or a poet. Or, perhaps, both.

In the year 1603, Yeyasu became the shogun of all Japan, replacing Hideyoshi, who had died suddenly in his sleep. Hideyoshi never had time to make his decision concerning Captain Iwata. The matter was passed on to the new shogun, Yeyasu.

He made Edo his capital and kept the emperor as a figurehead, just as Hideyoshi had done. He became the complete ruler of Japan, even stronger than Hideyoshi. Yeyasu believed the social classes of Japan had to be stratified carefully if Japan was to grow strong. He felt the samurai were his greatest asset and that nothing could be permitted to harm their integrity. His rule depended on them and their military skills, but also their virtues.

Yeyasu dispatched the three samurai to Korea to bring an end, one way or another, to the Captain Iwata affair.

Eight

The Visitors

Korea's early morning magic transacted its charms. Soft but jagged strands of fog wound gossamer webs onto the valley floors and began working their way higher and higher up the mountainside. They reached for the summit, a goal they knew was never achieved. But they realized the beauty they were creating was itself a greater goal, and they turned away from the summit. The sun, still below the horizon, poised itself to destroy their misty art.

The mudang had been awake for hours. She had a mudang's ability to sense when a change in her affairs was about to take place. Her anxiety wasn't only mental for her body ached with dull pain, her head warm, not with bodily illness, but a fever of the soul. She remembered feeling this way on that morning - oh so long ago - when she sent Dolsun's father off on a trip. He returned sick and died a few days later.

She got out of bed, dressed quickly, and walked outside into the cool morning darkness. The village was quiet and the only sounds were faint animal murmurings, some beasts feeling the pulling of the sun that was soon to pop out of the eastern horizon. When the mudang came to the end of the village she took the path leading up the mountain. The top of the mountain greeted the sun long before the lower earth. An eerie effect was the result, a plastering of light that did nothing to reveal the land below, a hard band of yellow across the upper earth. The wind blew softly, and yet as gentle as the wind was, a harsh enchantment appeared above her on the rising trail. Three small swirls of dust twisted around and around forming three small funnels. The swirls bowed, mocking her, and she felt danger. A cruel laughter floated on the morning mist.

The mudang stared at the swirling dust until her vision blurred and then, in an instant, the sun peeked over the edge of the land at the point where the horizon ducked into the valley between two mountains. Sunlight flooded onto the path and the glare blinded her. When she regained her sight the dust funnels were gone and in their place were three men in strange clothing. They were climbing down the trail toward the village. Long swords swung at their sides. Jet-black hair, woven into tightly pulled braids, hung down their backs. They looked foreign.

The three strangers were momentarily startled when they saw her, as was she to see them. But then, realizing she was alone, they relaxed and talked to each other in a strange language meaningless to her. They bowed toward her ever so slightly and the one in the lead, palm upturned, gestured down the trail and toward the village. The message was plain enough. She bowed, turned and walked slowly back toward the village and the three men followed. Tendrils of white-gray mist lapped at their feet as though to hold them back, but they didn't stop.

As they entered the village a farmer was on his way to the rice paddies to start his day's work. His eyes followed the four figures silently walking past him. The three strangers appeared alien and mysterious, their garments colors contrasting his own gray work clothes. Their swords frightened him. The village dogs slinked away. Even the birds were silent. The farmer shuddered.

The mudang knew who the strangers wanted to see. She took them directly to Iwata's and Dolsun's house. Iwata was in the courtyard washing his face and preparing himself for the morning. He looked up as the three men approached and a calm hint of recognition - and then resignation - crossed his face. The mudang saw it. Iwata glanced at the house, his home, where Dolsun was sleeping. Then he spoke to the strangers in the same strange language she had heard earlier. They answered him. A bow from Iwata and answering bows from the three told her they were greeting each other peacefully. At least for the time being.

Captain Iwata turned toward the mudang and spoke in Korean. "Woman, listen to me very carefully. Bring us four mats. I will sit with these three men on the porch of my house. We have some talking to do. Bring us food and tea. But most importantly, take Dolsun to your house and do not let her return here unless I send for her. I will not explain anything at this time. Do as I say and do it now!"

Iwata spoke with total authority. And she obeyed.

She brought the tea and food and quickly left the men, taking Dolsun with her back to her own home. Dolsun asked no questions, her mother's stern manner overcoming her curiosity. By now the morning mist was spent. The four men, now alone, ate and drank in silence. And then a polite, formal, but deadly, discourse began. The subject was no less than life and death, integrity, honor and dishonor, loyalty and treason. The subject was Bushido. Iwata spoke of beauty and poetry and other loyalties beyond that given to military commanders. He spoke of teaching others the Bushido code and how the result might be order and justice and structure for the whole world. He spoke of Bushido not having national boundaries.

The three strangers spoke of war and battles and victory and virtue. They spoke of integrity and honor, just as Iwata had. But then they spoke of justice. They spoke of a justice that had no turns or bends, a justice hard and necessary for preserving order and structure, the order and the structure of their shogun and Japan. Even civilization itself.

But most of all they said, "Bushido is Japanese."

Back and forth, back and forth. The sounds of the words were peaceful enough. Then bows and hand gestures. But the bows and the gestures were only a dance, a deadly dance, a formula being acted out. Their words spoke of death and their bows and gestures could not hide it. The talking went on and on and when the sun had climbed directly overhead the mudang appeared with more tea and food. The men hardly acknowledged her presence so she left her wares and departed. Dolsun was nowhere in sight. At least that part of Iwata's order was being obeyed. After eating, the talking resumed and lasted into the early evening. Iwata then went to Dolsun. The three strangers walked back up the path and onto the mountain where they planned to spend the night.

No one - neither Iwata, the mudang nor anyone else - could change their minds. In a strange land amongst strangers samurai warriors sleep alone and take care of themselves.

Iwata and Dolsun were alone. The room was still and tense. Husband and wife and unseen baby. So much to talk about. So little time to talk. But talk he must. So Iwata told Dolsun about Bushido and about the honor of samurai. He also told her that samurai honor was, in his mind, more than the honor of the battlefield, and he thought he could convince the three strangers of this.

Dolsun grasped Iwata's hand. She wanted to run - run - run. They must flee from these samurai visitors. But Iwata said no, that would be false and cowardly. He was sure he could convince them his Bushido honor was intact, that it had simply taken him in another direction. Just wait. She would see. In the morning it would be different. He wrapped his arms around Dolsun and assured her everything was fine, that the strangers would see things his way. Perhaps if he went up the mountain with them they would see the beauty of Korea and realize Bushido should live here, too, and that he was still a samurai but with a different mission than theirs. Yes, they would see it all clearly. He just had to take them up the mountain. Dolsun kissed Iwata gently on his lips and his cheeks and as she lay pressed against his body she felt the baby move inside her. It kicked once, and then again. Iwata felt it, too. For the first time in this long and weary day he laughed. And he fell asleep. But sleep did not bring comfort.

A dream began.

He is at the secret place and he is alone. And time is bending. It bounds forward. There is a gray and hazy monument, and the wind is blowing, a small white scarf floats out of the sky and onto the mountain grass, and he hears sounds of someone climbing off the trail and down to the secret place, and a child appears, a beautiful woman-child. She looks at Iwata and her eyes bulge with surprise. Iwata thinks he recognizes her but no, for she doesn't exist yet. But somehow he does indeed know her. Her image floats in and out of itself, pulsating like a candle flame. She is phantom-person-phantom, changing and changing. Finally she bursts into flames and her sparks shoot off in all directions. The largest flash jumps over the mountain, over the sea, and then over time. But the child is real! She exists. Some day. He knows this somehow.

Iwata awoke with a jolt. Dolsun held him tightly, offering comfort. Then he remembered, the child in the dream looked like Dolsun, and yet it was not her. But Dolsun had been there. Somehow.

Several days earlier Saja had spotted the three strangers as they traveled east to west. They stayed off the main roads and never entered any of the villages except at night when they looked for food. Their meals consisted mainly of eggs, vegetables and dried fish, with an occasional chicken. Their progress was slow but steady. They were making their way toward Iwata's village. Saja guessed they would arrive there in about three or four days. Saja planned to take a better look at them when they came closer. In the meantime, he would enjoy his life. Since returning to Korea, since being blown back from Japan, the fox with the white scarf had talked to him only once, when he instructed him to direct Captain Iwata's makeshift raft toward the Korean coast saving his life. That had been an easy job. He had no idea when the fox would call on him again, but he was ready. As for now, he would keep an eye on the three travelers in the strange looking clothing.

Saja flew to his usual sleeping shelter. There were several nests that Saja called home but this was the one he liked the best. It was on the east side of the mountain, away from the village, and was splashed with the first morning light that sprang out of the mysterious land the fox had called Japan. The trip to and from Japan had brought changes in Saja. By now he should have felt the urge to seek a wife, but no such craving came to him. His life mission had been altered. If he was to have a wife she would come later. Celibacy seemed for the moment natural to his new duties even though so far he wasn't sure what those duties might be.

When the three strangers got closer to the village Saja planned to sleep on the west side of the mountain, facing the village, to be nearer them and Iwata. The idea had just floated into his mind. But he knew it was important and must have come from the fox.

Magical things happened every so often. Sometimes when he was hungry a nice, juicy fat bug might suddenly appear. When he was ready to sleep a soft, fragrant pillow of moss might await his head even though a moment ago it was not there. Sometimes he awoke to the clear and beautiful smell of a flower growing close by, a flower that had not been there the night before. And sometimes an idea would suddenly enter his mind from nowhere, but with the feel of the fox about it. But the fox himself had been absent.

Once again a clump of moss. Once again a nice fat bug with an especially tasty flavor. A snack before retiring. Saja was ready for bed. The sun disappeared and the stars came out. The moon would arrive later. Saja looked into the deep vault of the sky just as a shooting star flew swiftly across the heavens and left, if only for a split second, a gossamer trail. As the webbed string of light disappeared Saja heard a sound he recognized. It was such a soft vibration it almost did not exist. He would not have noticed anything if it had happened before his trip to Japan and back. But now he knew who it was.

A silent paw had stroked the mountain rock near Saja's head. The fox with the white scarf had come for a visit.

"Saja, I am very happy to see you again. And, of course, it is always nice to come over here to your beautiful Korea." The fox spoke slowly and clearly as though he feared he might scare Saja by his sudden appearance. But that was not the case for the fox's appearance made Saja happy, not fearful.

"Yes, Mr. Fox, I am also happy to see you. Since I came back here to my home I've thought quite a bit about our talks in - Japan? - Is that what you called that place? I always have trouble with it, such a funny sounding name. I feel I am now fated to be more important than just being a cuckoo bird."

The fox interrupted before Saja finished his thought. "No, no, Saja. That is not exactly correct. What do you mean just a cuckoo bird? A cuckoo bird, every cuckoo bird, is very important. It is only that your duties have changed. That's it, new duties. But always remember, the duty of being a cuckoo bird is also important. A natural importance.

"And I am here to talk about a duty you must perform. I see you have noticed the three strangers who are traveling across land, east to west, and heading for Captain Iwata's village. The message was at my prompting, no words, a special communication. They will arrive there soon."

The fox paused for a moment and the two animals looked up and watched as yet another shooting star left yet another silver trail across the night sky.

"These three men are good men. They are samurai and they are true to their nature. But Iwata's nature has been altered. He is still a samurai, but his duties have changed. Iwata has a mission even he is not sure of yet. He is to bring to Korea, this wonderful country of yours, the Bushido code. But only a part of the code. Iwata is samurai now, but he is no longer a warrior, no longer a man of the battlefields. Now he is a poet, a warrior of words, and it will be his mission to bring the Bushido code of honor and purity and cleanliness of thought and loyalty and hard work to Korea. But not the killing of the battlefields. You see, Saja, there is good and bad in everything and everyone, even you. There are many kinds of warriors. They do more than fight battles and kill, and their enemies may be more than other warriors. True warriors fight many battles. The battle for good. The battle for beauty. The battle against ugliness and evil."

Saja listened intently. He understood most of the fox's words. But he had questions. "What does this have to do with me? What do you want me to do?"

"The strangers are samurai and Iwata is samurai. They

will try to take him back to Japan with them. And if he refuses to go they will try to kill him, or ask him to kill himself. They call such a thing seppuku. A ceremony of honor ending in death."

The fox's words chilled Saja. The wind stopped. The night birds fell silent. Insects stilled their rubbing legs. Even the stars dampened their twinkling. What is wrong with these humans? Why do they look for ways to push their fellows into unhappiness? Saja remembered the veiled scene at Iwata's secret place. He had stolen a look. Iwata and Dolsun at their secret place making love. Saja was confused. Is it the only happiness for these humans? And he knew he must help Iwata. He thought of Dolsun.

"Yes, Saja, you must help Iwata and Dolsun." The fox with the white scarf had read his mind. "They are one now. Their lives and fates and missions are one. It is up to you, Saja, to warn Iwata not to go with the three samurai, not to go anywhere. Not to go to Japan or up the mountain or anywhere else with them. You will know what to do when the time comes. I will tell you what to do."

No words were needed, no words at all. Thoughts and feelings were enough. And yet the meanings and sensibilities were crystal clear. Saja looked up at the full moon. It had just made its appearance from behind a large, fluffy cloud where it had been hiding since nightfall. When Saja's eyes returned to the mountain ledge the fox was gone.

Nine

Endings

The next morning Iwata and Dolsun arose early. The rosy sun had not yet bloomed. It sat below the eastern horizon. Iwata stirred first. Then Dolsun followed him with jerky, anxious movements. Iwata decided to walk through the village and Dolsun accompanied him. They held hands, walking along in silence, in darkness. Iwata thought about the three strangers who had agreed to join him at the sun's rising. The four of them would climb up the mountain and continue their discussions there. Iwata hoped the beauty of the mountain would influence their decisions. Dolsun sensed his preoccupation. She returned home to make tea and breakfast, leaving him alone on the village path. When she got back home the mudang was waiting for her.

"Daughter. Keep your husband away from the mountain today. There is danger. These strangers didn't come to our village for any good purpose. I feel very strange about this whole matter."

"Mother, there is nothing I can do. My husband will do what he must. I am sick in my heart. But this matter between him and the strangers must reach its own conclusion. The end will come, whatever it is, for happiness or sadness. We must pray. We must wait and see." Dolsun rubbed her teary eyes.

"And Mother, there is more. Last night my husband tried to explain to me what the strangers want from him. He thinks he can satisfy them. He is ready to face them, and I know there is nothing I can do but wait. And I will wait for him. I will wait forever."

Forever. Forever. Forever. It echoed along the village road and up to the mountain. The mudang now knew what the ending would be. Her soul became as heavy as a mountain boulder. She looked away from her daughter because, perhaps, *forever* was written in her eyes and she didn't want Dolsun to see it. After all, she was the daughter of a mudang and had special capabilities.

An interlude came on. Existence paused. Such a thing happened to a mudang from time to time. The mudang wished she could walk into the time-mist, that she could move about rearranging events, even history. But she couldn't for she was bound tightly within a strange stillness and could do nothing.

And when time moved again at its normal pace nothing had changed.

At daybreak the three samurai walked into the village and went directly to Iwata's house. Iwata was there waiting for them. Dolsun peered out from inside the house where her husband had ordered her to remain. He had eaten breakfast with her and afterwards not much was said between them. They gazed deeply at each other and the baby looked through his mother's eyes and saw his father. Three people declaring their love for each other.

The child let his presence be known with a big kick and for a moment, forgetting their troubles, Iwata and Dolsun laughed.

"I will be back, my precious love. Remember this, I love you." He spoke the words in the language of Korea. Then, as though remembering his samurai code, he spoke the same words again, but in Japanese.

The four samurai had been climbing for an hour. When they reached the point along the trail where it passed by the secret place Iwata waved them to a halt. He led them down the slope and through the trees and brush. The three warriors followed him without question even though they thought Iwata was leading them off the edge of the mountain. And several minutes later they were standing on the small plateau and gazing down into the valley below.

Iwata looked in silence, his mind buried in thought. He remembered making love with Dolsun at this very spot, and then looked at the beauty of Korea stretching out before him in three directions, the mountain at his back. He saw the sea in the distance, the sea that had brought him here to a new life, the sea that sent him to Dolsun and her mother. He thought of the battle with the strange turtle ship. It seemed a long time ago. He thought of the young kicking human man-child, his son, living and growing in Dolsun's body.

The four men unpacked their small loads and shared some tea that, by now, had not even a hint of warmth to it. For several minutes they were silent. The wind wept. The peaks above them stood at attention and the valley below waved proudly through the thick air. Iwata hoped the magic of Korea was working its enchantments Then the talking resumed.

And nothing changed.

The three strangers were interested only in the honor of their shogun, the strength of Japan, and the strict honor code of Bushido. The more Iwata presented his case for the universal application of Bushido into lands other than Japan and for disciplines other than war and battle, the more ardent and unmoving the three samurai became.

Several hours later Iwata surrendered to the helplessness of his situation. The only decision to be made was resignation or combat. He stood at attention in front of the three visitors from Japan as they lined up in a straight military rank, the four of them proudly wearing their samurai clothing. But in a neat bundle on the ground behind the men lay a samurai uniform of sparkling white material. The samurai uniform of Death.

Ten

Honor

Two days passed and Iwata did not return home. The mudang said nothing. The abbot Keeyong visited the mudang on the afternoon of the second day of Iwata's absence. She welcomed him more warmly than usual. She needed a friend.

"There is something wrong here. Does it have anything to do with the three strangers?" His question was motivated by concern for his friend. They had their battles but he, like her, thought they were pleasurable battles and added a spice to life. Many times they spoke of matters other than the everyday transactions of life and tongues in cheeks were common to them.

"How do you know about the three strangers? How do you know about matters here in the village, monk? Did you see them in the spinning of your prayer wheel?" Even in her misery she baited her friend.

"No, no. Please. Let me help. Everyone knows about the strangers and their funny clothes and their babbling language. You and I can fight later. But let me help you now."

She glanced over her shoulder. Dolsun was not in sight. A broken dam of emotion burst out of her soul and she cried. The abbot took her in his arms and placed the broad palm of his right hand on her back. The mudang sobbed into his chest sending a small pool of moisture onto his gray monk's robe. Tears for Iwata. Tears for Dolsun. Tears for herself.

She told the abbot the entire story. How Iwata came to the village several years ago, how Iwata became like a son to her, how Dolsun and Iwata fell in love. And now a child living inside Dolsun. She told the abbot about Bushido and about the three samurai. She knew more than Iwata thought she knew. And she told of her own misery.

The abbot thought that the end of her story could only be a sad one, but he didn't tell her that. What he did do was tell her it was time to go up the mountain and look for Iwata. He suggested they leave at once, and without Dolsun. But that was not to be. When Dolsun found the two of them preparing to leave she gave them no choice. If they didn't take her she would go alone, and carrying her baby inside.

The path up the mountain was not as friendly as usual, its beauty unnoticed. And which path should they take, for there were so many possibilities. One wrong choice and the day would be wasted. But Dolsun said, "I can show you where he is. I know where he has taken the three strangers." And of course she was right. Dolsun knew the place where she had given her love to Iwata that first time. Why is it, she thought, that many lives have a focal point on this earth where very important things happen again and again? Giving herself to Iwata was the grandest thing she had ever done. And now the secret place was drawing her once again. But for what? What would she find there? Life or death?

The mudang and the abbot followed Dolsun's instructions without comment. They climbed slower than usual because of the baby. Up the mountain ever so slowly. Onto the trail that moved to the left and along the face of the peak. Then they came to the point where the secret place lay off to the left and down from the trail. Dolsun stopped. She was afraid to move any further. The abbot was surprised when she told him to climb to the left and down. He expected to fall off the mountain, but when he saw the hidden path through the bushes and trees his fear subsided. He grabbed the mudang's hand and pulled her after him. Dolsun did not follow. They paused and looked back at her. She waved them on.

When the two, still holding hands, came upon the hidden plateau, the secret place, the mountain gave a sharp jolt. On the trail above where Dolsun was waiting she too felt the shock. Then another jolt, this time more violent. The mudang let out a weary moan. Dolsun heard her and knew at once what they had found. She climbed down to them as though swimming through a thick, murky pool of water, slow motion, like in a dream, ghostly dream-fish nipping at her legs.

Captain Iwata was on the ground, his face pointing up to the sky. His eyes were closed and his hands were placed across his chest. They saw his clothing, it was different. Not the usual uniform of a Japanese samurai, not the clothes of a Korean man. He had on a pure white tunic and trousers the same. Around his midsection he wore a black waistband, pulled tightly and neatly, no creases spoiling its blackness. A military bearing. An honorable bearing. Two large swords, one on each side, were fastened onto his waistband. A dagger was there, too, its handle sticking proudly out for all the world to see. His hair was braided in the back and hung over his left shoulder and across his chest.

Captain Iwata was a beautiful and honorable samurai warrior even in death.

Dolsun's breathing was slow and labored. She was unable to control the movements of her hands and arms. She collapsed to the mountain grass. Night was approaching but it made no difference. Night and day were the same. She was aware that her mother and the abbot were with her, but they blended into everything else. The mountain, the sky, the mudang, the abbot. All the same, all the same. The universe was gray and cold and damp and sad. Someone was talking to her. Listen! Listen! It might be important. She forced herself to pay attention.

"We must get his body off the mountain. Have some monks come from the temple to help us."

No! No! This is his place. This is our place. He must be buried here.

She heard her own words but didn't know if she had spoken or thought them. But her mother, the mudang, heard them and knew that it must be so.

The abbot, the mudang and Dolsun stayed with Iwata all through the night. The abbot prayed, the mudang sang her ancient bewitchments of sorrow, and Dolsun just sat by Iwata's side, all the while loving and crying and touching his face and hands as though she wanted life to move out of her and into Iwata. Or perhaps, yes, perhaps his death moved into her. It would be acceptable to her either way.

Morning arrived with a whisper that seemed to be apologizing for imposing itself upon the humans. The tendrils of foggy mist were not the same as on other mornings, for they lay flat, hugging the earth, trying not to disturb the sorrow of the secret place.

The abbot realized there were things to be done. Iwata could not be unattended indefinitely. He went down the trail and then doubled back up to the temple where he met with two monks, picking his closest friends, and after swearing them to secrecy, brought them back with him. They buried Captain Iwata there - at the secret place - in a deep, deep grave with a mound of earth piled above it as is the tradition of the Korean people. Dolsun knew he loved Korea, and it was a good thing to do.

On the morning that the three strangers approached the village Saja was up early, but that was not unusual for a cuckoo bird. He sat on the edge of his aerie (he always called any nest of the moment an aerie since his childhood with the eagle family) and looked down. As the fox suggested, he had slept on the west side of the mountain, the side facing the village. From there he watched the three strangers getting closer and closer. He awaited the fox's instructions. In the meantime, there was a fat, delicious looking bug begging to become his breakfast. Saja never questioned these fine culinary surprises. He ate the bug.

He saw the three men enter the village and he saw them sitting all day with Iwata. They were talking and talking. When night came the three strangers climbed a mile or so up the mountain and made camp for the night. The next morning Saja sat there thinking and waiting. No message yet from the fox. Later, the wind gusted in a most extraordinary pattern. It rushed toward the side of the mountain and then, just before it smacked against the rock, veered straight up to the sky without touching the rock face. Most unusual. Its velocity increased as it moved upwards. Saja knew this kind of wind would send him soaring higher than he had ever soared before. Perhaps he could ride this wind. He thrilled at the thought. But what about the fox? Should he wait for a message from the fox? What about just a little flight? When the fox sent his message he could quickly return to earth.

Saja jumped off the face of the mountain and in a second was shooting up at a faster speed than ever before. The swiftness of his ascent increased and before he knew what was happening the mountain became a small bump on the face of the earth. The wind was driving him faster and faster, up, up. And now he was even above the clouds. The sky was bathed in strong sunlight. Saja had never been this high before, not even on his trip to Japan. He tilted his wings and soared back and forth, content, but afraid to go higher. He forgot about Iwata and the three strangers.

The voice of the fox came to Saja.

Hurry, Saja! Hurry, Saja! Stop your playing. You must return to Captain Iwata at once! He is in grave danger. Stop him from going up the mountain with the three samurai. Stop him! Stop him! There is grave danger! There is death!

Saja dove. As he raced down a jolt of force smacked into him, and then a second, the same that were hitting the secret place. When he reached the village Iwata was nowhere to be found. He became desperate and circled the village again and again hoping Iwata might magically appear in one of the places where he had already searched. He became sick in his stomach. But he kept circling and circling the village, Iwata's house, the paddies, the mudang's house, the roads, the cemetery, over and over. Voices came to him.

Poor Saja, poor Saja. Now redemption is necessary. No matter years nor centuries, no matter time. Redemption is needed. Brother, we love you. We are sorry for you. But redemption is needed. You have failed your mission. Foolish bird.

A month later the three of them met again at the secret place, Dolsun, the mudang and the abbot. The abbot had made an obelisk and they placed it above the grave. There was writing on one of its sides and the abbot carefully placed that side facing southward so that the strong northwest wind would not wear upon its surface. The message on the monument was unadorned. Dolsun had insisted on that. It said,

Captain Iwata, Samurai Warrior
and Poet, Loved by Dolsun.

There was no date on the stone because Dolsun said she would love Iwata forever and that his death ended nothing.

Many years later and after hundreds of trips up the mountain to the secret place, Saja finished adding several characters to the obelisk. He had to do the job over a long period of time or his poor beak would have been worn away. The calligraphy was not artistic, but its simple message was plain to see.

I am sorry, Saja the Cuckoo.

Eleven

Samurai

The samurai Iwata lies on the mountain in his samurai uniform with his Bushido code intact. His white blouse and pants, death's glory, glisten in the sunshine and his black sash adds sparkle. Soft, fleecy clouds rub the blue of the sky as though wiping tears away. The wind whips a sad dirge along the edge of the mountain, its music rearing and bucking above the secret place. Insects stop rubbing their legs and birds stop singing. A lone wild boar climbing on the mountain above the sad field of death looks across the valley toward another string of mountains and sees three men crossing an arete. He fears for his blood. The three men are heading toward the east where the Sea of Japan waits for them. They are dressed in samurai clothing. Swords hang at their sides. They walk along the trail with the jaunting motion of warriors and yet with sad ghosts of lost comrades lingering about. A sound comes on - more sadness - a wind roaring across the arete with a melancholy voice. As it hits them they drop to their knees to keep from falling off the mountain.

A few days later the three men arrive at the great sea.

In their minds' eyes they see Japan sitting past the horizon, past the rising sun. Home. Their shogun waits for them. And their women also wait.

A Korean fisherman discovers his boat is missing and blames a neighbor whom he had fought with earlier in the week after a night of drinking hot rice wine. His friend swears he knows nothing of the missing boat. Perhaps the boat became untied and drifted out to sea. They wonder if it will drift all the way to Japan. And the matter is soon forgotten.

"History may judge us harshly but Bushido is the only way. The world is madness. Bandits roam our countryside and pirates sail our seas. Foreigners want to pollute our Japan with their mysterious ways and their strange religion of weakness. And they want our women. Even our Buddha cannot save us. Some of our citizens don't believe in him anyway. They just accept the Buddha as a social tradition. Others do believe but they constantly fight among themselves as variations of faith come and go, change upon change. And if you read the pure words of the Buddha he is saying that nothing matters anyway. Of course, if that shade of meaning became universal, the Buddha himself would be our downfall. But those thoughts will not prevail. We are too selfish for that.

"Only our Bushido code saves us. If one grain of Bushido is broken our nation will collapse into chaos, an end to Japan, yes, Japan will die. Iwata was not meant to be that fallen grain.

"I loved Captain Iwata, and I still love him. But now I love him even more. He chose to die for Japan, and for his shogun. You three warriors did well. You laid him down on the mountain in his white samurai garments of death and put his swords at his side. Thank you."

The three men listened intently to their shogun. At his "thank you" they were driven to tears. A shogun seldom said such words to his samurai. They did their duty to him and Japan and that was reward enough. Nothing had to be spoken. But now their tears came because they felt the shogun's love for Iwata, a man who was a Japanese samurai, a warrior, to the very end of his life. A man who had calmly met his death for Bushido, for Japan, for his shogun, for the life of the nation, and at the cost of his personal happiness.

The shogun continued. "I tell you this. No! I order you, do not talk about this matter. Not to anyone. This also is Bushido. Silence. Now go back to your duties. Love Japan and your shogun. You are samurai!"

Shogun Yeyasu sat alone after the three samurai left the room. He instructed his servants not to disturb him for anything or anyone, not even the emperor himself.

Yeyasu had never known Iwata personally and had only met him at a few military meetings here and there. But he knew all about him. He knew of his intelligence and leadership. He knew of his fighting skills. His predecessor, Shogun Hideyoshi, often had spoken of Iwata as a father speaks of a son.

Yeyasu looked across the room and out the sliding doors that led to a verandah. The doors were open permitting the sweet morning air to enter. The mountain loomed beyond and was so close that seeing the summit from the room was impossible for only a blanket of green filled the space created by the open doors. Yeyasu's mind drifted away from Captain Iwata and the three samurai.

All he could see was greenery but he knew that under the emerald blanket lived millions of living things, small animals, large animals, birds flying around in the sky and insects buzzing in the ground and trees and air. Were some of them the animal equivalent of samurai? Did they have an animal shogun? An animal emperor? Was their society as complicated as Japan? Had they created an animal Bushido to defend it?

Oh, if I could walk away from it and climb up the mountain and leave China and Korea and all the rest of Asia behind, even Japan, and forget the battles and the decisions and the deaths on the fields and seas of war. If only I could live with the simple animals of the mountain, large and small, and see for myself if their Bushido is simpler, perhaps even better, purer, than ours. No soldiers. No monks. No shoguns. No emperor.

Iwata, what pain you have caused me.

Then the powerful shogun, leader of samurai, turned his mind back to Iwata. The man had indeed transferred his loyalties to other people and to another country. But he asked the three samurai to tell the shogun that Bushido could live on, that he had changed his loyalties because that is where life led him and where love awaited him. And that he had not done it at the expense of Japan or his shogun. They would always be a part of him, but a part that existed in his past and not his present. He would still love them and never do them harm by word or deed. But they were in his past. A cherished memory. His Bushido was undamaged.

It was Iwata's original intention to fight the three visitors. He knew Bushido would order them to fight him one at a time, not all together, but warrior to warrior. He had a chance. A chance for a new life with Dolsun, a new life in Korea.

He shouted out to them. "I will fight!"

But the conclave at the secret place changed everything. Iwata understood the importance of Bushido to the civilization of Japan, to the life of Japan, to the future of Japan. Iwata realized that even though he thought himself loyal, even though he saw no immorality or treachery in his actions, even though the happiness of Dolsun and his unborn child was at stake, there was really only one answer. There was only one decision to make. The Bushido of Japan must be protected. It must be kept intact. As for Dolsun, she deserved a noble husband, a loyal knight. And that is what he would be. To die for his friends, to die for Japan, to maintain his honor, that would be the greatest gift he could leave his son. But the thought of leaving Dolsun almost overpowered him. He must act quickly before changing his mind.

Iwata did not really fight. It was more of a ritual. They killed him and then lay him down on the soft grass of the secret place. The grass was lush, dark green, with heavy blades that bent into semi-circles as they grew out of the mountain earth, their coiling shapes giving a spring to the grass that seemed to raise Iwata slightly off the surface of the mountain. But it was just an illusion.

They took off his multicolored samurai uniform, washed his blood-stained body, and dressed him in the white garments of an honorable death. For he was an honorable samurai warrior. Very carefully and with reverence they placed his swords at his sides. They fixed his hair in the manner of a samurai. And they left him there in the open air for his loved ones to find, and to bury.

The three hardened warriors, men who had killed often in battle, quietly cried. They saluted a fallen comrade and turned away. They left the secret place, but a part of Japan remained.

Turning toward the rising sun, toward Japan, they traveled to the east, to the sea, to their shogun, to home.

Twelve

1945

Japan

The little girl ambled along the dirt path. She was very pretty and every passerby gave her a glance and a smile. One old man even stopped her, picked her up and gave her a hug and a kiss. She was hard to resist. Her new silk dress had many colors, making her look like a small, walking rainbow, and her round face and chubby body singing and dancing, her dark eyes wide and sparkling. She looked like a baby doll.

"Sunae, Sunae. I bet I know where you are going, to visit your grandmother, right?" The old man knew her well for Sunae took this short walk down the village path almost every day. Halmoni - Grandmother - would be waiting patiently, looking out her window, hoping to see her coming down the road. Sunae looked at the old man. She knew the village people liked her and her family. It was a pleasant home for a child. The Japanese people living in this part of Japan didn't have as strong a prejudice against Koreans that existed in other areas of the country. For in Japan Koreans were not treated as full citizens. The law said they were, but that didn't matter.

Sunae's Father had relocated from Korea to Japan when he was a teenager. And now he had his own family. Sunae's mother was Japanese.

Japan had been at war for Sunae's entire young life, first in China and now with America and England. But for a six year old girl the war was remote, something her mother and father whispered about at night. The big American bombers flew over the city of Kuré quite often but never dropped a bomb. They were on their way to Tokyo.

Kuré was located on a natural harbor in the inland sea. Mountains arose into the sky both north and east of the city. Sunae's small village was on the slope of one of these mountains. It looked down at Kuré and the whole scene was like a painting of the beauty of Japan, except that it was real. The people of the area, both Japanese and Korean, were mostly Buddhist. They believed in the power of karma as an all powerful force in the universe. Most of them were stoic about the great war thinking it inevitable, caused by things from the distant past, a national karma. And because of their strong belief in karma they were called "the people of bowing" for they bowed stoically at many things that happened to them, good or bad.

For a small child in Japan in the early 1940's, life was almost normal, but not completely so. In school they were taught that the Americans were horrible barbarians and that to become an American marine you had to kill your mother and father. And so the war was justified. For

Japan and all of Asia had to be saved from these western devils.

Sadly, the war was not as remote for the children of Tokyo. They were bombed regularly. The children of Kuré, however, were more concerned with school and family life. Father had a good job at an electronics plant. He came home only a few days every month. Sunae missed him when he was gone. But she had Mother and Sister and, just down the village road, Halmoni, her grandmother. Father's engineering education, and the fact that he was Korean, had so far kept him out of the Japanese army. The family thought this was wonderful and except for the war and Father's long absences life was fine.

Hiroshima, the city where Father worked, a larger city than Kuré, lay thirty miles to the northwest. Hiroshima was the center of Japan's electronics industry and an important part of the war effort. While Kuré was never bombed by the Americans Hiroshima was attacked several times. Hiroshima's people lived in fear that someday their city would receive the same treatment as Tokyo. They prepared by crisscrossing the city with fire walls and hoped they would never be needed. They waited and prayed.

"Oh, Sunae, my precious baby, my angel. Hurry inside. I have a special treat for you, honey and rice cakes." Sunae's face grew rounder with a big fat smile that puffed out her rosy cheeks even more. She ran up the path and flew into Halmoni's arms. Her mother would scold her later for eating too many of the cakes, but that was later, and now she was with Halmoni. She must not make Halmoni sad, she must eat as many cakes as possible. It was her karmic duty to do so.

When Sunae returned home Sister and Mother were in the kitchen preparing the evening meal. "Sunae, why did you stay so long with Halmoni? And I know you ate too much. If you ruined your dinner I'm going to make you go to bed early." Mother was not in a good mood. The two girls decided to be extra careful.

Mother continued. "And another thing, stop speaking in Korean so often. It's bad enough that some people don't like Koreans. You don't have to keep reminding them where Father comes from." Mother had met her husband in Kuré when he was a young engineering student there, and they had fallen in love. It was a good marriage but, once in a while, Mother remembered that most of the Japanese people were not as tolerant as she was when it came to the Koreans.

The land was enchanted. In the mornings, especially the early mornings, it was said that magical things happened. The children believed the tales of magic related by the old people. Halmoni told the story of a magic fox who could speak human words, but only to the little ones. Halmoni said the fox wore a white scarf to show everyone that he was no ordinary animal, but a magical fox. Mr. Fox traveled around Japan and let himself be seen now and again, but only by the children. It was said that only the children were innocent enough for this fox.

One morning Sunae was peering out the window of the house. Soon she would walk down the road to visit Halmoni, so she checked to see if the weather was wet or dry. How should she dress? She could decide such things for herself. She was a big girl.

Mist was hanging on top of the ground but it disappeared at the edge of the forest beyond the road. Was there magic here? Suddenly a face appeared through the thick underbrush. Sunae rubbed her eyes. Was she dreaming?

It was a fox. And he wore a white scarf.

Sunae ran out of the house and to the very edge of the forest. The fox with the white scarf looked at her and she looked at him. He yawned just as cats and dogs do from time to time, although he was a fox. Sunae's eyes almost popped out of her head. She spoke to him.

"Hello, Mr. Fox." She could think of nothing else to say. After all, what do you say to a fox wearing a white scarf?

The fox continued looking at her. "Yes, you are the one. You are the one I have come to visit. I have something to tell you." He spoke in Korean much to Sunae's astonishment. After all, he was a Japanese fox. Then she remembered that he was also a magic fox according to Halmoni.

"Sunae, I want you to know that you are very beautiful. But that is not the least bit important. What is important is that you must be beautiful inside. Your soul must be beautiful. That is all I have to say. Good-bye. Good-bye. I'll visit you again some day."

Such an abrupt message! The fox with the white scarf who spoke Korean jumped up and - in midair - turned completely around before his paws hit the ground. He bounded into the forest and was gone.

No one believed Sunae when she told them what had happened.

One morning Sunae was alone at home. Mother and Sister were at the market. They would be gone for a short time. She pretended she was the mistress of the house. She could do anything she wanted, and what she wanted to do was eat something sweet. And what is sweeter than sugar? Mother kept the sugar in a large jar on a shelf that ran the length of one side of the kitchen. It was too high for Sunae to reach. But if she got a chair? Yes, that would do it. One more glance out the window and down the path to make sure Mother and Sister were not in sight gave Sunae the courage she needed. But even with the chair under her small feet she could just barely reach the large jar. After a struggle she finally grasped it in her chubby hands. The jar was much heavier than Sunae had thought. The chair wobbled beneath her and she lost her balance. She hit the floor and the jar of sugar flew into the air, the lid popping off and the sugar flying out. Sugar, sugar everywhere! But most of it landed on top of Sunae. The fall to the ground didn't do her any harm. Her chubby little behind, a good pillow, saved her. She was fine. But there she was sprawled across the floor covered with sugar!

At that moment Mother walked into the kitchen with Sister. At first they were concerned for Sunae's safety. It didn't take long to see that she was not harmed. Then Mother got angry.

"Sunae, you are a bad girl. What shall I do with you? Is this what your Halmoni has taught you?" Mother picked little Sunae up into her arms, checked one more time for injuries, and when she saw that there were none turned her over and gave her several whacks on her fat rear cheeks. Sunae cried. But her tears were those of disappointment in getting caught and having no sugar to eat, and not tears of sorrow or contrition. As for Halmoni, she gave Sunae an extra portion of honey rice cakes the very next day, just to make up for the lost sugar.

The American bombers flew over Kuré on their way to Tokyo. Sometimes the planes came in so low that the children imagined they saw the pilots peering at them out of the cockpits. "Look! The Americans are like animals. They have horns and their skins are like leather and their noses are elephant noses. And look, they have tails!" The children acted bravely. They knew the American pilots were way up there in the sky and couldn't possibly hear them.

One day a plane was shot down near the village and the pilot captured alive. The soldiers paraded their prisoner through the village on their way to the army base at Kuré. The children raced out to see this monster. Oh, they were so brave! This was as close as most of them would get to the war, except for those families who lost sons. But to their surprise the American looked human. No horns, no tail. The children were disappointed. Sunae had run down the road with the rest of the children. As she stood there on the pavement the American came by surrounded by his Japanese captors. He was dirty and there was blood on his shirt. But his eyes sparkled and his teeth were as white as snow. He looked down at Sunae and winked. She was crying and Kwinam, her sister, lifted her up and hugged her tightly. They rushed home. Halmoni was waiting for them and in an instant she broke the American's evil spell.

"Halmoni. What will happen to the American? Will he come back this way again?"

"Why, little angel, do you want to see him again, is that it?" Halmoni spoke tenderly to Sunae, her voice giving security to the child. It is the same as when, at a young age, you are half asleep in the bedroom but can hear your parents talking quietly in the next room. It is a wonderful feeling. Love and safety.

"No, Halmoni, not that. But he didn't look like an animal to me. He looked afraid. What will they do to him? Will they hurt him?"

Mother had been listening to the conversation silently. Finally she said, "Child, the American pilot is not our concern. I am sure that for him the war is now over. That's not so bad, is it? Someday, after the war, maybe you will meet an American. But be careful of them for if they can bomb the people of Tokyo they may not be too nice. Be careful of them. Father will be home in a few days, and now we have an interesting story for him."

"Mom, please let me tell Father about the American winking at me. Let me tell Father that, please. I'm not afraid anymore." Sunae hugged Halmoni a little harder, just in case.

Thump! Thump! Thump! The thumps were coming up from deep in earth. It was a little after eight in the morning. Everyone in the village felt the thumps. They were somehow different than a regular earth tremor. Deeper, sadder. Minutes later the wind blew strongly out of the northwest. It came into the village, swirling and stopping and moving and churning, and making a very strange noise. At first it was quiet, a soft whistle, but then louder and louder. It began shouting! It was a Japanese wind, but as it sailed through the village it spoke Korean.

Ssaammaanngg, Ssaammaanngg, Ssaammaanngg.

It was quite clear to Mother and Halmoni. Samang. The Korean word for death.

Sunae was visiting Halmoni when the first thumps

came. Dishes shook on the shelves and the walls shuddered. Chickens in the front yard cackled with fear and the village dogs barked. Cows mooed. Pigs squealed. Birds stopped singing. Then the wind came and the house rattled once again. Halmoni listened carefully to what the wind was saying. Sunae asked her, "What is it?" But Halmoni didn't answer.

After twenty minutes the wind stopped. Silence dropped on the village like a heavy wet blanket. The silence terrified Sunae and she cried. Halmoni tried to comfort her, but failed for her own fears were too great. Slowly the people gathered at the center of the village and just stood there, no one speaking. When talk did begin, it was quiet and subdued. Then someone turned on a radio and they listened to a special news broadcast from Tokyo. A very large bomb had destroyed the entire city of Hiroshima. One bomb, one airplane, had done it. Halmoni squeezed her grandchild so tightly that Sunae gasped for air. Mother and Halmoni were crying and moaning, as were many others. If Hiroshima was totally destroyed then what about Father? For that's where he worked.

Destruction and death. Thump, thump, thump, and the wind spoke. "Samang, samang." The war became real for Sunae and the other small children in the village.

There was never a funeral for Father. A sad ceremony at the temple was all for there was no body. He simply disappeared off the face of the earth.

Soon the war was over. But for Mother and Halmoni, for Sunae and Sister, things got worse, not better. Peace came, but without Father. He was gone. Japan was a defeated nation. Many cities had been devastated by fire bombs. People were missing. Destruction and death and unemployment were common conditions.

The Americans came. They were not the monsters Sunae's teachers had talked about, but they were still conquerors, and the villagers felt as humiliated as the rest of the nation. But for the Koreans living in Japan the end of the war gave them a choice. Korea now had independence from Japan for the first time since 1910. Many Korean families decided to return to their homeland, to become once again fully Korean. Others, feeling Japanese after so many years, decided to stay in Japan.

A family meeting was held. The Korean side of the family was represented by Sunae's uncles and cousins with Halmoni having a major voice. Mother was the strongest presence from the Japanese side. The discussions lasted into the night. The Korean side wanted to go, but the Japanese side wanted them to stay. Finally thousands of years of oriental civilization and culture prevailed. A father was the blood! A family belonged with a father's blood. And for Sunae's family the blood and veins were in Korea.

And it was decided, Sunae, Sister and Mother would go to Korea to be with Father's family. They would be welcome there. But Halmoni was old. Her son had brought her with him when he came to Japan, and now she was a widow and didn't want to start over again in a country that would bring her hardship. She was too old for that. Korea was her homeland, but that was a long time ago. She decided to remain in Japan.

Halmoni anguished for days thinking of separation from Sunae and Kwinam. But she realized that the family's plans were not going to change. Her son's homeland was the proper place for his daughters. Preparations were made, possessions packed and letters written. Halmoni cursed the war that had caused her to lose her son, and now her grandchildren.

Mother put on a brave face and acted as the leader of her family. She didn't want her children to feel her fear and apprehension. She was Japanese and really didn't know what to expect in Korea, but she also felt the children belonged in Father's country and the family would have ended up there sooner or later, war or no war.

They left for Korea in a sea of tears and sorrow.

Thirteen

Pusan

First moments. Terror and despair. Hopelessness. Emptiness. Gloom. Desperation. But such feelings can pass quickly for a child and the joy of childhood return. As a small girl - spawn of happiness - is sure it will.

I remember the small details but not the big ones. The name of the ship is gone from my memory but I remember the grain of the wood on the benches that were placed on deck to accommodate an overflow crowd and give us fresh air. I remember the foggy morning breath that came out of my mouth. I remember the colors of the Korean clothes I wore. I remember the reds and the blues and the whites and the greens. I remember eating cold rice on a windy deck and watching a foamy sea.

Halmoni insisted that we wear Korean clothes and not Japanese, and I remember her saying, "You are going to a new country, your country, and you must wear Korean clothes. You are finished with Japan." Halmoni was crying as the ship tooted its horn telling us it was time to leave. I remember a tear rolling down her cheek and how silvery it looked against her wrinkles, but I don't remember what day it was. Monday? Tuesday?

I remember my grandmother crying. Childhood memories can be so precise when it comes to small details. I look back now, back to that day that may have been the most important of my life and remember the colors of clothes and a lonely tear flowing down my grandmother's cheek and the grain of the wood on the ship's benches. Even today, when the weather turns cold and steamy ghosts are created by my breath, I feel the ship rolling under my feet those many years ago when I was eight years old and on my way to the country of my dead father. In my mind I am once again with Mother and my older sister, Kwinam, sailing across the Sea of Japan into an early autumn swell. How long was the voyage? I don't remember. But I do remember the thin, tiny wooden boxes that held our lunches and I remember the shining silver skin of the small fishes and the whiteness of the rice in those boxes.

Our first look at Korea was in the early evening - that's when the ship sailed into Pusan harbor. And what I remember most is a million small fires scattered over the hills behind the harbor, sparks of light dancing like fireflies, the flaming tongues climbing up the hills and back down into the valleys. We could smell the woody smoke as our ship approached the dock. Later, we knew that the fires were really many families cooking their meals out in the open, families like our family who had no place to go, waiting for someone to show up looking for them, waiting for something, anything, to happen.

Then the ship stopped and we were told to disembark. The three of us clutched our documents and our small satchels and we were pushed down the corrugated sheets of metal that acted as a gangplank. I remember the smell of the metal and the sea salt mixed together. We had been told by the sailors to leave our bigger bags and boxes on the ship and to come back for them after we cleared customs. I don't remember the details of this but I was told the story many times by Sister. I don't remember everything that happened next, only some of it.

When we set foot on Korean soil everything changed. The orderliness of our past Japanese village life changed. People were running everywhere and going nowhere. Babies were crying and men were fighting. There were no government agents to greet us and ask for our documents. No one to tell what to do or where to go. It was impossible to return to the ship. Everyone was pushing and yelling and grabbing. I lost my small bag and the papers that were in it. We soon forgot our papers and our bags and simply tried to stay together. If we separated it might be impossible to find each other again. The scene was a riot of humanity, the crowd moving first this way and then that way with no apparent purpose or destination.

The mob had moved us against our will to a point about half a mile from the ship, but we were still together. At least we had that. We hugged and grabbed at each other in desperation. Then we heard the ship's horn blaring out once again. The mob stopped for a moment and an eerie silence hit us, and we could hear our own breathing. Suddenly a rougher noise came on. It started with a murmur and got stronger and stronger. Everyone was yelling and screaming. The human river had stopped moving and now turned around.

The ship was leaving, and taking our bags and boxes

with it.

The mob immediately realized what was happening and turned, now flowing back down the road, back toward the ship. We were carried with it. We had no choice. I remember a cold sweat racing over my body and sharing my panic with Mother and Sister. Whenever I remember the terror in Mother's eyes and Sister's sad crying I have to steady myself even though it happened so many years ago.

The next few minutes are a blur, both then as it was happening and now in my memory as I try to think about it. We had lost everything but the clothes we wore. Our trunks and bundles were sailing out to sea, and far from our reach. But we were not alone. A common groan of misery and despair was rising out of a thousand mouths.

We wandered several miles from the dock area, walking as if drugged. Night came on with a cold and clammy stillness that I can also remember as if it were only yesterday. Again, small details so clear, large things, important things, so murky. The first pangs of hunger reminded us that we had no money, no notion of where to go, and no idea of what to do next. Ahead of us lay an open field that smelled like cattle and hay. But no cows and no people in sight. There were some empty metal drums scattered about. Mother and Sister pushed several of the drums into a small circle and we sat inside their metal ring. Our roof was the black night sky. We huddled together as closely as we could and the cold night air was made warmer by our pressing against each other. The wind seemed to know of our discomfort and decided not to blow. Mother started to cry. And the three of us simply went to sleep. Easy for me, a child, but more difficult for Mother and Sister.

The fox with the white scarf came to me from over the sea, all the way from Japan, all the way to Korea. He came over the top of the empty metal drums and stood beside me. Mother and Sister were sleeping and the sound of their heavy breathing is clear in my memory. Waaa, waaa. Waaa, waaa. I remember that the sounds gave me comfort and I forgot about our troubles as I listened. The fox looked at me with big, black eyes that sparkled with the light of the moon and the stars even though the night was ebony black. And, just as in Japan, he spoke to me in Korean.

"Well, here you are, little Miss Sunae, my love, my delight. Things look pretty bad, don't they? But it is all passing. Troubles come and go, yes, they come and go, come and go. But listen. Mother and Sister are sleeping so soundly. Hear how heavy they are breathing. Now, do you think they could sleep so well if they were worried about tomorrow? And now you too, Sunae my joy, go to sleep, and tomorrow will take care of itself."

Just as he had done on the Japanese mountainside the fox jumped up and darted into the black night. He was gone. I blinked my eyes and the dust of a moon that was still out of sight blew down and put me to sleep.

Morning. I awoke and realized I was hungry. But Mother and Sister were still sleeping, so I closed my eyes again. A voice came from beyond the drums.

"Hey, what is this? Three fine ladies in such beautiful clothes sleeping in my field and hiding behind my empty drums."

La, la, la, la, la, la. Up and down, up and down. The voice spoke Korean with the same lilting tones as Halmoni, and the same as I did since my grandmother was my teacher. (I realized later that this was the accent of Father's province, his home sounds.) The man was young. Perhaps five or six years older than Sister. But to me, a child of eight, he was definitely a man.

The stranger moved one of the drums aside and towered over the three of us as we lay huddled together on the ground. We were all awake by now as he looked down at us bending forward and examining us closer. I remember him as being the roughest looking fellow I had ever seen. He had a face that was as dark as a sun-burnt log and his hands were marked with the signs of hard work. His nails were dirty and his breath, as he got closer to us, smelled like last night's rice wine mixed with tobacco. I remember thinking at the time that he was a rather ugly guy.

But I was a bold child. I said, "Mother. I'm hungry. Please ask uncle where we can get some food." I referred to the man as my uncle, a customary Korean politeness.

"Hush Sunae, have some manners. First we have to introduce ourselves." Mother spoke in Japanese for that was more natural to her. As had happened several times on the ship, Sister proceeded to translate Mother's words into Korean, but her Korean came out with a heavy Japanese accent. I laughed and repeated what Sister said in perfect Korean and, better yet, with the same lilting singsong of the stranger which I somewhat overdid. Looking back, I hope he didn't think I was mocking him. But perhaps I was.

The man reached down and patted me on the top of my head. "Well, what do we have here? A little angel who speaks Korean with an accent like she has lived in my home province her whole life. You just may be the perfect translator we need."

It was love at first sight. I immediately liked this sort-of-ugly stranger. And he magically became handsome in my eyes. And as I looked up at him my stomach growled so loud that the man heard it and laughed. He said, "Is that another ship coming in or is it time for breakfast? Come on ladies, let's get some food."

That is the story of how we met the Cowman.

The restaurant was a dismal place. Its floor was simply hard packed dirt and the table a metal drum similar to the ones we had used for our shelter but with a sheet of plywood for a tabletop. In spite of all that, the food was a real feast. Steaming rice and a hot soup made with small bits of beef and bean sprouts, and kimchi, two different kinds. One kimchi was made of fresh radishes with the greens still attached. It's called "bachelors' kimchi" because it's easy to make, even by a lone man, and another the daikon kimchi that is a staple at most Korean meals. I ate like a little pig and that made the Cowman happy. Mother and Sister also ate their fill, but with more refinement. It had been over twenty-four hours since the three of us had eaten. Every time the Cowman looked at Sister she placed her hand delicately in front of her mouth, the universal act of feminine shyness in Korea and Japan, but one that women can also use to send silent signals to a lover. Later, later. But of course, that was not Sister's reason for she was simply shy. I remember the Cowman glancing at her quite a few times.

His real name was Yi Jongsu. Mr. Yi. But he told us that everyone called him the Cowman. Mother and Sister were quite surprised to hear his name was Yi. Our Korean family name was also Yi. But the Japanese didn't let us use our Korean surnames and gave us a Japanese one. To them, I was Miss Iwata. But I guess they considered only surnames important for they never bothered me about my given Korean name. I was Sunae Iwata.

The hot barley tea that came with our food made us feel a lot better and Mother and Sister began telling our stories. Father's death at Hiroshima made the Cowman frown. He listened intently and clicked his tongue several times as a sign of his concern. Now and again his eyes flashed to Sister and every time he did this she not only covered her mouth but also looked down at the floor. Double modesty!

Mr. Yi - or Yi Jongsu - or the Cowman - we could decide later what to call him, told us about himself.

"I am from a small village but my cattle business takes me all over the land, even up to Taejon, Suwon and even Seoul. My father was in the cattle business, that is, he bought and sold cows, a broker, we are not farmers. It was a good way to make a living and the Japanese didn't bother us. I guess they needed our cows to feed their soldiers. I hear that up north, in Seoul, they bothered the women a lot, but not down here in the south. At least not in my village. We seldom saw a Jap.

"Anyway, my father died suddenly last year and I am the only son. So you see, as young as I am, I am now running the business, and doing very well, thank you. In fact, I am expanding my company. That field you slept in last night, I own it. It's used as a marketplace for cows when I bring them down to Pusan from up north. Three days ago you would not have been able to sleep there. We were very busy and there were cows all over the place. As you noticed, their smell remains. And where are you fine people going?"

Mother answered, "My husband's family village is somewhere northwest of here, perhaps a hundred miles or more, I'm not sure. I sent letters that we were coming, but I guess they never got them. Now I know why. This country is in turmoil."

"No, no. It's not as bad everywhere as it is here. This city was always crazy, even before the war, what with the sailors coming in and out. And the Japanese Navy added to the foolishness. Now the regular people who live here, the Koreans, have caught the same madness. It's contagious."

When Mother asked about his home village he answered, "My village is Daebong-Dong, a long drive from here. And what is the name of yours?"

When Mother told him the name of her husband's home village the Cowman opened his mouth and we got a good look at his long white teeth. They made his face appear longer than when his mouth was closed. He looked like a horse. He should have been called the Horse Man.

"Your village is just about three miles from my home. We are neighbors. And with a name like Yi, why, we might be cousins. But I hope not." As he said this he looked long and hard at Sister. She blushed a deep red.

Mother commented that the chances of our being related were very slim even though we shared the name Yi. There just aren't that many surnames in Korea. The most common one, Kim, is held by forty-two percent of the population. And Yi is the second most common. The names go back thousands of years. But each name has many clans. If the name is the same but the clan is different there is no family connection. In fact, later we learned that the Cowman was indeed from another clan and not a relative of ours at all.

"I will take you to your village. No arguments accepted. It is my duty to the royal house of Yi. Now let's go to a bathhouse and wash up." And looking quickly at Sister he added, "Separately, of course. We are not Japanese here. We are ladies and gentlemen. We bathe separately. After our baths I'll finish my business and we can be on our way home."

Mother said softly, "We have no money. We lost everything."

The Cowman looked quite handsome in spite of his horse teeth. He said, "And now you have me."

Fourteen

The Village

The village was nestled between two mountains whose peaks and ridges looked like swirls of green and brown paint rubbed onto a canvas with the heavy trowel of an impressionist. The highest peak guarded the village's thatched roof houses and stone walls on one side while the other, almost as tall, defended the other side. Animals - pigs, chickens, cows, dogs, cats - roamed about freely or lived in pens. It was similar to hundreds of other Korean villages. Almost every home had a father who was a rice farmer, the luckier ones possessing an ox to help in the fields and paddies. But those without a working beast didn't complain and did the extra work themselves, or a friendly neighbor with an ox helped. And at the time when the rice seedlings were placed in the communal seedling paddies, and then again when the seedlings were transplanted into the regular paddies, the whole village - men, women and children - worked together as a village, some of the women with babies strapped to their backs. Although their lives were filled with hard work the people were happy. Weather and the growing season, health and sickness, birth and death, marriage and babies - these were the things that mattered most.

The Cowman had hired a taxi to travel to the village. The ride from Pusan was hours long and the road bumpy. And in spots, no road existed at all. Several times an army truck forced the taxi to leave the narrow road and wait in a field or dry paddy while the truck passed by. In the area near Pusan soldiers were everywhere, some still wearing parts of their old Japanese uniforms and others with their new Korean uniforms starched and pressed, and mixed with American army shirts and pants that were invariably too big for their Korean bodies. But as the taxi got further away from Pusan fewer soldiers were seen for the great war that the Americans called WWII was now over. Korea was free, the Japanese gone, and the only reason for a new Korean army was because the Americans said one might be necessary some day. But most of the people just wanted to get on with their lives, the farmers simply wanting to work their rice paddies and have babies and live as Korean rural people had done for thousands of years. Armies and kings came and went but their lives remained the same.

The taxi finally arrived at its destination. As it entered the village it was greeted by a throng of children who followed it into the village square. They ran along the rutted road even faster than the taxi could drive, laughing and yelling with excitement as they greeted the travelers. The taxi stopped and out tumbled the Cowman and three ladies dressed in fancy, if somewhat wrinkled, clothes. Mother, Sister and Sunae had arrived. The driver, who by now thought that he was a member of the family, sat for a brief moment inside the taxi. But then he, too, got out and set his feet onto the dust of the village street. Unpaved and dusty as it was. By now the crowd was more than children. For a taxi pulling into the village was not a common thing and several farmers, both women and men, walked in from the closest paddies to see what was going on.

The news of visitors quickly reached the mayor's house and mayor Yi, who had been taking a nap, rubbed his eyes, brushed his hair with his hands, put on his pants, shirt and shoes, and walked swiftly to the square. It was one thing for the weekly bus to pull into the village, but a taxi, that was another matter! The mayor wanted to know what was going on and who these new arrivals might be.

Mother was bewildered. Father had relatives in this village but none of her letters had been answered since the end of the war. What if they were no longer here? Had the Americans bombed Korea? Were Father's people dead? The Cowman told her not to worry, that he would help her find them. But who was this Cowman? Mother had many questions. The five travelers stood in the square, close to the empty taxi, its motor still running. Mother looked at the Cowman, her eyes pleading.

What next? What next? Here we are, but what next?

Suddenly she saw him. Yes, his walk had the same lilting sway and his hair the same early invasion of widow's peaks. She could almost hear his voice and was sure it too would be the same. But he was dead, vaporized by the Americans, evaporated at Hiroshima. The ghost approached. He ran to her.

"Kyesu, Kyesu! Oh my goodness!" Mayor Yi came to them and hugged Mother, Sister and Sunae all at the same time, as he cried and moaned. "But where is my brother?

I have received no mail from anyone for two years. The Japanese isolated us from all news. Where is my brother?" He called Mother "Kyesu" again and again, for it meant a younger brother's wife in the dialect of the area. Mayor Yi was Sunae's uncle

The Cowman stood back. He was content to watch this family reunion that he had done his best to bring about. He walked along the edge of the small crowd that was gathered in the village square and got into the tax. The taxi moved away. When Sunae heard it leaving she ran toward it and saw the Cowman looking back at her out of its rear window. He grinned waved his hand. A bump in the dirt road bounced his head up, smacking it onto the roof of the taxi, and he chuckled as he rubbed it with his rough hand. Sunae laughed. She knew the Cowman would be back.

The Cowman was neither tall nor short. But he walked with a slouch that made him appear shorter than he really was. His clothes, especially his shirts, were always one size too large, their looseness adding even more to the illusion of shortness. His hair more often than not contained an excess of grooming oil and had a messed up look because the oil succeeded only in creating clumps. Each clump was neat enough when seen in isolation but together, clump added to clump, made a series of planes shooting off in many directions. His hands and nails were dark, no doubt from his work around the cattle. And his teeth were crooked and large. But clean and white. Sometimes he wore an American style hat that he tilted in a rakish way. And sometimes a red bandanna was wrapped around his neck. His friends said he fantasized himself as an American cowboy. But they loved him. He was their natural leader. And he was a comedian.

When his father died he took over the family cattle business and his success was remarkable, and unpredictable. He worked very hard. He was a shrewd businessman and his natural skill at making people like him compounded his other assets. But he also liked to play and spent time, perhaps too much time, drinking and carousing with his friends. He tended to be a cynic on certain serious matters, such as religion, philosophy, and education, and his defense when things got too profound for his taste was laughter. When it erupted, for instance in a pub, it could be heard way past the tavern's walls and the villagers would know who was laughing. It was a signal to his friends that they were being too serious for the Cowman.

The Cowman fell in love with Sister in Pusan within that forlorn circle of metal containers, her utter helplessness adding to his emotion. He decided on the spot that he would help Sister and her family even if he had to carry them to the farthest corner of Korea. When he learned their village was just a few miles from his own he was convinced that a mountain spirit must be at work and he really had no control of the situation. For her part Sister liked the Cowman right from the beginning, too. But *like* is not *love.* That came later, it took her a while to get past his rough appearance, his rough talk, his rough beauty. But get past them she did, and when it happened they both hid their feelings from their families. They would sneak off together walking up the mountain single file, around the bend in the trail, and once beyond, hand-in-hand.

But he was a cowman. Not exactly the favorite profession a well-bred Korean family looked for in a husband for an eldest daughter. What was wrong with the cattle business? Everyone ate beef. Was it the slaughter and blood? No one knew for sure, or where and when the prejudice had started, but there it was, and as with many things of Korea, no explanation was needed. For there it was, and that was that! Confucian ethics assigned roles carefully and relentlessly. And sometimes ruthlessly.

Fifteen

The Obelisk

Life in the village settled into an ancient rhythm. The radios that were now ubiquitous, and the small tractors that ran around in the rice paddies and belched smoke out of their diesel engines were different; and the modern pumps with their chugging motors that delivered water to the village square and, more importantly, into the rice paddies, and the modern drugs, few as they were, that lined the shelves of the small pharmacy that also sold small packets of cigarettes, perhaps all of these things were different. But the people were the same. They worked and loved and fought and married and had babies and died. After working in the paddies and, for the women, working in the kitchen, they sat around and gossiped and played games and complained. Laughter was passed around, savored like wine. The people did worry about their families and the future, but the worrying was not overdone. If they happened to be poorer than their city cousins they didn't care one way or the other.

Sister and Sunae went to the school a mile down the dusty road that was also the main street of the village. It was halfway between their village and the next. The girls dressed each morning in their black skirts and snow-white starched blouses, their black stockings and black shoes, and joined the parade of boys and girls walking to school. They seemed to lose their identity - the children all dressed the same - but only if they kept their mouths shut for they had a Japanese accent. As they mastered their new language (of course, thanks to Halmoni, Sunae was quite good at it already in spite of the accent) it became apparent that Sunae and Sister were born leaders. They took command at most games. They answered most of the questions asked in class. The other children came to them with their problems and sometimes asked them to settle squabbles. In the evenings, homework done, the family sat together and talked about the day's adventures and problems.

Their small house, next door to the mayor's modest but larger home, was pleasant enough. It had two big rooms and a kitchen. The kitchen had a dirt floor with the oven and stove built into the wall facing the rest of the house. A flue ran from the oven and under the floor of the two rooms and then to a chimney on the other side of the house. This system heated the house very nicely during the stark Korean winters, and sleeping on the floor was wonderful because no matter how much the wind howled and no matter how much the snow swirled the floor remained hot, sometimes very hot and demanding them to turn during the night. They slept together, all three of them, burrowed between thick quilts. In the morning the quilts were neatly folded and stored out of sight, transforming the room from bedroom to living room. The other room was a storage room and study for the girls and

Mother. And available for overnight guests.

If the weather was warm the family ate their breakfast on the wooden porch that ran around three sides of the house. No shoes were ever worn on this porch or in the house. Shoes were lined up neatly where the porch ended, but close enough for the overhanging thatch roof to protect them from rain or snow. Sometimes in the winter they washed their shoes, bottom and sides and brought them inside the house.

The day was special. No school. A holiday of some sort. Best of all, the Cowman was going to visit. Mother planned to come home early from her small, one room pharmacy, or yak-kuk, as it was called. She started the business soon after the family arrived from Japan and the villagers, only too happy not to have to walk two miles to the next village for a pack of cigarettes or an aspirin, made Mother's modest venture into capitalism a modestly successful one. The family was financially independent. Sister helped Mother occasionally at the store but Sunae was more trouble than help. Sometimes she ate the candy Mother had for sale. Without permission.

This evening Mother wanted to make a special meal for the Cowman and she sent Sunae down the road to a farmer who was slaughtering a cow that morning. Pulkogi, a delicious, spicy roasted beef, along with many savory side dishes, all items especially liked by the Cowman, were on the menu. And plenty of steamed rice. Sunae was excited about both the food and the Cowman's visit. He was like an uncle to her. But the Cowman's thoughts of Sister were quite different. He didn't want to be Sister's uncle. Not at all.

The meal was excellent. Mother and Sister had brought their cooking skills with them from Japan. Their hot and spicy Korean dishes, with an occasional Japanese treat thrown in, were a marvel for those lucky enough to be invited to their home for a meal. The Cowman ate his fill and even sucked his lips and belched a few times to show his pleasure. Now he sat back and enjoyed a cup of hot rice wine that a proud Sunae served him. She impatiently watched him drink, eager to refill his cup.

The Cowman said, "Sunae, some day you will make a good kisaeng. The way you keep my cup full! All you have to do now is sing me a love song. But be careful, I may fall in love with you and carry you away from here."

Mother pretended to be mad. "No daughter of mine will ever work at such a job! Don't even talk like that. From now on you can pour your own drink. No daughter of mine will ever be a kisaeng. Not even for you!" But as she spoke Mother leaned over, picked up the bottle and refilled his cup.

"Mother, now you are acting like a tavern girl, like a kisaeng."

Sunae ducked as Mother cuffed the back of her head for such a remark.

Then Mother corrected her. "And your Korean is all wrong. A kisaeng is not a tavern girl. She is like a geisha, you know, a Japanese geisha, and very proficient at many things besides serving drinks."

They laughed, and Mother too. Sunae wondered what was so funny.

"Well, Sunae, what have you been doing with yourself other than school and getting Mother mad at you? Tell me about your adventures." The Cowman was smiling and, as usual when that happened his teeth and face seemed longer. Sunae resisted the urge to call him the Horseman. But she knew he wouldn't think that was funny, especially when Sister was present. He lit a cigarette, leaned back, and waited to hear of Sunae's latest exploits. She always had something new to tell him, a fight with a neighbor child, a joke on Sister, or a new song she wanted to sing for him.

"Cowman, I think I have found a buried treasure. Halfway up the mountain I found a stone monument with some Chinese characters on it. I couldn't read them, they were so worn away. They looked very old. Of course, I could have read them, otherwise, if they were not so worn."

She overstated her ability to read Chinese characters. Sister and Mother and the Cowman accepted her exaggeration and said, "Of course you could have, we believe you." He overdid it, unskilled at such irony, and she realized his true thoughts.

"No! No! It's true. The stone shaft was hidden by weeds and moss had grown all over it. I only discovered it because I dropped my scarf and the wind blew it off the main trail. I remember exactly where it is. Let's go up the mountain. I'll show you."

It was early in the afternoon and the Cowman planned to spend the day with them. So he and Sister and Sunae set out, climbing up the mountain to find Sunae's treasure. About one hour later they came to a withered tree that had no leaves. There were several silk strips of cloths tied to its lower branches placed there by someone seeking a favor from the mountain god. The ribbons would stay there until the favor was granted or the wind - or a

Buddhist monk or Christian missionary objecting to what they considered false religion - tore them down.

"This is the place, right past this old tree. Hurry!"

Sunae was excited. Just as she had told them, the spot she was leading them to was off to the left and below the main trail. They left the trail and climbed down to the left. It was a sharp incline and the Cowman worried about the young girl. But there was no danger. The truth of the matter was that Sunae was a better climber than Sister or the Cowman. She loved the mountains and many times had come up here by herself in spite of Mother's warnings. And they didn't have far to go. A thick clump of vegetation, scrubby and tough looking, lay directly in front and slightly below them. They pushed through, and beyond lay a natural terrace.

"Here is where my scarf landed. And here is the monument!" Sure enough an obelisk about six feet tall stood in the middle of the small table of land, its stone surface well worn and covered with moss. The elements and time had had their effect. And there was indeed writing, old Chinese characters, on the side facing south and away from the westward wind that most days blew across the Korean peninsula.

"Someone sure knew which way the wind blew when he put this marker up," the Cowman said as he ran his hand over the writing. He then stood back. "Yes, there is writing here. It's quite old. Sunae, you were right. It does appear to be Chinese characters but not what I am used to reading. This is really old stuff and the calligraphy style is ancient. I can't read most of it."

Sunae glanced at Sister and then at the Cowman. Her story had been factual and she wanted a moment to gloat. But the Cowman was too excited to notice. He saw the marker as having historical value and was planning to return tomorrow with the necessary things to make an ink rubbing of the characters directly off the obelisk, and then take it to Taegu City where the university would have someone, perhaps a scholar specializing in ancient Chinese characters, who would be able to read it.

And that's what the Cowman did. The next day he and Sunae again climbed up the mountain and he carefully pressed a special paper against the obelisk and rubbed it with a charcoal ink rubbing pencil until a copy was made. The next day he took the bus to Taegu and showed the impressions to a certain professor of antiquity at the university who got so excited he wanted to go back to the village with the Cowman immediately to see the obelisk for himself.

Professor Kim had written several books about Chinese influence on Korean history and culture. He specialized in Chinese characters both ancient and modern. The Cowman's story animated him and he wondered what it might mean and what he would find on the mountain. He noticed that the characters on the obelisk appeared to be similar to those used around the fourteenth and fifteenth centuries. This was the time that the Korean phonetic alphabet - Hangul - had been created by the great King Sejong. But Hangul didn't catch on with the common people until several hundred years later. And scholars, even to this day, continued using Chinese characters. It was more scholarly, they said.

The Cowman took Kim up to the monument, just the two of them, for Sunae it was a school day. Kim made his own copy of the writing using more professional equipment than the Cowman. Now it was evening, and they were sitting in the mayor's house. Professor Kim was ready to give his report on what he had discovered on the mountain. Sunae, Sister and Mother were there, too, for Sunae was the one who had found the treasure in the first place. They all were waiting anxiously for Kim to speak.

"And what does the writing say? I am sure that is what you all want to know, isn't it? Of course it is, yes, yes." Kim was talking to himself as much as to the others. "Well, the answer is quite simple, yes it is. Even though I cannot make out some of the characters because of terrible weather erosion, you see, wind and rain for hundreds of years is a powerful force, an erasure, I can read quite a bit of it, yes, yes, and I can guess at some of the missing parts, but this symbol here gives me trouble." He stopped talking and pointed to a certain character on the sheet.

"The figure doesn't mean much in our language of today. But I showed it to a colleague of mine and he reminded me of a simple fact. It is a name, yes, a name, but not a Korean name, and that is what confused me. It is a Japanese name. And the obelisk is a grave marker. It is the grave of a man named Iwata. It is a Japanese name, not a Korean name, yes, yes, and that is what confused me." In his excitement he was repeating himself.

Then he continued, "Yes, yes, but what was a Japanese man doing so high on the mountain, a Korean mountain, three or four hundred years ago? It doesn't make sense. In the village cemetery, I could understand something like that. But high up on the mountain? And that is not the only mystery. It appears that the message is signed by a Korean lady named Dolsun and that she loved this fellow Iwata."

Sunae, Sister and Mother looked at each other wide-eyed. For Dolsun was Mother's Korean name, and Mother was Japanese, and the Japanese name Iwata had been assigned to Sunae's father by the Japanese, a Japanese name and a Korean name, and a Japanese man in Korea and a Korean woman in love with him, and what else? Did this strange story out of the past have a connection to the present, a tie involving people and nations and names and languages and times past and present?

But Kim was not finished. "There is yet another mystery. Several characters are different than the rest. A different writer, in fact, a different hand. I can tell by a change in the style. They appear to be sort of childlike."

He looked at the Cowman and then at the others. "See these smaller characters? They were not made by a chisel and I have no idea how they were made, but they are different, the cutting of them is different, cruder. They say something about a bird, a cuckoo bird, who is sorry for something or other and is apologizing to this fellow Iwata. I'm not exactly sure, but it says something like that, something like an apology. Perhaps it's just a poem. And if it is nonsense it's very old nonsense. And one more thing, there is no date on the stone. Rare indeed for a grave marker."

Sunae noticed Kim's hands trembling. He arose and mumbled, "Thank you and good-bye, and yes, yes, thank you and good-bye." He spoke too quickly, mixing his words and repeating himself, for he was in a hurry to return to his books. Sunae laughed and the Cowman frowned. Some of the others looked shyly away. Then Kim went to his car, mumbling all the while to himself, and drove away from the village and back to his university.

That night as Sunae lay in bed next to Sister she thought about the things that had happened since she told the Cowman about the monument. It was all so strange. The name Iwata, a lady named Dolsun, a grave marker without a date, ancient Chinese characters, and a strange message from a cuckoo bird.

The temple bells were ringing far up the mountain. The monks should have been asleep two hours ago. There must be a special event taking place. Sunae wanted to sneak out of the house and climb up to the temple to see what was going on. She could even stop at the secret place and see the grave marker. That's what she wanted to do. But instead she went to sleep.

Sixteen

The Professor

When Professor Kim was excited he stuttered and said "yes, yes" much too often. If he was talking to someone he would mumble the last word of a sentence as though he couldn't wait to get on to his next thought. The news that Grandfather had found old family journals with the samurai's signature on them meant Captain Iwata was now more than just a name on an old tombstone. Kim felt as though he had discovered Iwata alive and could interview him about life in the past. He wanted to ask Iwata what a Japanese samurai was doing in Korea in those days, and how he got to be buried on the mountain at such a most unlikely and hidden spot? He stuttered in his thoughts although no one was listening.

He returned to the village for a second visit.

As the car entered the village it kicked up clouds of dust. Grandfather, the mayor, the Cowman and Sunae were waiting in the square. The Cowman insisted that Sunae be there. After all, she was the one who had originally found the grave with the ancient marker. She looked like a doll as she stood among the men. But she felt as big as a giant. Her black school uniform had been neatly washed and ironed to perfection by Sister. At first Mother objected to her missing an afternoon of school to meet Professor Kim, but to no avail. For both the Cowman and Grandfather (who was really Sunae's great-grandfather and a man to be honored) insisted she be there.

Kim wanted to see Grandfather's findings, an ancient journal. And now he was holding the three scrolls gingerly, as though fearing they might crumble in his hands. He wanted to give them a quick examination before deciding what to do next. He peered at the first page of the first scroll and took notes on a small spiral pad that mysteriously jumped out of an inside pocket of his crumpled suit. He read the scroll very slowly because the writing, as he already knew it would be, was as difficult as the writing on the obelisk. Calligraphy evolved, changed, as the centuries moved ahead.

When he finally finished his first, quick look at this treasure from the past, an examination into a life lived long, long ago, his eyes moved down at Sunae. He studied her face, and then leaning closer to her, his eyes narrowed.

"Yes, yes. I can see it. I can see the Japanese blood in the little girl." At these words Sunae frowned. She was a little woman, not a little girl. And Kim, oblivious to her displeasure, continued. "Little girl, you are the kinsman of a Japanese samurai. There is no doubt in my mind. After all, these scrolls were found among your family's records."

It seemed like Kim's face would burst open with delight. He could hardly contain himself. His entire academic career was tied to the period of time when Iwata had lived and died in Korea. Now he felt that he was about to meet someone from the past, someone to talk to, someone who could talk back to him. A time machine at his disposal, that's what it was.

"I want to take this journal back to the university with me. Please. Please. I cannot take no for an answer." Anxiety raced across his face. Sunae looked at him and thought that if he were not given the papers he would grab them and quickly run away, back to his university.

The mayor, (Sunae's uncle), agreed to the request, as Grandfather had previously ordered him to do for Grandfather respected Professor Kim's credentials as a scholar. The journal was placed into a special container built to safeguard old records from heat and humidity, and a seal of wax was applied across its lid. Then both Grandfather and Professor Kim pressed their personal signets into the wax. Kim signed a statement of responsibility agreeing to return the scrolls safely several months later and handed it to Grandfather. As Kim realized what had just taken place, that he could now examine the journals slowly and carefully in his own office, his stuttering returned. He bowed a nervous, jerky bow and said, "Ttthhhank yyyou all vvvery mmmuch."

Sunae laughed. The Cowman scowled at her and slapped the back of her head.

Several weeks earlier Grandfather had started this chain of events as he spent a day going through some old trunks and boxes that had been sitting in a secret and dusty storage space built into the roof of the Yi family ancestral home, a place where family records were stored. After wiping spider webs, cobwebs, and years and years of dust and grime off the boxes, he opened one of them.

There were three scrolls inside, each wound upon itself in tube-like fashion. Antiquity and historical treasures are found everywhere in Korea, an ancient country with a written history far older than that of Europe or America. Grandfather instinctively knew to be careful, that the scrolls might crumble in his hands if not handled properly.

Now in his own study, surrounded by his books and charts, Grandfather wondered if there might be a connection between the journal and the old grave Sunae had found on the mountain several months earlier. He didn't know where the thought came from. It just suddenly arose in his mind. Then he heard a cuckoo way up on the mountain singing away. The wind had carried the bird's singing down to the village.

Grandfather understood a few of the old characters on the scroll, but others appeared a mystery. The Professor had pointed out during his first visit to the village to see the grave, how some old characters had swirls and strokes close to those used today, and how others differed. The writer's name was Iwata, and he was a samurai. That much was clear to Grandfather. Yes! Same as the writing on the obelisk. Why were these ancient scrolls locked up in the attic of his home along with other Yi family records? Grandfather wondered if the man might be an ancestor. That evening he walked to the home of the village mayor, his grandson. As Grandfather entered the courtyard where the mayor and his wife were having a cup of tea, the two came to their feet and gave a low bow. His age alone would have warranted this special courtesy, but it was more than that, for Grandfather was the oldest living member of the Yi family.

"Grandfather! It is an honor for you to visit our humble home." The mayor continued bowing and didn't straighten up until the old man was comfortably seated on an ornate pillow that was hastily set down for him. He was offered food and drink by the mayor's wife but the old man refused and waved her to sit down. Grandfather looked at his grandson's face, studying, looking for a trace of Iwata.

"Yes, you do have a certain Japanese look about you. I always said that somewhere in our family tree there was a Jap hiding."

The mayor's wife blushed and covered her mouth with her hand. The mayor answered, "No, Grandfather, I am as Korean as the kimchi I eat three times a day. No Japanese blood in me! We got rid of the Japs at the end of the war, and I don't want them back. Not here, and certainly not in my own blood!"

He said the words quickly, perhaps too quickly. He gave the old man three low bows hoping to restore any breach of respect his harsh tone might have given.

Grandfather laughed. "Well, like it or not, I have important news to tell you." He then related the story about the old papers and how they might fit in with the grave on the mountain. The name, Iwata, was the same, the reference to a samurai was there too and, since the journal had been sleeping among other old family records, why not a connection to the Yi family bloodline? Existing Yi family records mysteriously stopped somewhere around 1630, and no one knew why, and nothing to preclude Iwata as a distant ancestor, perhaps their earliest ancestor. A new arrival from a foreign land. The start of a new ancestry, a new family, a new bloodline.

At a family meeting, but including the Cowman who had become as close as family to them because of his rescue of Mother and her daughters at Pusan, they decided to tell Professor Kim about the journals and invite him to see them. The Cowman telephoned the next day. Kim stuttered on the phone, the news exciting him beyond his control. He immediately decided to travel to the village and examine the journals, but told no others at the university for he wanted Iwata's journal all to himself, at least until he had a chance to read them.

He traveled once more to the village and brought the journals home with him. And then, finally, back at the university and safely in his own study, Kim gingerly unwrapped the box containing Iwata's writings.

The three scrolls lay on his table, placed there as though an offering to an ancient temple deity. Professor Kim might have appeared as a stuttering old fool to others, but he knew his trade. He knew exactly how to proceed with papers as old as these. Always begin with reverence. Even a prayer. He slowly unwound the scrolls. The first thing he observed was that they were numbered. The writer had indicated the order in which he had written this journal. And Kim thought that logical. He called to his wife to bring him a fresh pot of tea and told her that he would not eat dinner that night, that he was too busy. Progress would be slow, he told himself, because the writing style was ancient. One thing he knew. Even though the writer of the journal was Japanese, the use of Chinese characters permitted him to read the documents in either Korean or Japanese. For both languages used the same characters. Professor Kim was fluent in Japanese, as were all Koreans who went to school during the Japanese occupation of their country. But whatever language he used it would not be an easy job. He started reading the first scroll.

My First Journal. I am Iwata, a Japanese samurai. Yes, I am a samurai. Here I am in the land of the Koreans, the garlic eaters, and I am not sure how I got here. I remember the enemy ships looked like turtles and there was a magic about them. Our cannon bounced off their sides without harming them. I remember being blown into the sea and then a dream. Yes, I remember the dream. There was a bird, a small bird, but I can't remember much more. The bird landed on my hand. The next thing I remember is being on the sandy beach with great pain in my shoulder. And then blackness. I remember someone approaching. And I was carried somewhere. I don't remember anything else. My sleep was deep and dark. But when I awoke I remember laughing at the sound of a strange language, and someone laughing back at me. Now I know it was Dolsun. Yes, now I know that. But I didn't then. I remember silver in her voice.

I remember how she walked.

Now I am in the home of the mudang and her daughter Dolsun. I am quickly learning the language of these people. That is good. I want to talk with them. I want to thank them. I want to return home to Japan. I am confused.

Slowly but surely I can speak. It is an easy language, but the sounds are harsh. I wonder if there are any poets here? Such harsh sounds. And the land, it is harsh, too. But not with the severity of pain. It is a harshness of angles and valleys and bare rocks and green colors and brown colors. It is a harshness of beauty. It lacks the roundness of Japan. What a stupid thing to say, but I know what I mean.

The mudang is a remarkable woman. She appears to be some kind of a shaman. She claims she can tell fortunes and she casts spells and talks to spirits. But I am not sure about that or what she really believes. I do know she understands people and their problems and she knows how to make them calm down. I better be careful. Perhaps she can read my mind. Perhaps she will put a spell on me. Maybe she already has.

Her daughter Dolsun is young and I can see beauty and grace when I look at her. But she is young. I will wait for her to grow a bit more, that is, if I am still here. I must be healthy to think of such things again. I am a young man even with my wounded shoulder.

Dolsun asks me millions of questions. She is very curious. That is good. This home is comfortable, but too small for my privacy. As soon as I am stronger I will build my own house, but it will be close by this one because, for the time being, the mudang and her daughter are the only family I have. It would be lonely without them. And their food is delicious, too. A consideration of importance. Samurai have to eat. The other villagers are a puzzle to me. I don't understand if they want me here or not. Perhaps they are afraid of me.

I have been training some of the village boys in

basic fighting skills, but I will not go too far with them. They might start killing each other. These Koreans love to argue and fight, and the women are the same way. I have shown the village men how to build a better plow. It will make their farming easier. I think the people like me better now than when I first arrived. The biggest change in my situation is my language ability. Now I can talk to them. In spite of its harshness I like this language. Some of its words have no equivalence in Japanese. It has more swear words than I have ever imagined possible. Japan's fighting men would love this tongue. If I go home I will teach them.

I am writing poetry. I am feeling that this harshness and beauty go well together. A strange thought? No, not so strange. The harsher a language, the harsher the contrasts. A pure and simple road to poetry, if you ration your words.

I have built my new house. It is made of mud bricks and has a thatched roof. It has a narrow porch almost all the way around and an outer wall that does indeed go all the way around creating a small courtyard. It looks just like the other houses in the village, but it is one of the smaller ones. I can always expand it later if I wish. In the meantime, I followed my secret plan and built the house close to the mudang and Dolsun. That's where the food is. Am I becoming a garlic eater? What would my shogun think of that?

Oh, I forgot to mention, the village men helped me build my house

Today I met the abbot from the Buddhist temple

on the mountain. I am not very interested in his religion, but he seems to be a good man. I like him. He doesn't hate the material world the way his religion preaches. That's fine with me. He appears to like the mudang and seems to be her good friend, even though they argue all the time. I think they both enjoy it. He invited me to visit his temple.

There was more to the scroll but Kim couldn't read it. The last page had decomposed so badly that the writing had simply disappeared into gray and white smears. Kim wrapped his large hands over his face, rubbed his bloodshot eyes, and wanted to cry. He knew there was nothing he could do to restore the scroll. Off in the distance, even though the university was in the middle of the city, he heard a cuckoo bird singing in the night. Or was the bird crying? The evening had passed swiftly as he struggled with the old-style writing from out of history. It was three o'clock in the morning. He decided to go to bed and save the second scroll for tomorrow.

His wife had his sleeping mat ready for him. She heard him come into the dark and his presence glowed across her soul. His small noises made her comfortable. She loved him more than she had a moment earlier. Her dear, obsessed husband. She thought, my dear husband, what have you found now? What mysteries have you discovered now? What ancient things have robbed you of sleep tonight? Well, good for you. I am happy for you. I know you are doing an important thing. But try to sleep. I know that you love this work of yours, and I love you, but sleep, my dear, sleep.

The Professor did sleep but his dreams might as well

have kept him awake, for he did not relax. He flew back to the sixteenth century and found himself at Iwata's grave, the dirt still fresh and brown. The obelisk that he knew would be there later was not yet in place. He stood in a dark and murky night existing in a time long ago. He looked down at the grave and asked what the last part of the first scroll had said. But there was no answer.

My Second Journal. Yes, I am Iwata, a samurai warrior. Is there more to it? Is samurai only a warrior? Why do I ask myself such questions? Why is my heart troubled? I should be planning my return to Japan. But deeper, darker thoughts roam about my soul. We lost the battle. Should I lose my life? It is such a foolish thing? Such a waste. What does my shogun want of me? What do I want of myself? I am confused. I think of honor and I feel I still have mine. But do I have honor or not? Are my feelings true or am I fooling myself? A samurai should know the answers to such questions. But I do not. I am confused.

Yes, I have my honor and I will keep my life. I will keep my life here in Korea. I am now a man of this country. Yesterday I climbed up the mountain and traveled on a different trail that led in a new direction. It was cold for it is late autumn, and I wore my white scarf, a present from Dolsun. I loosened it for a moment and the wind blew it off. It flew down and to the left. As I chased after the scarf I discovered a small, hidden trail that wound below some trees and through an overgrowth of shrubs. I thought the trail would fall right off the face of the mountain, and me with it. But it didn't. It led to a small, flat piece of land that can not be seen from the trail. It was so beautiful hanging there in the sky that I decided to spend the night. A strange emotion overcame me, a complex emotion. As the sun set into the sea I felt two contrasting sensibilities. I felt as though I was alone, the only person in the world, and at the same time I felt as though others were with me, talking to me. Is this possible? I have no explanation. But I can tell you of these strange feelings, here in my journal, because you cannot argue with me. Will anyone read my words?

At this point the style changed, a different mood, a different sensitivity. Kim noticed the change immediately. It frightened him. But he continued reading.

I have not written in this journal now for several years since my last entry. It didn't seem important to write everything, but now it does. My life has changed. I am still a samurai, but I do not feel Japanese. When I climb up the mountain by myself the universe talks to me and says that my world is here, and not in Japan. Honor and duty are part of a warrior, but also part of a poet. I am happy here and it is here I want to live.

When did this change in me take place? I really do not know. I have even had the ridiculous thought that the mudang is casting a spell on me and that she is turning me into a Korean, a garlic eater. I must admit I do love this garlic, and the hot, red pepper, and the fluffy, sticky rice. But of course, there is more to this than food. The air enters my body and tells me I am home. The mountain dirt clings to my shoes and says the same thing.

The weirdest thing is the language. I am thinking in Korean, and sometimes even dreaming in it. When did this happen? When did it begin? I forget.

I am in love with Dolsun. She is no longer a child. She is no longer a girl. She is a woman. I have known of my love for quite some time but was too stupid to admit it to myself. Then one day as I watched her working in the kitchen she cut her finger. My finger ached at the same time and at the same spot. She saw me flinch and turned her face. A mudang's daughter! Was she the one casting a spell? That night we made love at my secret place on the mountain. I will say nothing more about such a thing. It is meant only for us, only for husband and wife.

The rest of the second scroll was filled with many things that were of great interest to a historian. Iwata wrote of village life in great detail, how houses and roads were constructed, what foods the villagers ate, what alcoholic drinks they drank, how the rice crop was harvested twice a year if the weather was cooperative, and what the people thought of the Buddhist temple that prospered up on the mountain. He described in great detail the clothing of the people, the materials, the colors, the designs, and the games and songs and poems of the children, working and playing. He described weddings and funerals and celebrations and sorrow. He told how the farmers loved to dance and how they played their drums and horns made of wood while they danced, jerking rhythmically at each drumbeat. These were things exciting for a scholar. Professor Kim became a time traveler.

Iwata talked in detail about the language of Korea, nouns and verbs and adjectives, and how the children studied it and loved to sing it more than say it. How they sang their everyday conversations from time to time. He talked about Korean poetry, and how he had taught Japanese poetic structures to some of the villagers and how they used the forms, but with their own Korean shadings. He talked about the animals and the birds, the streams and the waterfalls, the trees and plants.

Again and again, he talked of harshness and beauty and how they were connected. In a playful mood, he said he felt no need to describe the country in any more detail because if anyone found his journal they would already be there and could see for themselves. Or, he said, if they weren't there, they could simply think of a Japan modified with humor and sharper edges.

Seventeen

The Journal Ends

Professor Kim was out of bed and working before the first rays of sunshine peeked through the window. His wife gave a sigh of resignation when she finally opened her eyes and saw speckles of dust shining like foggy silvery stars floating across the bedroom. She turned away and buried her head once more under her blanket. Kim, at his desk on the far side of the room, didn't notice her movements. For he sat there in a trance, his eyes fixed on the last scroll, Iwata's words talking to him.

My Third Journal. I am Iwata. My wife is pregnant and we are very happy about that, but I have a rather strange prescience that something troubling is about to happen. I do not know what my feelings are trying to tell me but I sense they have to do with Japan. Thoughts float toward me from across the sea. They do not bring physical fear but sadness, changes from my present happiness and calm, changes I do not want.

I had never thought happiness was such a simple

thing as I know it to be now, here, with Dolsun. But it is. I now believe happiness and simplicity must live together if either is to exist. I feel it when I look at Dolsun as the sun shines onto her ebony hair and bounces back at me. And the moon. It is then that her hair looks so clean and deep as though it could exist without her, as though it were a pool of raven silk woven by a mountain god. Her skin is smooth and creamy with a touch of bronze that has a ruddiness about it sending a signal of activity even when it is motionless. And her beauty is overpowering. When she works in the kitchen, or in the rice paddy, I like to sneak up behind her and look at the back of her neck, at her arms, and turning her around, at her brow. In the heat of summer if there is dampness on her body it is like small drops of purest silver that glisten and cool. Everything is clean - clean - clean. Work makes her pure. Every smell is scrubbed and unspoiled. The scent of woman, the scent of musk. It is strange that the other women of the village do not appear like this to me. Perhaps I am not looking at them with the same eyes.

Even the movements of Dolsun's clothes as she walks release emotions inside my heart. We talked in the kitchen last night and she lifted her arm to reach for a pot sitting on a shelf above her head. The sleeve of her dress pulled upwards and toward her body and the movement of the cloth danced with beauty and grace. I heard music that sounded like the chatter of happy animals. The way they talk as sunset comes on and again when it goes away. I can only compare the shift in the fabric to watching her as she walks, efficient movement, so like a poem, though without words, but never without purpose, never without meaning. Sometimes Dolsun gets angry with me for as we walk along together I like to stop and let her move ahead of me, and watch her. She says this embarrasses her because a wife should always walk behind her husband. At least some things are the same in Korea and Japan.

Are these thoughts important enough to be put into my journal? Yes, because I have never felt this way before, and what is life if not all these small things bunched together into small rhythms of movement and thought, mixing together and becoming human, defining what we are, how we love?

When we make love the physical pleasure is greater than I have had with any other woman. In seeking her own pleasure Dolsun achieves an increase in mine that I do not wish to explain. A samurai journal is not meant for such matters. Who will read this journal someday? Strangers? I do not know. So enough of this talk of the bedroom.

The Professor shyly lay the journal aside for a moment, he was concerned for the privacy of the man. He looked across the room at his wife and turned to his work.

I have spent days trying to understand my new feelings about Bushido and honor. What is a life without honor but an empty movement through a universe of mud and dirt. These are not simple questions. I am a warrior and will always be a warrior. But I did fight honorably. After the battle nature, or the gods, or God, put me here in this land and gave me Dolsun. I feel strongly that I've maintained my honor. But another, an additional matter of honor has come to me. And it is part of my Bushido now.

And here I am! I have never been disloyal to Japan or my shogun. I love them both and always will. But I now have another attachment, an additional loyalty, a new love. There is only one way to proceed with my life and that is to assume that this change is made for all eternity even though I sense something about to happen, a danger. But a man cannot be terrified of danger! Worrying about the future is not an acceptable road to honor.

Kim stopped reading. Danger was leaping out of the scroll and onto the top of his desk. He wanted to warn Iwata and Dolsun and the mudang, and especially tell Iwata that the grave on the mountain was waiting for him. Kim felt a deep sadness for the samurai. Brother for brother. Then, remembering Dolsun, he glanced across the room at his wife. His despair thickened and clung to the desk and the chair, to the walls and the diplomas hanging there, and even to the vase of flowers his wife had placed on a small table in the far corner. She knew her husband loved flowers.

This man Iwata, this Japanese samurai, had been dead for over three hundred years but Kim lost himself in the warp of time and planned a warning. But then reality took hold and melancholy replaced his scheming. He was powerless. He could not warn the samurai. Too many centuries between them! He damned his inability to act. It was more than he could stand. He wanted to be with his wife. He gently woke her and lay down beside her putting his arm around her warm body. He smelled her woman musk. She knew his discomfort and said nothing. She placed her head upon his chest and felt his breathing falling across her cheek. They lay together as the morning sun grew stronger and stronger, finally overpowering the silvery dust, finally destroying it with pure light.

Later in the morning Kim returned to his work. The journal now went into a rather long section on the history of Japan and in particular the story of the flotilla of cruisers that had been sent to destroy any Korean navy that might exist. It explained why Korea was important to Japan, and why it was needed as a base for the conquering of all of Asia, and how the Japanese nation believed it was their manifest destiny to rule Asia, especially China and Korea. It told of the Japanese fleet's defeat at the hands of the Korean navy, an unexpected outcome caused by Japanese cannon balls bouncing harmlessly off the sides of the Korean ships. Professor Kim, being a historian, was fascinated with the details.

He came to a section on Bushido. It was quite formal and explained the loyalties owed to Japan and shogun by the samurai. It contained little of the passion and emotion Iwata had expressed earlier in the journal, but now was like a fixed presentation, a catechism, a textbook. But then the journal moved back to Iwata's personal story, and a chill ran down Kim's back.

I am Iwata. Time has passed since my last entry in this journal. There are three visitors. They are samurai from Japan and have come to see me, Iwata, also a samurai of Japan. We have much talking to do and until our discussions are finished it will be peaceful. After that? I cannot say anything about after that. We shall see.

Iwata was moving from peace to anguish, from happiness to danger, crying for help. A controlled desperation was flowing into the journal, that's what Kim thought, and he felt helpless. He began reading again.

A good battle. Love is strong enough to overcome danger. Even death. It is strong enough to live alone. It has life regardless of all else. It is like the mountain snow that lives and then dies in the spring only to turn into water and return to the sky, and then to the earth, over and over, alive again. The whiteness of snow on a mountain, what is more delightful than its elegance and simplicity? Its value is in its own essence. Love is the same, and contains it own wonder. I walk on the mountain in winter because the coldness and whiteness burnish my face with existence. Love is the same. Explanations are not needed. It is there. Feel it. Hear it. The sky shouts it! It is the answer to everything. Existence is love and beauty, elegance and simplicity, but mostly it is love.

I must go. It is time. The samurai have come for me and I will not make them wait for they are noble men. I will try to show them beauty. Perhaps I will succeed and, if that is the case, my journal is not finished. But if I fail. I must go with them now. The journal can wait. Or end.

Professor Kim came to an empty space on the scroll. Then it started again, but with a different brushstroke, a changed ink, a short message, the style staccato, Kim's eyes filled with tears.

This journal ends.
My husband is dead.
Our son was born today.
Perhaps someday he will write his own journal.
He is a handsome and healthy boy.
His name is Bongchae.
He is Korean.
He is Japanese.
He is the son of Iwata and Dolsun.
And he is a samurai.

Eighteen

Mother

Mother's love for her daughters was fierce and protective. That's why she took them to Korea when the war with America was over. Father's family would provide a degree of security that was not possible in Japan. For she saw the prejudices of the Japanese against anything Korean. Japan had lost the war and the Americans were beginning to arrive. The people had been told the Americans were animals who killed for fun alone and raped women at will. Korea would be safer for Kwinam and Sunae, and even for herself.

When they arrived in Korea Father's family gave them love and support. Grandfather (Sunae's great-grandfather) was the most honored member of the family. He received first place at family meetings and festivities. The family treated him as a monarch and spoke only the most honorific language in his presence. Sunae took advantage of his love for her. The two of them spent happy times together talking and playing. Grandfather read to Sunae and taught her poems and songs and bought her candy and toys. They climbed the mountain hand-in-hand, but never too far up the trail for he was an old man. And he always took Sunae's side when Mother scolded her.

Grandfather was sad when his daughter (Sunae's grandmother) did not return to Korea. But he understood. The great war was over but the world was still a turmoil. And he gave little Sunae an extra share of affection because of his missing daughter. He was Halmoni's final gift to Sunae.

Mother was Japanese and she missed her homeland. Her small pharmacy kept her busy as did working in the rice paddies along with the other villagers during transplanting time, and then again at harvest time. Hard work was good for her. No time for sadness. But often she remembered her home village up on the mountain, the sea and the city of Kuré in view down below. She thought of the gentleness of Japanese formalities which because of their constant use became ubiquitous, the bowing and nodding, and the good manners. She ached for the softness of the Japanese language and the musical quality in many of its words, and for the sweetness of the food. But she knew her decision was the right one. Her daughters had Father's Korean blood and now they were with his family, exactly where they belonged.

The Korean language was no problem for Mother. She was quite intelligent and spoke it well enough even while in Japan. And now she was quite proficient at it, but with a Japanese cadence that was delightful to hear. Mother wore her accent like a badge. She was Japanese! But the truth was that her speech, when mixed with the already strong provincial sounds of the village people, sounded like a full orchestra.

Some of the village women thought Mother to be an

unyielding lady, but not those who really knew her, those who realized her hardness was a way of protecting her daughters. As for the men of the village, when Mother first arrived, several of the widowers quickly noticed her grace and beauty. But Mother would have none of it! She was a well educated lady from a fine family and her husband had been an engineer. No village farmer for her! The men never gave up and sometimes threw wistful glances at her when she passed them along the village paths.

Her charm and loveliness increased as she entered middle age. She was slightly taller than most of the village women and her slim waist gave her a cosmopolitan look even if she wore baggy work clothes sewn out of discarded brown army blankets. Her cheekbones were sharper than most Japanese and, at first glance, her face appeared more Korean than was really the case. Her soft black hair, always neatly prepared, and her olive skin, somewhat lighter than Korean, completed a picture of aristocracy even while she lacked wealth. Mother knew fashion and could make the most common clothing fit and look fine, and with perfect color combinations. She taught her daughters these same skills. And when she wore a traditional Korean dress with its high waistline and tightly fitting bodice, she took on a soft sensual appearance that excited the men even more.

Mother's small pharmacy business gave her and her daughters a degree of independence. But it was good to know the family was there and willing to help if needed. It was a comfortable little business and the villagers welcomed the conveniences it offered them. The pharmacy sold the usual over-the-counter medicines and patent cures, snake oils and bandages, along with tobacco and candy. And rice wine, but only those brands made by top companies for special occasions. Perhaps not medicinal, but close. For their regular drinking the village men usually brewed their own drink at home or went to the local pub, a tent having rough wooden benches and a dirt floor, where they drank, sang, played chess and solved the world's and the village's problems.

Sometimes in the heat of summer as Mother worked in the pharmacy drops of moisture formed on her upper lip, looking like tiny pearls and causing heat to flash over the brow of a male customer. And the man would buy more than he needed. Mother indeed had an effect on men.

In spite of their animosity toward Japan, Mother was completely accepted by the village people. They were wise enough to realize that a person can be loved without loving a whole country. On a more practical matter, the women had no qualms about coming to Mother for instructions when their husbands craved a Japanese meal that they didn't know how to prepare. Also, Mother taught those who wanted to know the Japanese tea ceremony, which became quite popular in such an unlikely place, much to the surprise of an occasional visitor.

She and her daughters had complete and loving approval from Father's family. They were embraced with love, and they in turn gave love back, family ties being more important than anything else in the world, politics or war be damned. When the mayor said a slurry word for "Japanese" in Mother's presence, a slip of his tongue during a political conversation, Grandfather quickly and vehemently scolded him. It never happened again.

But there were hard feelings against Japan everywhere

in Korea, for the Japanese had gained control of Korea early in the 20th century until the end of the war with America in 1945. They even had banned the teaching of the Korean language but their order was ineffective for the Koreans simply taught their children at home. And, of course, they continued to dream in Korean, awake or asleep. And sing, and laugh, and make love.

The Japanese built Shinto shrines around the cities and countryside, ordering the Koreans to worship the Japanese Emperor Hirohito. But this didn't work either, and became a joke as the people cursed at Hirohito with choice Korean words that the Japanese could not understand.

But now, the war over, it was a love-hate relationship, this feeling between the two countries. They shared many common customs and ethics and Japan, indeed, had stood up to the mighty western nations and fought bravely and almost won the war. The Japanese occupation of Korea was at times benign and at other times brutal. They stripped the land of its natural resources and offered no payment. They took coal and lumber, and left a scourge of floods and mud slides caused by missing forests. Now, years later, Korean students from high school through college demonstrated against any hint of Japanese influence in their beloved land. But as the students grew older their animosity faded, some of them even working for Japanese companies that invested in Korea, and, all the while, Japanese songs were played in the tea rooms, and Japanese movies in the theaters.

Mother was not concerned with the politics of nations, not at all. Her world was her family and even though she missed Japan and her Japanese family and friends she knew coming to Korea with her girls had been the right choice. When it was discovered with the help of Professor Kim that the grave up on the mountain was that of a Japanese samurai who was, perhaps, the patriarch of Father's family, Mother felt a swelling pride rising in her breast. She examined her two daughters looking for samurai virtues, albeit feminine ones. A samurai was an important person, a giant step above the ordinary, and Japanese! These two young ladies, Sunae and Kwinam, had the best of both countries. But now they had a double share of the good things of Japan. Yes, a samurai was very special.

The family accepted the Cowman the same as if he were a kinsman. For he had saved Mother, Sister and Sunae when they arrived at Pusan and they faced disaster. Perhaps he had saved their lives. And he was the one who brought them to the village. But as his interest in Sister became more than friendship Mother reacted harshly. If the Cowman came a little too near Sister Mother's face hardened and her voice raised a notch. The question of his name, he was a Yi, was Mother's constant and overplayed theme. It made no difference to her that he was from a different clan, meaning his name had no legal block to marriage with Sister. But legalities did not prevail. What was best for her daughter came first. She used his name as an excuse. Her real objection was the Cowman's profession.

A cattle worker, a slaughterer of animals, was just a step above grave digger, professional athlete, prostitute! It didn't matter that he was quite successful and made a lot of money. Korean society (and Japanese society too, for that matter) was a highly structured thing. He was simply not good enough for Sister. Grandfather and the mayor agree with Mother. Sunae, too young, was not asked her opinion, but she would have taken the Cowman's side. Always. She loved him.

The Cowman seemed to be two people. They treated him as a good friend of the family most of the time, but when the subject of him marrying Kwinam came up, he became an outcast. The role he was playing at any given moment decided his acceptance or rejection, but only for that moment. If Sister walked into the scene it went one way, and without her, another. This manipulation of acceptance and rejection, this bouncing of emotions backward and forward, up and down, may only be possible, at least to this extreme, in the highly structured societies of Asia. A monument to Confucius, a living haiku, harsh and striking. But family politics were beyond Sunae's grasp. She was still a child and loved the Cowman, and she delighted in his company and accepted his discipline and correction without argument. He could do no wrong.

As for Sister, she loved the Cowman. And the Cowman, he loved Sister. The matter heated up just as the red peppers ripened and the time came for their harvest.

Nineteen

The Chungmae

The village was too small to have a doctor. When someone got sick they ran to Mother's pharmacy for help, or consulted a mudang, or talked to an old woman. And the old women usually knew what to do, especially in the case of a female matter. Birthing babies was easy for them. Sometimes the new mother was back in the rice paddies working alongside her husband the very next day, the new infant strapped to her like a backpack. The old crones knew their business. For the men it was another matter. Depending on their ailment, most decided to suffer silently rather than let the old women pry and poke at their bodies. If possible, that is, if death itself was not knocking on the door, they waited for a traveling doctor to arrive in the village. Or they would ride on the back of an ox cart thirty-five miles to the nearest hospital, usually arriving at the hospital sicker than when they had started out.

The village did have a fire department. It consisted of everyone - man, woman and child. The mayor was chief. The fire department was efficiently and quickly assembled when the fire alarm went off, the fire alarm being the yelling and screaming of the whole village. Since there was no crime, none at all, the county policeman didn't come to the village very often, that is, except on holidays when he expected to be fed by the villagers. But he did show up once when there was no holiday. That was the time Kim Manbuk got drunk and beat his wife. She then set fire to their house. The policeman came to arrest her. But the old women of the village chased him out of town along with Kim. Kim came back three days later, rebuilt the house, and in nine months his wife gave him a new son. There is no record anywhere, village or county, that the fire ever took place.

Some of the village men, especially those who had no male children, thought about the beating and the fire. Was it a remedy? Should they also try it? It turned out to be only idle talk at the pub. There was no rash of arson. They continued trying other solutions, nature's own, and, in time, that always worked and a son was produced. But they loved to discuss and joke about setting fires and beating wives. The women laughed at them.

One thing, or one person, the village did have was a chungmae. A chungmae was one of the most important citizens of the village. He didn't work for the government - village, county or national - but he was still an official, and an important one at that. Sometimes he performed his duties without leaving the village. But mostly he had to travel to other villages and sometimes all the way to Taegu City. Once he even went as far away Seoul on a very special mission.

A chungmae is a marriage broker.

Being a chungmae was his profession, just as it had been for his father and his grandfather before him. In a small Korean village where many people are related to each other in some way (cousins everywhere), marrying off a daughter or finding a good wife for a son is quite a project. Marriages within the same clan were forbidden and clan records went back a thousand years. A very narrowing situation. This made an efficient and hardworking chungmae a very important person.

For mothers and grandmothers the search for proper spouses was a major activity. After their daily work was done the village men headed for the pub to drink their rice wine and smoke their long stemmed pipes, but the women sat at home and talked for hours about prospective husbands and wives for their unmarried children. They talked of reproduction and housekeeping and cooking and education, or lack of it, and wealth, or poverty, and land ownership, especially land ownership. All the while, the young people in the village talked of looks and fashion and sex, especially sex. The young people, from time to time, would go to the home of the chungmae and tell him what they thought about a proper marriage partner and ask him to influence their parents in such a direction. But since these young people were not his paying customers, their parents handled the money, he listened to them but nothing more. He was polite, yes, for they were his raw material. But he never remembered what they said. Nor did he really care.

There was a connection between hot peppers and the young people's conversations of marriage, love and sex. When the time of the year arrived for the shiny red peppers to be placed on straw mats and left in the sunshine to dry, and then ground into a fine dust for making either a red hot pepper powder or an even hotter pepper paste, it was then that the torrid talk of love, in all its varieties, escalated. The hot sun dried the peppers, wrinkling them like prunes and sending their acrid peppery smell into the air. The whole village became hotter when this happened, especially the young people. The chungmae knew that his business would increase during pepper drying season. Young people talked to young people, young people talked to their parents, and the parents talked to themselves and to other parents. And everyone talked to the chungmae.

Many of the young people fell in love while the peppers were drying, for the pepper dust intoxicated them. They noticed each other in a different way, not like it had been in primary school where boys and girls were different species. Now it was different, a species united in love and lust. The peppers saw to that. And they noticed bumps and turns and sly smiles and secret signals. This made the chungmae very nervous for if any of these liaisons blossomed into true love, and then into marriage without his special services being contracted, he would lose his professional fee. And his wife would be very unhappy about that.

His fee was set by tradition at ten thousand Won and the price of a cow. The cow made the formula safe from the scourge of inflation.

Sister knew the Cowman wanted her for his wife. They reviewed their problems for the hundredth time. First, he was a cowman and that was not good. Second, his surname was Yi, the same as hers, and that too was not good. But their clans were different. That offered hope. And he had money, that too was a positive.

When Sister announced to her family that she wanted

to marry The Cowman all hell broke loose. Grandfather screamed and Mother's face changed to granite and she fainted. The mayor, still the mayor, a powerful voice in the family, yelled "NO, NO" as loud as he could. He quickly walked three miles to the house of the Cowman, and in a very loud voice shouted "NO, NO" once again. Both villages heard the commotion. That night at supper, young unmarried girls were sternly reminded that their parents would pick husbands for them with the help of the chungmae, and not the girls themselves.

The next morning as she worked in the kitchen with Mother Kwinam didn't say a word. She worked quickly and furiously. As for Mother, she never stopped talking. How could her oldest daughter think of marrying the son of a cowman who was himself a cowman? And what about his surname, the same as hers! Was he a distant cousin? Mother knew this was not the case, but if it helped her argument she used it. What would happen to her if she married a cowman? And a cousin? She talked of six fingered hands and idiot babies and a brow with one eye. No! It was decided! They would see the chungmae that very evening and do things the proper way. The chungmae would be very scientific and find a proper match, one that would quickly lead to love, and give harmony and compatibility both to her marriage and her mother's happiness. Yes, that is what they would do! Go to the chungmae.

But the peppers were burning Kwinam's eyes, and her soul as well. She had never been as miserable. She loved the Cowman. She silently cursed the chungmae, the monster who would separate her from her love.

The poor chungmae! He only wanted to do his job.

Then Mother expanded her plan. Yes, she would place an order with the chungmae to find her daughter a proper husband. But there was more to be done. Mother knew what unrequited love can do to a new marriage before time offers its remedy. Her plan was simple. She would pay the chungmae to find a suitable mate for the Cowman as well. That would end this ridiculous matter once and for all at both ends of the problem.

And so Mother went to the house of the Cowman and presented her plan to his family. The Cowman's mother agreed because she considered it to be the best way. For she was a very traditional lady and wanted the old way, the best way, for her son. Now he would get a fine wife and a mother-in-law more to his liking, one who would not harp on him for the next fifty years, and one who would not faint every time she was displeased. And one who was not Japanese. But she would not agree to Mother paying the chungmae's fee. That was out of the question. She would pay for her own son's wife. The cattle business being very good. And she, like Mother, also offered to pay both fees. Mother thought it a stupid idea even though she had, in fact, proposed the same thing herself a moment ago.

The chungmae was delighted with this turn of events. Now he would not lose a fee because of the unfortunate love affair. In fact, he would gain a double remuneration. Further, such a solution would discourage other young people in the village from shunning his services. Much was at stake. He must give the matter special effort and find a partner of the highest quality for each of them, partners compatible with each family's interests. He would consider all aspects. social, financial, education, temperament, for this was a special case. Doubly important. He decided to go all the way to Taegu City for his raw material.

The two lovers met halfway up the mountain. They didn't worry about explaining their absence from the village for only the moment was important to them. Their kisses were long, and mingled with salty tears. They pledged their love for all time. Then they made love. At least this, the first time for both of them, meant they would deny the chungmae his usual guaranties of virginity, although no one would know this part of the contract had been broken. Afterwards, as they sat on the edge of a jutting cliff, the lovers momentarily thought of a permanent solution to their anguish. But then they realized there was a better way. They would let the chungmae begin his work. It would buy them time. And before the chungmae's plans could mature they would run away to Taegu City, or even Seoul. They didn't think of money or food or shelter or anything else. Not even what would happen to the Cowman's business. For who could think of cows at a time like this? They thought only thoughts of love. And the weather was hot.

But events moved ahead faster than anyone expected.

The chungmae returned from Taegu triumphant. Rarely had he been as successful. Two excellent pieces of raw material. One from a family of some means, a husband for Sister, and the other from a good but less socially acceptable family, a wife for the Cowman. His traveling bag contained two sets of pictures, family charts, birth certificates, educational accomplishments, and short statements from two sets of parents describing in most glowing of terms how wonderful their children were.

But the most important papers in the bag were four single sheets, each one containing the name of one young person, and basic information, but nothing else. When the chungmae got home he would follow a procedure that never varied in his long career as a chungmae. He would staple together the sheets that were to marry each other. For him, his staple completed the contract in permanence and destiny, two lives sealed together forever by an office stapler. Never to be broken. The chungmae had visions of twenty thousand Won and two cows. One trip, two staples, double remuneration. A trip to the bank and a trip to the cow pasture.

But something was in the air. He had noticed it in Taegu City. There was a fever going around and many people he met had it. They called it by a most formal name, Asian Flu, as though it were a person. Those who had it wanted to die. They were miserable. Their skin ached and their bodies were covered with a sticky sweat. Most stayed in bed and, even though the weather was hot, they couldn't get rid of a chill and piled quilts on top of themselves, feeling so bad that death itself presented no fear. The chungmae was happy when his search was done. He started back to the village and away from the city's malevolence, this evil thing with such a funny name, this Asian Flu. What he didn't know was that it had hitched a ride on his body. It traveled with him all the way back to the village.

The wife of the chungmae was concerned for her husband, but also for the business at hand. He had been in bed for three days, not saying a word, but moaning and groaning every few minutes. He was covered with sweat.

For the last three days the two families came to the house and asked what his trip to Taegu City had brought them. Much was at stake.

The futures of Sister and the Cowman! Four very important sheets of paper, perfect mates, perfect raw material. The next step was to clip them into pairs, and thus produce two new marriages, two new families, two new babies with more to follow. But for the time being the chungmae only knew that he wanted to die.

The chungmae didn't get better. The two families got very impatient. Of course, they felt sorry for the chungmae and his wife. But something had to be done. They finally asked his wife to open the small pouch and give them the contents so that they could proceed with these most important of matters. The wife of the chungmae understood their impatience and also thought about the twenty thousand Won and the two cows. But she refused to act while her dear husband was on his sick bed.

When she was alone she emptied the four sheets of paper out of the pouch, along with the personal letters and pictures and other documents. She put everything on her husband's small desk. Neatly placed and ready for action. She asked him what she should do. The chungmae instructed her to give the families nothing, nothing at all, until he was ready. He didn't want to lose his double fee. So he struggled out of bed and crawled over to the desk where he formed the four special sheets into two piles. Before he could staple the couples together his coughing and weakness returned and forced him back to bed. He could staple the proper documents together later. Husband and wife. Wife and husband. A staple or a wedding band were the same thing to the chungmae!

Two days later the chungmae died.

The funeral was an impressive one for the chungmae had been an important man in the village and he deserved a grand funeral. There was singing and eating and drinking. There were drummers and whirling dancers. Many chungmae from all over the county, even several from Taegu, came to pay their respects. And professional mourners were wailing and moaning and crying. Everyone had a great time. The festivities lasted for three days. Then everyone walked slowly along the winding road that led to the mountain, and then up to the village cemetery just beneath the summit. The chungmae was laid to rest under a mound of earth that was high and grand looking.

Village life returned to normal. But there was one (or was it two?) matters that needed attention. Papers and staples! The papers were still in two neat piles on the chungmae's desk. Three days went by. Then the two families appeared at the door of the house. When the chungmae's widow looked out she saw two cows and twenty thousand Won in her mind's eye. She smiled as well as a new widow can smile the week of her husband's funeral and told the two families that she would gather the documents together and have them ready by noon tomorrow. They agreed.

She closed the door to be alone with her memories, at least for a day longer. She loved her husband and wanted to be with his spirit in this, their home, as long as possible. This man, who did so well for others, had done the best job for himself. His wife was very special to him. Their love had grown, just as he always promised other couples. Somewhere in the house, stored away in a secret place known only to the two of them, was the simple document he had written listing his own wife's qualities and assets. And, true to his profession, his own sheet was securely stapled to hers. Of course, he had listed his own many fine qualities on his sheet. Indeed, the match had been perfect and had led to a deep love.

For the time being, the other four documents remained on the chungmae's desk. They were safe there. The families would just have to wait. The widow could staple them together in the morning.

Saja had been watching all of this. He sat in his nest on the mountain and thought how strange these humans were. Then a voice came from across the Japan Sea. The voice told Saja to do something. True love must win out. He must help the Cowman and Sister. He flew down to the chungmae's house and looked into the window. There on the desk, in their two piles, were the four documents wrongly matched. But they were not stapled together yet. There was hope.

Saja formulated a plan. It was a good plan but it had to be carried out in a very precise manner. There was no room for error. Saja had no idea where the plan came from. It just popped into his head. The wind would do his work for him. But first he had to fly to Mount Paektu - faraway at the very northern end of the Korean peninsula. Saja worried. Did he have enough time to get there?

As had happened to him once before a long time ago, when Saja flew into the sky a strong wind came out of nowhere. It blew south to north, which was a very unusual thing on the Korean peninsula, and carried him at an astonishing speed. Before he knew it he was standing on the top of Mount Paektu. Saja knew what to do next.

He flapped his wings as hard as he could with a strength that came from outside his body. Then at a very exact moment, a scientific mathematical moment, he stopped his flapping.

A weather scientist in California looked at his reports and noted that a sudden wind somewhere on the northern end of the Korean Peninsula had grown stronger and faster as it traveled southward. It raced through northern Korea and moved southward. The northern mountains slowed it but it still continued racing down the peninsula creating eddies here and there and blowing dust into the eyes of farmers and city folk alike. By the time the wind reached the chungmae's village it was still strong enough to make the dogs bark and the cows bellow. It was still strong enough to push open the window at the house of the chungmae. It was still strong enough to ripple across the chungmae's room. It was still strong enough to blow two neat piles of important looking papers onto the floor. The next morning the chungmae's wife got out of bed very early. She wanted to prepare herself for the visit by her husband's final clients. This would be his last act and she wanted to be ready. She walked over to the small desk in the room where her husband had kept his books and business papers. Papers were scattered all over the floor. She had no idea which were which.

"Oh, dear husband, what shall I do? Please guide me. Who marries whom? Whose paper should be stapled to whose paper? Husband! My dear chungmae husband, guide me!" She reached down and picked up the four papers. But she had never learned how to read!

"Oh, please, my dear husband, make this right, make this right. Please match these young people together into perfect families, just as you did for so many others your entire life." She was moving as though in a trance. She barely looked at the four papers. The only thing she made sure of was that they were matched male and female in both cases. That part was easy for the chungmae had always used a different color paper for each sex, white for the bride and gray for the groom. She heard a voice. "Do not worry, my sweet, you are doing what has to be done."

She stapled a white paper to a gray one, then the third paper to the remaining one.

The two families arrived right on time and were greeted at the gate by a nervous widow. They took off their shoes and sat on the floor of the main room where the chungmae had greeted them many times during his lifetime. But this was business and so, after a pot of tea, the chungmae's wife produced the stapled papers. She handed the top pair to Mother. The second set of papers remained on the desk.

Mother read the paper and immediately turned red, a deep frown flashing across her face. She groaned and let the papers drop to the floor. When the Cowman's mother looked at the papers she too trembled, the scowl on her face even topping Mother's ferocity.

Utter chaos!

Mother screamed. "What is the meaning of this? What kind of a horrible joke is this?" Thick veins throbbed on her temples and her lips quivered with anger.

For the top paper had Sister's name on it and, stapled safely to it, the bottom paper contained the name of the Cowman!

Far up on the mountain Saja was laughing at the scene

below. And he felt a great sense of accomplishment. Magically, for he was far, far away from the humans, he viewed the scene at the home of the chungmae, and heard every word that was spoken. He knew there was one last thing for him to do. He needed to flap his wings once more, this time to help the wife of the chungmae. He flapped them weakly at first, and then a phantom took over and carried this new wind down to the village. It was a soft wind but it contained a special power. The wind blew into the ear of the chungmae's wife. She heard the message as clear as a cuckoo's call on a silent mountain that had no breezes wandering about to soften it. And she became a giant cuckoo bird and beat her own wings, gently but with authority. Mother fell back, and the Cowman's mother too, both dumbstruck. They had no choice but to listen to what she had to say.

"No, No, No! This is what my dear husband has done. He was the very best chungmae this land of Korea has ever known. This is his decision! He gives you these life partners. These belong together. This is the way. Here is a new family and love will surely follow. (But, of course, it already had.) Trust my dear husband, my dear chungmae husband. He must have had his reasons for this matching. Remember, he was the best. This entire village - yes - this entire valley, is filled with happy husbands and wives and lots of healthy children. This is what he left us! This was his profession! If you go against his findings I cannot tell you what harm it will bring to your daughter and son," she glared at both mothers, "and at the cost of wonderful grandchildren." She did not blink or turn aside. She spoke with softness and loudness and with an authority that she had never known before. Somewhere, somehow, the chungmae was laughing. And so was Saja.

Years later, three sons and one daughter later, the Cowman's business had grown. He was an important man in the valley. But more significantly, he was an excellent father and husband. And Sister's family was very happy that the wife of the chungmae had been such a strong person when she defended her husband's honor. No question about it. The Cowman was a member of the family. And Sunae, at first she was jealous because her wonderful Cowman had married Sister. But that soon passed and she welcomed him into her family. Now the Cowman was her brother.

As for the chungmae's wife, she lived to a ripe old age and never married again. The villagers treated her with deep respect and honor because of the good things her husband had done for them. His legacy was the many happy husbands and wives and their children all through the villages and countryside, and even some in Taegu City.

Ah yes, even Taegu City. The chungmae's wife had taken the second set of stapled papers back to Taegu where a happy couple had no idea of the intrigue and mystery that had placed them together. But they also found love. Such was the skill of the chungmae even from the grave, but now with the help of Saja. Their first child grew up and became a distinguished artist. Her most famous work is an oil painting of a magnificent cuckoo bird with wings clapping in happiness. It is hanging in the National Art Museum in Seoul to this very day.

From time to time when the chungmae's wife went up the path leading to the mountain and sat before the mound of earth containing her husband's bones, a lone cuckoo bird flew in and sat on her shoulder. She once told Sister and Sunae, and she swore it was true, that the bird winked at her when Sister's first son was born.

Twenty
War

The seeds of yet another war were planted in the soil of the Korean peninsula at the end of the Second World War when the Russians sent their army into the northern half of the country and the Americans invaded the south. The plan was for an election, and then for one government to run a united country. But it didn't happen that way. There were disputes concerning which political parties should participate in the election, and what form the economy should take. The Russians backed out of the agreement and set up a communist regime in the north headed by Kim Ilsung. Kim made Pyongyang his capital city and publicly declared his intention to unite the entire country, north and south, by arms if necessary.

On the morning of June 25th, 1950, masses of communist North Korean troops invaded the south and swept deep into the poorly defended country. Seoul, the capital city, was quickly captured and the Red Army moved into the southern provinces. There were few American soldiers in Korea at the time, but many more in Japan, just across the Sea of Japan. The Americans sent troops from Japan to help Korea defend itself. But they were no match for the well-trained and well-equipped communists and their Russian T-34 tanks and MIG fighter planes. They fought bravely but were quickly driven back. The communists didn't slow down until they reached the Nakdong River just north of Taegu. A small American combat intelligence unit, six men, were ordered to slip behind the battle line and determine the strengths of the advancing communist army. Small planes were usually employed for such purposes, but there were no small planes for they had been destroyed by the MIGs at the Suwon airport, south of Seoul.

The young American lieutenant and his men were exhausted. They had walked all night to reach the village, avoiding communist troops who were moving relentlessly southward. The nearby mountain offered an advantage, for from the high ground they would be able to see in all directions and get an idea of how many trucks, tanks, artillery and soldiers were coming along behind the enemy shock troops. The lieutenant planned to send his men up various peaks with their radios. He himself would stay in the village as the enemy got closer and attempt to identify their unit designations. His army, the Americans and South Koreans, had set up a fixed line to the south, near Taegu. They wanted to make their stand there and hold out until fresh troops with tanks, artillery and planes arrived from America and other United Nations countries. In the meantime they wanted to know what they faced.

"You know what to do. Let's do it right, and for God's sake be careful. Check your radios, make sure they're working. I'll be coming up the mountain myself later, so look before you shoot. Remember! I'm the American.

The others are the bastards." The men shook hands and several hugged the lieutenant. Two weeks earlier they were living like tourists in Japan, now bonding as warriors, brothers, have done for thousands of years. Joe watched as his men walked toward the mountain. He immediately felt lonely.

The village appeared to be deserted, but it was not. Some farmers had remained, hiding within their houses as if the mud walls and thatched roofs could protect them from bombs and bullets. The government radio said the communists had been stopped and these simple country folk wanted to believe their government. They were not wise to the ways of war and propaganda. They were confused and afraid.

When Joe appeared he added to their consternation. He walked through the village looking for a place to set up his post. A few villagers emerged. When they realized he was an American they greeted him with a babble of noise that meant nothing to him. It wasn't anything like Japanese which he didn't speak either.

War is noise, very loud noise, a lasting impression civilian-soldiers bring home with them when the war is over. This intensity of war noise cannot be described to others. And it never leaves the memory of those who hear it. The war arrived in the small farm village as noise. A communist patrol had spotted the small band of Americans and guessed correctly where they were heading. Their artillery lobbed shells into the village. The explosions were thick and hot and pushed the air apart with gigantic booms. The noise terrified everyone, including the lieutenant. Then a large shrieking orange ball formed in the village square and raced toward Joe. He thought of a supernova exploding in outer space. A moment later the light disappeared and was replaced by a blackness that was as dark as the orange had been bright. A pain shot through his left shoulder but it soon disappeared along with the rest of the world.

When Joe awoke he heard men speaking Korean and without understanding the words he knew they were military men. Their voices were loud, shouting, ordering. He was inside a hut of some sort, and they were outside. He curled tightly into a fetal position as though that would give him safety. He knew he must be totally silent if he was to live. He was laying down on a rough wooden floor, his body covered with coarse dirty rags. Someone had hid him. His shoulder pain was agonizing and he reflexively worried about the cleanliness - or lack of it - of his wound. Then he realized the wound had been bandaged, perhaps coarsely, but it had been done. He smelled alcohol.

The shouting became louder and closer. He heard a door open and a voice popped into the room. Then the voice withdrew and rejoined the others outside. And after a long, unbearable moment the voices moved away. Hours passed. No more voices. His bandages became wet with blood, and he was thirsty and hungry. His head pounded and kept perfect time with the blood thumpings in both wrists. He passed out.

A small voice spoke and a gentle but firm hand shook his arm. "Hello. Hello. American soldier, wake up. We go to san, no, no, mountain, yes, san, the mountain. Wake up. We must go mountain."

Joe rubbed his eyes. The room was dark but with tiny slivers of moonbeams squeezing through a broken window near the top of the back wall. It was a storage room and contained old tools, a rake, a hoe, a shovel, and some bolts of cloth stacked in one corner and broken furniture in another. Dust floated in the air. A musty smell lay flat and heavy. His visitor was a young Korean girl, perhaps thirteen or fourteen years old. Her clothes were made out of rough gray cloth. She wore a gray bandana on her head made of the same material. Her face was dirty, a war-face, but he saw beauty under the dark and the dirt. Her appearance saddened him. She was a war-child with a war-face. He thought of his sisters living in another world with their clean faces.

"The soldiers go away leave village. They sleep very close. Please, silent. No talk. No talk. I take you up mountain. Good place hiding. I know. I know. Come with me. But no talk. No noise. Soldiers close." She ended her instructions with a smile that dark and dirt couldn't hide. Moonbeams bounced off her snow white teeth.

They left the small hut and walked along the dirt path that led to the edge of the village, and then up the mountain. But a noise and activity ahead brought them to a halt. Fear came to Joe and his skin became cold and clammy. The pain in his shoulder increased and flowed into his entire body. He closed his eyes and the red color of war returned.

"We go back. We go back. The soldiers come again." The girl tugged on Joe's shirt and turned him back to the hut. He never opened his eyes until they were inside. They waited. The noises finally got quieter, but didn't go away.

In several hours it would be daylight and chances were the communist soldiers would begin a careful and systematic search of the village looking for food, medicine or anything else of value. The girl thought of a plan. She told Joe to wait, that she would be right back. "Don't worry, American soldier, I will go, no, I will come, yes, I will return." Joe smiled in the dark - in spite of his situation - at the broken English coming from this little Korean girl who was so intent on saving him from the enemy. Her words sounded better to him than even Shakespeare might have written.

Sunae, for that was her name, left him waiting in the darkness.

And with danger time seems to slow down. Perhaps this is nature's way of helping humans think things out, letting their bodies and minds adjust to menace. But a slowing of time does nothing to soothe mental anguish. Alone in his hiding place, alone in the middle of an Asian country with enemy soldiers just a stone's throw away, Joe thought of death, his own death. Would the girl return, and if she did, what was her plan and would it succeed? A small insect buzzed in a corner of the room. Joe visualized it, a small life caught in a spider's web singing its funeral dirge. He wondered if it was time for him to sing such a tune? He closed his eyes and prayed. The pain once again centered itself at his shoulder. That's it! He concentrated on his aching wound and blocked out the rest of the world. An old samurai trick he had read about when he was a boy.

About an hour later he heard someone approaching the hut and his fear came back. But it was the girl, and she carried a bundle of clothes and a small flask of water.

"Hurry! Hurry! Put this on. Hurry! We go now mountain. Please bend low when walk and hide face. Here. Wrap scarf on face. Hide face. We go."

The clothes Sunae brought were traditional Korean funeral clothes - pants and shirt made of a gray material resembling cheese cloth and a black hat that stuck up rather high and looked vaguely like an old formal top hat. There was no time for argument or discussion. Joe changed into the outfit. He quickly thought of the rules of war. By putting on this civilian outfit he became a spy and probably would be shot if he were caught. But what did it matter? They might shoot him anyway.

Sunae checked to be sure that the scarf was pulled tightly around Joe's face. She again told him to stoop over when he walked, to look like an old man. Then they left the safety of the hut and once again started up the path leading to the mountain. In the darkness Joe looked like an old Korean country gentleman going to a funeral very early in the morning, no, in the middle of the night. They traveled no more than fifty yards when a loud voice boomed out of the darkness.

"Stop! Who are you? Stop!" But it was in Korean and he didn't understand. Two communist soldiers pointing their guns approached them. One was a captain, the other a sergeant.

Sunae was ready with her answer. She had rehearsed it in her mind many times in the last ten minutes. "This is my grandfather and he wants to go up to the Buddha's temple on the mountain this early morning. Today is the one year anniversary of my uncle's death and he wants to pray for his son with the monks. Please let us pass."

The sergeant barked, "Are you crazy! Are you stupid? We should shoot you for being out here. Get the hell into your house and stay there!"

Sunae broke into tears. She looked at the soldiers and

said, "Please, my grandfather is an old man and he is terrified of this war. He just wants to go and pray for his son at the temple. Please let us pass, I beg you. We have to leave this early in the morning for my grandfather needs a lot of time to travel up the mountain if we are to get back before nightfall."

The sergeant took a step toward them and lifted his rifle in a menacing gesture. "Let me see this grandfather of yours."

"No. No. Please. He is old, he is harmless and he is so afraid that I worry he might get sick with fear. Please let us pass." As Sunae spoke, Joe, although not understanding a word, knew the danger had reached its crest. The very next moment would bring life or death. He felt sorrow for the little Korean girl and the danger he was causing her. He wished the scarf were tighter around his face. He wished he could disappear and take her with him.

The communist officer saw the girl's horror. He saw the fear in her eyes in spite of the darkness of the night. He remembered that she was Korean just like himself. He remembered his young sister back home. "Sergeant, we will let them pass. An old man and a young girl. That's all they are."

"But sir, no one should pass. There may be enemy soldiers in the area. I say no, They should not pass."

"You say no? Shut up and do as I say. This war is bad enough. We don't need to hurt our own people." The communist captain took his pack off and rooted through it. He took out a small package and handed it to Sunae. "Here, girl, here's a bit of boiled rice. Give it to your grandfather to eat while he climbs up to the temple to pray for his son."

The two communist soldiers turned and moved into the night. Sunae and Joe stood still and didn't budge until the noise of the soldiers' steps disappeared.

Joe didn't remember much about the climb up the mountain, just that they finally came to a place where she said he would be safe. But he did remember her forcing him to eat the rice and telling him that it was the only food he would have until she returned the next day, that is, if she could return at all. And he did remember her changing the bandages on his shoulder, winding the fresh ones tightly. And he did remember her leaving him a flask of water and warning him not to get too close to the edge of the mountain. That's when she tied his foot to some kind of a stone that stood there tall and straight, just like a monument.

Then the night closed in. Even with the danger and the pain in his shoulder reminding him of the war below, even with the occasional sounds of battle far away, and the occasional flashes of artillery across the mountains and valleys, a feeling of ease came over him. The mountain performed its magic. He fell into a deep, deep sleep. No dreams. No thoughts.

The mountain separated him from the rest of the universe. He was in an unconnected place. No war. No pain. A separated place. The mountain formed a trinity with the quiet and the dark.

Time passed. When Joe woke up it was still night. Or the next night, he was not sure.

Twenty-one

The Phantom

It was the darkest night of his life. When Sunae left him on the mountain she promised to return the next evening with food and water - if she could - and he trusted her. But now he was alone and the deep mountain blackness closed about him tightly, wrapping him in fear. There were no stars, no moon, the world silent except for an occasional artillery thump or the pop of a rifle shot or the rippling of a machine gun far off, perhaps five or six valleys away. His shoulder ached and he felt fresh blood soaking into his bandages. He imagined the red blood overcoming the stark, clean whiteness of the cloth.

His loneliness was overpowering as though he was the only person in a solipsistic universe. The stillness moved, first expanding outward and then bounding back. It happened over and over again, its movements making him dizzy. The calm became clamor, and yet remained unruffled. It was thicker than the dirt and rocks of the mountain only to shoot out again and become thin. He fell asleep, but it was more like walking on the edge of existence, a fog, an unbalancing. He tried to steady himself, not fully asleep and not fully awake, fearing he would topple one way or the other.

At first the intrusion was subtle and he didn't react to it. It sort of became part of everything else - the stillness and the calmness and the clamor and the thickness. But soon it assumed a separate identity and he knew something was changing. It was sound. It was music. The drum beat had a hollow, earthy tone. Not too loud but easily separated from the other instrument, a wooden flute of some sort. It resembled the farmers' music he had heard many times in both Japan and Korea.

Then came the grandest instrument of all - human laughter. And the movement came out of the darkness and joined the laughter. At first he saw it only in the corner of his eye. The motion approached and he blinked his eyes but it didn't go away. And he was too astonished to doubt what he saw. He knew he might be imagining it but the magic of the mountain was overpowering his doubt.

The sounds became a man, a most unusual man, a man dancing above the ground. Joe sat up and, ignoring the pain shooting through his wound, turned his body as his eyes followed the dancing man who was circling above him. The source of the music was not apparent. It seemed to come from the mountain itself. But the man - or phantom - his outline was clear and crisp for one moment only to become misty the next, and then, in a twinkle of time, clear again. Joe wondered, was this reality or was it the effect of his loss of blood?

The dancing man had on white pants and blouse. And in the sky, no moon, no stars, only a deep darkness that made the whiteness of the cloth dazzle his eyes. Wrapped tightly around the man's waist was a sash blacker than the darkness but with a shininess that separated it from the night. The phantom's hair, as black as the sash, was pulled behind him and hung in a pigtail dangling halfway to the ground. He was dancing and laughing as he moved about. Joe noticed a red stain on the dancer's left shoulder. When he realized it was blood and was oozing out of the same spot as the blood on his own body a fright came to him. But the laughter of the dancer brought with it an inexplicable humor and easiness, a rough, mellow ease. Joe tried rising but a tug reminded him that the little girl, Sunae, had tied his right foot to the mysterious stone obelisk. The dancer looked at his roped foot and his eyes followed the cord to where it was securely tied. He laughed even louder. Then he stopped dancing and floated over to Joe, hovering a few inches above the mountain earth.

"Your foot is tied to my monument."

Joe looked down at his foot and at the rope. He blinked several times and when his eyes moved up to the dancing man, the phantom, if that's what he was, was still there. The two stared at each other, irresistible grins spreading across their faces. A deep laugh came up from inside his belly, bursting out like a volcano, uncontrollable. The two men, still glaring at each other, but they were both laughing hysterically, so loudly that sleeping animals and birds, silent a moment ago, made small noises and moved small distances further away from the two of them.

"You are a warrior, aren't you!" the dancer said. It was a statement and not a question. "So am I. At least I was. No, I yet am, I will always be a warrior."

"Who are you? Am I dreaming? Where am I? Am I still on the mountain?"

The dancer shrugged a dramatic shrug. Then he said,

"I am part of your past. Perhaps not yet, but I will be. The blood has not mixed yet. But it will, yes, it will. As for now, I want to dance and laugh. I am happy, brother."

Brother!

The music started once again and the man danced just as before. Again, Joe wondered where the music came from. But it didn't really matter. The pain in his shoulder had stopped and between blinks of his eyes the blood on the shoulder of the dancer disappeared. Now the snow white material of his blouse became pure in its whiteness, unstained, glistening with power. The unseen drum and the flute played their strange sounds over and over and the tempo became faster and faster. The man continued laughing and - just as before - it was contagious. Joe sat there, tied to the strange obelisk, laughing away and away at what he was not sure. Time stood still and Joe knew for certain that it had also stopped for the communist soldiers down in the valley. He wondered if they could hear the music and see the dancing phantom.

As he followed the movements of the dancing man he felt himself dancing. Everything was so real. But then the music, very slowly, became softer and the man's image blurred at its edges. Slowly, slowly, both the music and the man faded into the night. But before it was all gone Joe heard the man say,

"I am a samurai and we are brothers. You will understand. It will happen, yes, our blood will mix, and you will understand."

What did it mean? He was alone once again on a mountain in Korea with blood seeping out of his shoulder and pain in his body and enemy soldiers below in the valley. Perhaps it meant nothing. Perhaps it was only a dream.

Bells were ringing somewhere on the mountain, higher and off to one side. It was the monks calling themselves together for morning meditation. The sun would not rise for three more hours but for the monks the day was already started. Not even a war in the valley below could disrupt their ordered way of life. The young American had slept well after the phantom dancer departed. He felt refreshed, in fact quite hungry now that the bells came down from above awakening him even more, in some way adding their energy to his body. This was a good omen. Appetite meant health. His shoulder ached but not as much as last night. He loosened his leg from the monument and walked around the small mesa where Sunae had hid him. Now the moon was in the sky and its strong light shone on his grassy hideaway hanging out from the face of the mountain. A small flask of water rested against the stone beside the loose rope. It was his only provision since the communist captain's rice had been eaten. He gulped at the water, not thinking of any future need. The little Korean girl would return. He had no doubt of that.

When daylight arrived Joe gave a furtive look over the edge of the cliff, down at the valley below and toward the village. He imagined a North Korean officer with binoculars scanning the mountain looking for American soldiers. The thought made him step quickly back a few yards. A moment later he heard the whine of a small plane's motor and ran for the cover of a nearby pine tree. It might be a scout plane or an artillery spotter. Then he heard a noise, a movement of branches and underbrush, coming from above, from the face of the mountain. He froze.

Sunae was true to her promise. She carried a basket of food and water, clean cloth for bandages and aspirin from Mother's pharmacy. But no medicine for infection. The North Koreans had taken that away for themselves. And the bells from above peeled away.

Her English might have been unsure and broken but it sounded beautiful to Joe. She scolded him, "You foot you untie. Be careful. Now you stay here. I go down again. You stay I tell you. I get you when, no, when, when, yes, when safe. Then you come down to village. I tell you. I get you, yes, I tell you when safe."

"Yes, my little sweetheart. I understand."

That evening there were loud explosions below. The fighting had picked up. Joe heard the whistle of incoming shells. The fighting lasted for about twenty minutes, and then deadly silence. It had no effect on the temple bells. They rang at seven and sent the monks to bed. Joe ate some of the rice and vegetables that Sunae had brought. Then he remembered her warning and tied his foot to the stone monument. He tried to sleep. The warrior dancer named Iwata did not visit him again.

The next day Sunae did not return. Joe was sorry he had not been more careful with his food and water, but he had been in a festive mood after her visit and had taken his fill. He waited and waited. Night came once more, again prefaced by the temple bells. Joe tried to sleep but now it was more difficult than before. He was hungry and lonely. His shoulder was healing, he knew that, for the wound itched more than it pained him. A good sign. He examined his injury and there were no signs of infection. Good.

Then he thought of the phantom dancer and the

Korean girl who had, at the very least, saved him from a North Korean prison camp or even death. He felt a connection between the phantom dancer and the girl but there seemed no logic to it for the dancer was only a dream and the girl was real. But what was real and what was unreal on this magic mountain? He gave up the idea of sleep and listened to the mountain sounds. The bells stopped ringing and were replaced by the whistling wind. Night insects played violins and bats shrieked across the sky. The Milky Way jingled and jangled. And then an adventurous cuckoo bird, wide awake, landed on the small mesa that was Joe's sanctuary and sang a song. It was happy and sad at the same time as all grand music can be. Mozart knew that, as did Beethoven, and apparently cuckoo birds. Joe couldn't see the bird in the darkness. But he sure could hear him. And then his eyes were heavy, his body weary, and his mind thick, as a mind can be when no thoughts, or too many thoughts, clutter it. The bird's song became quieter and quieter. Finally, sleep arrived as a friend in the night.

Saja sang a last few notes, a coda, and flew off to his own nest and a good night's snooze of his own.

Sunae didn't return until the afternoon of the following day. By then Joe was hungry and thirsty and his bandages needed changing. When he heard Sunae climbing down the path from above his stomach growled. And when he saw the girl he knew something was seriously wrong. She carried her basket of supplies - food, water, bandages - but her face was unsmiling, her eyes red and wet with tears.

"Mother, my mother is died." In spite of herself she broke into Korean. "Omah chugosoyo! Oh maná, oh maná" Back to English. "My Mother is kill by bomb. I am not happy." She burst into tears and ran over to Joe and put her arms around him. He held her tightly. The sounds of fighting that he had heard two nights ago were indeed just that. It appeared from Sunae's account that an artillery shell had landed in the village and destroyed the pharmacy. Mother was inside at the time.

She quickly returned to the village and he understood.

Three days later she came back and told him the communists were gone from the village and it was safe for him to return. The American and South Korean army was attacking the enemy and the communists were retreating northward to avoid encirclement.

Sunae was quiet during their trip down the mountain. When they reached the village it was in a turmoil. Several people had been killed along with Mother. Dead animals - cows and dogs and goats and pigs - were scattered on the ground. Many houses had been destroyed along with the pharmacy. Several rice paddy walls were destroyed and the escaping water left thick mud in its path. People were wandering around in a daze, but others were busy cleaning and rebuilding. Work sounds filled the air, boards being nailed, earth being shoveled, ruins being torn down, paddies being rebuilt.

Some of the people began singing. It started with a slow tempo, sad and soft wails, but then it got louder and clearer. They mourned their dead but they were alive and there was work to do.

Then it was time for Joe to leave the village and look for the American army. The people gathered around him wishing him well in their own language, but he understood. He spoke in English, telling them he loved them and thanked them for saving his life. A few of bolder young kids who had studied English at the primary school translated his words into Korean as well as they could. And it was sufficient. Many heads nodded in approval when he promised to come back some day. But he wasn't sure about that.

Sunae came forward with a basket of food. He thought, she is always taking care of me. She offered it to him and he accepted it. Then she gave him a handwritten note on paper that was ragged on all four sides. It was probably all she could find to write on in the rubble of the village. The note was written in the precise and neat script of a student seeking her teacher's approval. Joe looked at the paper and its words confused him. The writing was in Korean. A puzzled look came to his face. Sunae reacted immediately and spoke. He listened carefully.

"I want to talk to you but it is, it is, yes, difficult my English for me. Please translate note later."

She gave Joe a hug and a kiss and ran away from him, back towards the mountain. The little Korean girl who had saved his life disappeared.

Several weeks later, back with his unit, Joe remembered the note and gave it to a Korean officer who spoke English, asking him to translate it. The note said,

Dear American Soldier,

I am very happy that I helped you. Did I save your life? I am not sure if I did or not, but if I did, I am now responsible for you for the rest of your life. That is Korean custom. Ha ha. Yes it is.

If you ever come back to Korea please come

visit with me. I will be grown up by then. You will find me here at this village. If I move away the village people will know where I have gone.

Your friend - Yi Sunae

Twenty-two

The Return

Joe's wounded shoulder healed quickly in the American army hospital in Japan. He was sent home, his life as an intelligence officer was over. He left the army. It is difficult to explain but he cried when he realized he was no longer a soldier. And this after years of complaining about army life. At first civilian life was confusing. He was homesick for the army, something he never imagined could happen. Joe went back to his university and several years later, with his degree in hand, went to work in the office of the steel company in his home town. But he was confused. As with thousands of men before him, no, millions, the experience of combat in a foreign land was the dividing line of his life in half. A sharp before and a sharper after.

Many nights he dreamed of Korea. The dreams were not nightmares. They were filled with things of nature and not war. And he thought that strange for the war had been a defining time in his life. But there they were, the mountains and the rice paddies and the small villages. Instead of the smoke of war his dreams had the smoke of village kitchens, women cooking meals for their families. Instead of soldiers his dreams had farmers and children as the actors. Several times he dreamed about the dancing phantom on the mountain and woke up still hearing the strange laughter. Once he woke up to his own laughter.

The little girl who had saved his life, she was in the dreams, too. Once he saw her walking up the mountain trail. And with her were two animals, a fox and a bird. He didn't know what kind of a bird it was until it sang its song. It was a cuckoo bird. The dream was strange indeed and its meaning, if it had any, eluded him.

An agitation came to his mind and body like a small or large rippling tide invading an ocean beach, a good metaphor because from time to time the waves, like his restlessness, were larger and then smaller. The discontentment compelled him to move around, mentally and physically. At the office his concentration collapsed unless he walked about the building once in a while. In the evenings he would leave home without knowing where he wanted to go or what he wanted to do. He usually ended at a bar and sat until the early morning hours drinking and smoking and talking and thinking.

He thought of what was good and what was bad about himself, and it was easy to be honest because no one else was listening. He was a complicated man, and sometimes two men at the same time. He believed in the good but sometimes did bad things because of the pleasure it gave him, either physically or mentally. Too often he played devil's advocate simply because he thought the argument itself more important than its content. It was a game. Everyone seemed to know him, some even to like him, some not. He had many acquaintances but few real friends because too quickly he saw the defects in everyone. Even his own. But the friends he did have were like brothers and sisters to him.

He read books by writers he disagreed with, but liked them anyway if the writing was good. It helped if their causes were unpopular. Another game, another conflict, that's all it was. Sometimes he loved the common folk and sometimes he laughed at them. He argued with priests simply to observe their reaction. He drank and smoked too much because he was told not to do so. But he had a strong sense of loyalty to friends, to family, and even to the Church that he so bitterly attacked from time to time. This was a puzzle to him. It was as though he knew the Church, the good old Roman Church, would be there waiting for him when he was ready for it. He was proud when he remembered the army and how, while a soldier, he had given complete loyalty and love to his country and to his army and to his fellow soldiers. If he passed a soldier on the street he felt like saluting. If the man was sloppily dressed he wanted to harass him. A officer and a gentleman to the bitter end, he kept his gig line straight even in mufti, and his shoes highly polished.

His curiosity served him well and led to a high knowledge of religion, philosophy, literature and music. In moments of conceit he fancied himself a renaissance man. And maybe he was, but he was not sure because it seemed a game was being played, and he was an actor and not real. But if anything tied it all together, it was his recognition of the importance of love. Whether he himself loved or not was not the point. He recognized its reality and power, *that* was the point. Perhaps it was a grace, a free gift, and needed no cultivation and it would freely come or not. But all his likes and dislikes, all his seeking and hiding, even his passions, had their beginnings in this feeling of love. Of a woman, a country, a family, God, even erotic passions. Everything somehow had its genesis, and its death, in love.

And when he got too serious about himself he fled to humor. He had the ability to make people laugh. And, indeed, he could make himself laugh. The world is a most ridiculous place, that's what he thought.

His discontent finally overpowered him. He decided to act. So he sent letters to companies that had operations in the Far East, especially Korea. He received several job offers, accepted one, and soon found himself on a plane to Japan to meet his new employer. Two weeks later he flew across the Sea of Japan to Korea to work in the company's Seoul branch. It happened so quickly. In a twinkling of time his life changed once again. He never had a chance to waver. New friends, new places, new customs, a new language to learn. For the first three months he was so busy with his new job and his new life that he had little time to think of anything else. It was quite an adventure, and a long way from the steel company.

The dreams that had haunted him back in America stopped as his activities increased. He forgot the restlessness that had prompted his return to the Orient. One night as he was studying a primary school reader - he found this to be an excellent way to go about learning the language - he came across a poem about a cuckoo bird who lived on a high mountain in a southern province of Korea. The bird looked for ways to help humans.

That night the bird in the poem came to him in a dream. He found himself climbing along a mountain trail at night. He had been here before. It was the same mountain where the little Korean girl hid him from the communists, but in the dream he was confused. He had to reach a place where he would be safe, but the mountain was dark and he was lost and didn't know which way to go. Every turn led either into the face of the mountain or off its edge. Then the cuckoo bird in the dream startled him by landing on his shoulder. Joe saw the bird's clear eyes looking into his, a hint of a smile on his beak. The bird's weight pressing against him reminded him of his old war wound with its pain and blood. Even in the darkness he saw every detail of the bird's feathers, feet and eyes, and the turns of his beak. The bird spoke -

Past - Present - Future.
The note will tell you what to do. Remember the note.
You must remember the note.

He woke, his body covered with sweat even though the air in the room was sharp and cool, like mountain air. The dream stayed in his mind and, unlike most dreams, did not dissipate. A note? What note? Such an unusual dream with such a strange message. But the cuckoo's words were not obscure, just their meaning. What note?

Then he remembered.

He remembered the note the little Korean girl had handed him when he left the village to look for his army unit. He remembered her name - Yi Sunae - and he knew he could easily find the village. After all, some of the most dramatic events of his life had taken place there. It was all burned into his memory to be recalled when he was ready.

A business trip had to be make to a southern province

to meet with government officials in a provincial capital city interested in buying printing equipment made by an American manufacturer represented by Joe's company.

Korean trains are clean and efficient. They run on time. It is a matter of pride. Uniformed attendants parade up and down the aisles hawking drinks and food and everyone feels free to talk to everyone else, stranger or not. In the first class section where Joe sat they didn't allow animals. But suddenly a pig ran down the aisle and was quickly followed by a farmer from third class. The passengers cheered him on and clapped their hands when he caught his pig. A similar incident happened two hours later but this time it was a chicken chased by a young farm girl.

The man sitting next to Joe was the president of an umbrella manufacturing company in Seoul, and he was intent on practicing his English. The man talked and talked but not in Korean. Joe stubbornly answered him only in Korean and when he realized they were communicating rather easily he felt quite proud. As did the man. He gave Joe an umbrella.

A government jeep was waiting at the train station. It took him to his hotel and, after a quick shower, he was on his way to a meeting with the governor of the province's middle-schools. The man was a stolid fellow who depended on his young assistants to do most of the talking. He never said a word in English, which was fine with Joe, this being his country. The business at hand was quickly settled because Joe had exactly what the customer wanted and the price had been set in preliminary negotiations. But every time an assistant translated something that required an answer from the governor - whose name was Yi

Yongsho - Mr. Yi had the habit of sucking air through his teeth with gusto. Joe found himself trying to guess when it would occur, and how many sucks per episode, and he became fairly accurate at it.

The governor was a short man, heavy, but not fat. He was thick and muscular and even in his dark suit and tie and crisp white shirt he had the look of a farmer. He smelled of tobacco and garlic. But his position was at the top of the provincial educational system and everyone who approached him bowed before speaking, and then spoke in the highest honorific form of the language. Proper verb endings, honorifics, accompanied the bows.

Once business was completed and the documents signed, Mr. Yi had a rather long discussion with one of his assistants. Every once in a while they stopped talking and looked at Joe. They talked quickly and with such a heavy provincial accent that Joe couldn't follow them. He guessed they did this by design. Finally there was a short silence which apparently signaled a decision had been made. The young assistant frowned and Joe knew he was translating a response in his mind before presenting it to him in English. (The wrong way to learn a foreign language, he thought.)

"Mr. Yi wishes to me that I invite to you to his home this very evening for a dinner and also for to drinking. If you do agree he will send to you, no, for you, his automobile to your hotel at seven this very evening. He hope very much that you can eat Korean food, you know, they is very hots. And, yes, for sure, it is has much garlics."

Joe's answered immediately, which was not exactly the way a Korean might have behaved. "Yes. Yes. I will be very happys to visit with you this evenings." And he was instantly sorry for his joke on the poor man. So he bowed a very long, very low, bow. For a moment he was tempted to suck his teeth, But he resisted.

Mr. Yi returned his bow, of course not as low as Joe's, and left the room quite suddenly. The assistant looked at Joe and spoke. "Please understand this is a most unusual happening. Governor Yi has never invited a foreigner to his home before. Here in Korea most entertaining is done outside, wives never participating. Perhaps you will meet Mrs. Yi, but perhaps not. In any event, you are honored." His English was much better this time. Joe had a feeling that he had just been told to behave himself, to be careful and not act like an occidental barbarian.

Back in his hotel room Joe looked out the window at the mountains that circled the city. It was early autumn and the mountain trees were changing their colors. Reds and oranges and many different greens splashed against the brown mountain earth. The traffic along the streets precluded any of the mountain sounds from reaching his ears. But his imagination raced past the busses and cars and people. He heard temple bells, musical winds, and insects and birds singing. Then beyond these natural sounds, he heard a drum and flute and a very faint trace of laughter. And he heard his own laughter, but from afar, coming from another place, another time, another mountain.

A neuron shifted in his brain, a chemical change happening way down at the level where the molecules talk to each other. Once again he remembered his dream, and Yi Sunae, and that other mountain, and the dancing phantom.

Twenty-three

The Mountain

The car arrived late, not an unusual matter in Korea, time not being the first measure of efficiency, and then after a fifteen minute ride they came to Mr. Yi's house. It was quite large and had a noble look to it. Its gray slate roof glistened in the last gleams of the setting sun. The black iron gate with its fancy grill work opened without a squeak after being pushed by an unseen hand just in time for the arriving car to enter. Apparently Yi was not only a high official of the Ministry of Education but also a well-paid one. Yi himself greeted Joe at the front door, bowing this time a little lower than he had earlier at his office. Yi's assistant, the one Joe thought had ordered him to behave, was also there. After removing his shoes Joe was ushered into a grand room decorated with Korean scrolls and paintings and several remarkable pieces of black lacquered furniture with inlaid mother-of-pearl formed into images of birds, flowers, dragons and tigers. It was an oriental palace.

Food was set on low tables in the center of the room. There were many heated bottles of the best rice wine.

Other guests had already arrived so the assistant immediately introduced Joe to them. The guests included several high officials of the Ministry of Education, a certain Professor Kim from the university, and several middle school principals. Professor Kim was the only man among them dressed in traditional Korean clothes. His puffy trousers, fancy vest and white booties were quite attractive. There were no women in the room except a serving girl. But Joe heard plenty of female voices coming from behind two large sliding doors off to one side. The doors were made of a delicate white paper framed into small panels by a lacework of shining black wood. They hid a room beyond. It was customary for women and men to eat separately. But it was a custom broken as often as it was obeyed, especially with the help of the rice wine. Later in the party the men and women would mingle freely. However Yi was old-fashioned when it came to these formalities, at least at the start of things, and so this is how the party started. Anything might happen later in the evening, but not at the beginning, not in this house.

Joe impressed everyone with his ability to speak Korean although they gave him more credit than he deserved and ignored his many mistakes. The Koreans especially liked his humor. They were astonished when he told a story they thought no foreigner had ever heard, a story about a bad Korean king named Yonsan who brought snakes to Korea in the 15th century, sort of an Irish tale relocated and reversed.

Before the time of King Yonsan, as myth had it, there were no snakes in the entire country. What his listeners didn't know was that Joe used this story over and over in his travels. He had made himself an expert on this one ancient king who was so bad that Korean history later demoted him to prince. Mr. Yi laughed and laughed and this meant that everyone laughed and laughed whether they thought the story funny or not, or even if they didn't understand Joe's Korean pronunciation. But it was a good tale and some of the men did indeed laugh so hard that a few women popped their heads into the room to see what was going on, one of them saying in English, and rather loudly, "The American is a comedian."

The food was excellent and the rice wine magnificent. Then the women, led by Yi's wife herself, a grand matron in her own right, entered the room en masse, the party becoming westernized. She didn't seek her husband's approval, simply came in with her friends when she thought the moment was ripe. No one complained.

And then a younger lady appeared. She looked to be, perhaps, nineteen or twenty years old. Her clothes were remarkable, traditionally Korean, a dress that flared out at the bottom like a bell and a top that pressed tightly into her bosom. The colors were a celestial blue with finely stitched designs made of gold thread. She wore pure white muslin booties. Her hair was blackest ebony, shining and perfumy, and her skin a soft olive, its color being presented at its best by a radiant face. High cheekbones, but not too radical, accented a soft beauty that did the impossible. It spoke of grace and passion, harshness and softness, and all at the same time. She was both beautiful and delightful, a wonderful combination.

Joe was stunned and struggled to act normally. But no introductions were offered, neither to the young beauty nor Yi's wife nor the other ladies. Joe glanced at the beautiful lady every time he could. He played a game in which his eyes swept around the room pretending to be observing the scrolls and paintings but always managing to pass by her. Sometimes when his eyes rested on hers she caught him looking.

The party lasted well into the evening and the men played drinking games. The women finally left them to their revelry and returned to the other room. As some of the men got drunker they sang Japanese army songs. This surprised Joe. No one else reacted. Many of the older men had served in the Japanese army and it was easy for them to separate present day bad feelings toward Japan from their youthful army days.

Joe got quite drunk and when he attempted to get up to go to the bathroom he fell back down to the floor. Instead of feeling shame he caught the spirit of the party. And the rest of the men, including Yi, were proud of him for he had partied well. As far as Korean custom was concerned the point of rigid formalism had been reached and passed. Mr. Yi himself came over and helped Joe to his feet, patting his back in approval. "Fine drinking. Well done. You are a good guest in my home. Well done." Yi insisted that Joe spend the night. He must not go back to his hotel alone and with a bad stomach. In the morning he would be fine. But for now he must stay and sleep.

Early the next morning Joe awoke and found himself lying on a wonderfully soft, thick Korean quilt that had been placed atop an ondol floor, a floor that heated the room from the bottom. The sun was shining into the room and its rays danced across the floor. A few flickers landed on the quilt and sank into soft oblivion. Suddenly a maid walked into the room unannounced carrying towels and soap. She went to a side door and flung it open revealing a room containing a large Japanese style bathtub. She pointed to the tub and said something in Korean that Joe couldn't understand, but it was obvious what she meant for him to do.

The bath was heavenly. He took his time and enjoyed every moment of it. The maid reappeared again, and again unannounced. She didn't consider the fact that he was stark naked. She carried a container of clean water, apparently meant for rinsing. She said another few words in Korean and left. A year later, when his language ability had grown, Joe recalled what she had said. "Tolbo." He was a hairy person. He dressed himself.

There was a knock at the door. He opened it and there stood the young lady who had spun his heart and head last night at the party. She carried a small table, a tray, covered with several small dishes of food. Rice, kimchi, soup, meat and vegetables. Joe paid no attention to the food. He looked at her. A strange emotion came to his mind. He felt as though he knew her even before last night's party. But when and where?

"Hello American soldier. I have brought you your breakfast."

Her words "American soldier" opened the door.

"Hello Sunae Yi. Or is it Yi Sunae. Now I remember you, but you're not a little girl anymore."

"Of course not. That was years ago. And you are no longer a young lieutenant. Now you are a man, a young businessman." She continued. "I recognized you last evening but then was not the time for talking. Now is the time."

"What are you doing here? Is Mr. Yi your father? And your English, it's so good, I really don't know what to say." And he added, "You are so beautiful. And you saved my life." He knew he was talking too quickly and was embarrassed.

And at his word "beautiful" she was discomfited. Her face turned crimson and her eyes looked down at the floor. Her hand, predictably, went to her face in a gesture of embarrassment. Then she spoke in a quiet, clear voice. "Mr. Yi is my older uncle. My younger uncle is the mayor of our village. For the time being I live here in Taegu with my sister and her husband. My mother was killed during the fighting in the village. I'm sure you remember that. I still miss Mother. I came here last night to visit my uncle. It was by accident that I was here. But when I saw you I knew immediately who you were. It is like a dream, but dream or not, I remember you very clearly.

"How is your shoulder?"

"Oh, it's fine. But you, are you married, or, engaged?"

Sunae laughed. Again, Joe heard the temple bells.

"No, I am not married. I am a student at Taegu University. That is why my English is better than before, better than at the village during the war. But I am not sure what I want to be. And I am not in a hurry to decide. I have thought about you many times. I wondered if you got home safely and if your shoulder healed. I am happy that it did. And you? Are you married?"

Joe decided to stay the rest of the week in Taegu so he could spend more time with Sunae. They met for dinner that evening.

The restaurant was on the edge of town, built on the early slopes of one of the many mountains near the city. It had private rooms with tatami floors to sit on and low tables made of black lacquered wood and mother-of-pearl. Joe and Sunae sat in the room alone. A young serving girl had just brought the food but he was more interested in Sunae. She wore a navy blue pants suit with a lighter blue blouse, and around her neck she wore a fluffy white scarf that reminded him of a foamy sea splashing against a rocky shore. Her western clothes, this was the first time he had seen her dressed like this, pleased him. She was a woman, a very beautiful woman. Oriental or western clothing, it made no difference.

They ate slowly and talked, but not about the war. Joe told her of his college days and Sunae talked about hers. He mentioned the deep restlessness that had driven him back to Korea and she told of the uncertainty of her plans. She didn't seem interested in continuing her education and really didn't know what she wanted to do with her life.

"But why did you choose Korea? There are many wonderful places in the world. You could have gone anywhere. You Americans are so free." She waited for his answer, her eyes becoming slightly larger. Like a child, but she was not that.

"Well, for one thing, I've been here before, and I liked it. The war wasn't a good part of it all, but the rest was. I really can't explain it, how I felt. I just knew I wanted to come back."

"Please try. Tell me. It is very interesting. Most Americans think of my country as a war land. They think of cold winter and blood and death. What is different about you, about the way you feel?" She leaned slightly across the table and Joe felt a double emotion. Again, like a child, but she was not that. No guile, but a simple curiosity. He wanted to touch her. And it was not time for that, not yet.

Joe thought it out and then words came to him.

"This land, it is harsh, but not with the harshness of pain. It is a harshness of sharp angles and sweeping valleys and bare rocks and green colors and brown colors. It is a harshness of beauty. Many of its people share that with the land. You do. And the language has the same, hardness and beauty at the same time."

A change came over Sunae, her face showing a bewilderment that was not there a moment earlier. She was breathing faster and a trace of fear clouded her expression.

"What's the matter? Have I said something wrong?"

"No. No. But what you have said, it has been said before, a long time ago. The words are not identical but they are close and the meanings are even closer. You see, there are these journals." She hesitated. "But wait. let's finish our meal and then I will tell you all about it."

Behind the restaurant and sloping slightly up the mountain was a large garden filled with trees, bushes, flowers and rocks arranged in the fashion of the Japanese. Sunae and Joe walked toward the top where a small greenhouse, or was it a tool shed, stood alone with a bench in front. Perhaps for workers. The view looked down on the city that was by now twinkling in the night. They sat in the darkness and watched the night sky playing with the moon and stars and meteors.

He kissed her for the first time.

Sunae told Joe about Iwata and Dolsun. She told him about the journals and how a man named Professor Kim had translated them into modern day Korean. She told him that Iwata was her family's progenitor, she had no doubts about that. She told him that she had tied his leg to Iwata's grave marker on that night of war up on the mountain. Then she said that the words he had spoken in the restaurant when he talked about Korea were very similar to Iwata's words in the journal.

"Professor Kim was at the party last night. I am sure you remember him. He was the man wearing traditional Korean clothes. It is strange. Since he first saw Captain Iwata's journals he always wears traditional clothing when he handles the journals or when he visits my family. He is very excited about the whole affair. But so are we all, my family and myself."

Sunae continued, "There is one other thing I must tell you and it is as unusual as your words about Korea. When I think about the journal, and about Captain Iwata, I always think," she paused a moment, then continued, "in my mind I always created my image of Captain Iwata as you. I always made him look like you, the young American soldier. That you are an American and he a Japanese didn't make any difference to me."

"But what about my appearance, my eyes?"

"In my mind I can change you and your western eyes very easily. But the changing of eyes is not important. There is more to it than that."

The car ride from Taegu to the village was long and dusty. The rental car, a small Datsun, greeted every bump in the dirt road with a bouncing echo of its own rattles and squeaks. So when they finally arrived at the village Sunae and Joe were exhausted. The mayor was waiting for them and greeted Sunae with a hug and Joe with a bow and a handshake. The village had no signs of war remaining. The houses and the paddies had been repaired or rebuilt. Even the little pharmacy had been replaced, but of course Mother was not there to manage it. Sunae averted her eyes as they walked past.

The mayor's home was bigger than before the war and Joe was given a room for himself. He was a guest of honor. A hot bath and a fine meal, and then Sunae explained to her uncle that they wanted to walk up the mountain to the spot where she had hidden Joe from the communists. The mayor said he would come along too, but Sunae shook her head. Remembering her stubbornness as a child, he decided not to pursue the matter. But he did press a flashlight into Joe's hands just in case they were caught by nightfall.

They walked slowly up the mountain, at first single file, but then hand in hand. It was the hour before sunset and the colors of the sky were changing. The sun's rays slanted off the buttermilk clouds in oblique angles that happen only once a day. Magic was in the air and as they breathed it into their bodies they became part it. They both thought of Dolsun and Iwata. And of themselves.

Shadows. All shadows. Even Saja had to look twice from his perch further up the mountain. Did he see two people, or four? The sun changed to a deeper red and anticipated its dive beyond the edge of the world. It decided not to watch. That is for the moon to do. The moon is for lovers.

As Sunae stopped and then moved to her left an abrupt recollection came to Joe. But the memory passed quickly and its blood red color (for memories do have color) flew into the sky and joined the setting sun. They stepped away from the main trail as though intending to leap off the edge of the mountain, but a hidden path awaited them. It had waited for over three hundred years, and then for more years. And there it was, the soft and gentle plateau, small enough to have remained what it was, a secret place. A mountain god or someone or something had guarded it and kept its secret for hundreds of years. And then a few more.

Joe was overpowered by Sunae and her emergence as a woman, with her touch, with her scent, with her beauty, with her heart.

In his eyes a poem took form, real, not metaphor. Her eyes and her lips, a verse, her hair and her skin, a verse, her lilting walk joining her sigh, a verse. A happy poem? Expectant? Sad? He wondered about an ending yet to be written.

The wind bent itself like a twig to fit between their bodies as it tried in vain to fill the tight space. It gave up and blew over them, refreshed, now a love breeze. A virtuoso cricket offered his violin concerto in a key known only to himself. The earth warmed and softened. A sacrament floated down from heaven and the world stopped.

Twenty-four

Saja's Message

Joe returned to Seoul. In two weeks Sunae was coming north to see him. In the meantime he had a lot of thinking to do, decisions to make. He welcomed two weeks by himself because things were happening quickly. He wanted to slow down. He was in love with Sunae, there was no doubt about that, but what should be done about it was another matter. As for Sunae, she had given herself to him at the secret place and that was that. There was no turning back.

Once again restlessness. Moodiness. Day and night he thought about Sunae and the very unusual circumstances that had twice placed her into his life. He tried to remember every detail of that night during the war when she led him up the mountain after disguising him as an old man mourning for his dead son. He thought of the communist captain and his gift of cold rice, and the phantom dancer who laughed so lyrically. Once in the middle of the night, half asleep, he even reached down to his ankle to see if he was tied to the obelisk on the mountain. Then he thought of the party the night when he had met Sunae - again - as if by magic. The mysterious qualities and coincidences of these events astonished him. He was stunned at the time, and still was. The affair was odd, puzzling, a process that could not be reversed even if he wanted it halted.

Then one night he dreamed about the samurai Iwata. Sunae had told him in great detail the story in the journals. And he recognized the samurai as soon as he stepped into the dream. It was a short dream, Iwata dancing to the drum and flute, but not for long. He stopped, looked at Joe and said, as he had on the mountain,

"I am a samurai and we are brothers. You will understand. It will happen, yes, our blood will mix, and you will understand."

Our blood will mix. Our blood will mix. My brother. The samurai's words had meaning.

Joe met Sunae at the Seoul railway station. But she was not alone. Kwinam, her sister, was with her. The two women were dressed in very royal looking Korean clothes, an aura of aristocracy about them. They carried a small basket of apples, each grasping one end of it, and explained that their province was famous for its very delicious apples. Their bags were carried off the train by a porter with a toothless smile. Joe tipped him an extra hundred Won for the dentist, and a few apples. Then they got a taxi and sped into the city, Sister giving instructions to the driver.

"Sister and I will stay at our cousin's home for the next two weeks. It's in the Shindang-dong section of Seoul. We'll go there now and then decide what to do later this evening." The taxi headed for a very fine section of Seoul where the homes were large and the gardens fine, the streets narrow but cleanly swept. In the meantime, Sunae was excited as she watched Seoul race across the taxi's windows, her eagerness having a childlike quality that enchanted Joe. The city had recovered from the war in spectacular fashion. Battle lines had passed through the city four times and much had been destroyed. But now much had been rebuilt. Some streets in the downtown area were still not paved and pot holes were everywhere, but the streets were crowded and busy with people buzzing about. Restaurants and bars were crowded, perhaps because prices were low and food, as was the case before and after the war, plentiful. Even though it was daytime they saw a drunken man staggering out of a local pub. Sunae let out a gleeful laugh. Then Joe, too, laughed when he saw the man moving comically along his way. The drunk walked with a bending and yielding rubbery motion, his body fitting into his pathway - up, down, around, over, under - and this precluded him falling on his head for down was always followed by up. He was harmless and happy, at least until he got home.

"Joe, do you drink too much? Like you did at my uncle's party? Do you drink often?" Sunae asked her questions timidly. But before he could answer Sister was talking very quickly and slurring her words, just like Mr. Yi's assistant had done attempting to keep Joe from understanding. Sunae answered the same way.

"Tell your sister that I don't drink too much, that I am a gentleman."

"What? What did you say?" Then silence by all three of them.

The evening was special even though Sister came along with them. Joe liked Sister, chaperone or not. Things were different here, this was Korea and not America. Sister was just fine with him. The three of them drove up to the Bear House, a secluded restaurant on the early slopes of the largest mountain north of Seoul. They had an excellent meal of abalone steak and a red hot beef and pepper soup, and then a carafe of hot rice wine for Joe and soda for the ladies. Then Sister showed her good intentions and suggested that Sunae and Joe walk around the garden that wound its way up the hillside behind the building.

It was a brisk night and the sky was a deep crystalline blue. Pinholes, really stars, perforated the blanket of the night and all of it, pinholes and blue, awaited the arrival of the moon. Joe wrapped his jacket around Sunae's shoulders and snuggled the garment tightly across her chest. She shuddered, but not from the cold.

They were half way up the hill to the top of the garden. Sunae looked quickly back down toward the restaurant. She reached her hand across his back and felt him bend forward. Their lips caused the moon to leap into the sky and her silvery waves splashed into their hearts. Then Sunae said in Korean, "Na-nun tangsin-ul sarang haeyo." It was at this precise moment that Joe knew there was no turning back. So he said it too, but in English. "I love you."

And all the while, several hundred miles to the south, on another mountain, a much higher mountain, a cuckoo bird named Saja watched the two with deep interest. The fox spoke to the bird all the way from Japan and told him what he must do.

Sunae and Joe set their plans. The first move was hers. She had to go back to Taegu and tell her older uncle, Mr. Yi, what they had decided. Sister planned on being with her, and helping. Yi was the head of the family, and even more so for Sunae because her father was dead. Yi had the power to say yea or nay. In fact, he was the one who should have picked a husband for Sunae, either on his own or with the help of a marriage broker. He would have wished a marriage that was good for Sunae, but also good for the family, and Sunae would have no say in the matter. That is the way it was supposed to be. Before Joe and Iwata came along.

On the train ride back home Sunae worried what her uncle's reaction would be. And more than once she wished that her other uncle, the mayor of the village, a calmer and more reasonable man, was in charge of the family. But that was not the case, and Yi, the hard one, would have to be faced. Joe was a foreigner and Mr. Yi was a very conservative man concretely set in his ways. When he wrote he used Chinese characters as did most traditionalists. He enjoyed reading about the old Korean kingdoms and their warring kings and queens. His manners in public were impeccably Old Korean. He had a chup, a second wife, as did many of his friends. Just like in ancient Korea. But that had nothing to do with his first family, his real family.

Koreans should marry Koreans. Or at the very least Japanese or Chinese, but never yellow dog of a westerner!

Boom! Boom! The sound of Mr. Yi's voice struck the walls and bounced through the house, room to room, out the front door and into the courtyard. Neighbors turned their heads to the explosion and muttered nervously to each other. Sister and Sunae were thrown backwards by the blast. But they landed on their feet.

"No! No! This will never happen. You will not bring a foreigner, an animal, not even human, a yellow stinking barbarian into this good family of ours!" The veins in his neck throbbed as he spoke, and his hands flapped about in a frenzy. For a moment Sunae thought he was going to strike her. She stepped back yet another step. She knew not to answer him. She kept her head low and stared at the floor. When he finished his tirade she dropped to her knees, bowed low, very low, and left the room, Sister following after her. In the courtyard the tears finally came and Sunae hugged Sister tightly and sobbed.

"What shall I do now? He will never change his mind. But I will never change mine either. What can I do?"

Sister was traditional in her beliefs. Most of the time. The big exception had been when her own wish to marry the Cowman turned into a family problem. But that issue had been solved in a manner more mysterious than anyone realized. And now her husband, the Cowman, was the center of her life. She did whatever was needed to make him happy, and she was happy too. Her answer surprised Sunae.

"You will do what you want to do, not what your uncle wants you to do. I never told you this before but now I will. My husband and I were prepared to do anything necessary to be together. Even leave our families. Maybe even leave this life. But things worked their way out for us and our families finally accepted us. Now it is your turn. Do what you want. Grab your own happiness. You know, my sister, we Korean women have been running things here for a thousand years. The men are just too dumb to realize it."

Sister gave a defiant pout and looked back at the house.

"But what shall I do right now, at this moment?" Sunae looked like a little girl asking an older sister for aid. Sister remembered Japan, and their anguish at Pusan. She remembered their childhood, little sister, the beautiful one, the cute one, the pixy one. And they hugged and cried. Then she gave orders for she was, after all, the older sister.

"Go back to the village. Go back to the mountain. Think about everything. Think it all out, and then make your decision. But be sure it's *your* decision and not someone else's."

They stopped sobbing, brushed themselves off, straightened up, and walked out of the courtyard and into the street.

The next day Sunae arrived at the village and went to the home of the mayor. She come alone for Sister sent her away telling her not to come back until her decision was formed. After a short rest she started up the mountain to the secret place. It was late in the morning and the day was clear and dry with a high blue sky. A few clouds, were far off to the west, distant and remote. A rumble rolled in from beyond the eastern horizon. At the edge of the village, as Sunae walked toward the mountain, she saw two frogs making love in a small pond of water that had drained off a rice paddy. The one frog was a darker shade of green than the other. But they didn't mind the distinction.

The secret place was unchanged except for a white cloth wrapped around the obelisk with large black letters on. "This is a national historical monument. Do not touch." The Professor had done his best to protect Iwata's monument. Sunae sat down near the marker. For a moment she thought of Iwata's body resting in the earth below her seat. And this gave her a vague comfort. Perhaps he would help her. She rubbed her eyes and stretched her body out on the soft grass. The hot sun made her think of sleep and, perhaps, a respite from her worries. Her eyes closed and a wave of gentle slumber floated in.

A noise. A small noise. Almost imperceptible, but then loud as its smallest parts were joined. Clawed feet landing on the ground. A scratching on the earth. A trampling of grass. Sunae opened her eyes and saw the bird. He stood perfectly still except for a balancing move as the wind gusted. Then the wind died. Silence! They looked at each other and a puzzlement came into each pair of eyes. Sunae expected the bird to quickly fly away. But it did not.

What to do? Neither seemed to know.

The bird's eyes moved away for a second, glancing into the sky as though looking for instructions. Then he looked back at Sunae and she read his mind.

This man is yours.
If he drinks too much, scold him.
If he fights too much, fight back.
If he strays, grasp at him.
Two frogs don't see the small differences in their green.
Neither should you.
Love between man and woman is everything.
It is above family and clan.
Love is a new family, but only if allowed to live.
Now it is up to you. Put your arms around it.

Melt into it. Become one.
Become one!

A philosopher bird no less! The bird jumped into the sky and even though there were no clouds and the sun was brightly shining he immediately disappeared. Sunae rubbed her eyes, glanced about one last time, and walked down to the village.

Twenty-five

Pulguksa

Before her trip home Sunae and Joe agreed to meet three weeks later at Pulguksa, an ancient Buddhist temple southeast of Taegu on a mountain overlooking the Sea of Japan.

Pulguksa Temple is famous throughout the world as a masterpiece of Buddhist architecture of the Silla dynasty. It was built in the eighth century AD. The main temple is located on a mound of earth and has two flights of stone steps at its front symbolizing the passage from a world of illusion into one of enlightenment. Several large bronze bells are scattered around the temple grounds. They, too, are very old. They differ from western bells for they are not flared at the mouth and are not sounded by an inside clapper. A wooden log held up by chains hangs horizontally next to each bell and is swung to and fro to produce the dull tolling.

Several pagodas of different sizes are placed around the areas in the front and behind the main temple building. They are valuable art pieces in their own right. The entire compound is a national treasure and is protected by the Korean government.

Sounds! Sounds! Temple noises are everywhere. If sound can be thought of as a part of the earth, the temple sounds are a continent. Not in size or loudness, in fact they are soft and subtle, soft bells and tender bells. Chantings of monks everywhere, one voice at times and many voices at other times, the same note - over and over and over - and then wooden sticks striking wooden blocks almost as fast as a woodpecker hammering on a tree, as a monk uses the soft and hollow clamor to send his mind away from this evil world, fleeing existence, seeking detachment.

Temple fragrances hang low on the ground. Incense clings to the trees and bushes and the mountain grasses outside the buildings. Rice in temple cooking pots has an odor even blander than that cooked in any Korean farm kitchen. No spices are ever used, nor is meat added to the pot. A musty aura hovers in the air inside every building and then soaks through the walls filling the entire compound.

Everything is ancient.

Behind the main temple there is small pool of water that fills itself from a spring flowing out of the mountainside. The cold water gathers itself in a pool, about four feet deep, made of granite. The source of the water must be from deep inside the earth for the water has that special coldness that seems to say the atoms have stopped spinning. If you drink or splash your face the water passes its coldness onto you and you feel as clean as if kissed by the angel of purity. Perhaps imagination, perhaps real, but the water seems to have that power.

But Pulguksa's most famous attraction is miles up

and near the top of the mountain behind the main temple compound. Sokkuram is small grotto, a dark cave. Inside the cave is an anteroom and beyond that is a larger domed chamber lined with granite stones so closely fitted that they have lasted over twelve hundred years protecting the contents of the holy of holies.

The walls of both rooms are dedicated to Buddhist saints, the most important being Kwanum, a bodhisattva who is a symbol of compassion. But dominating the main chamber is the Buddha himself carved from a massive block of white granite over ten feet high. His pedestal is a lotus and his robe is so delicately carved that it is a ripple in a breeze that is not there. The effect is one of grace and perfection and peace.

The cave faces to the east and looks toward the Sea of Japan. In the morning, but only on certain days of the year, the first rays of the new sun enter the cave, pass through the first room and into the main chamber and sparkle off the eyes of the Buddha. The eyes spring to life for a moment, and then quickly revert back to complacency, back to serenity. It is believed that a prayer quickly said while the eyes are glowing with life will be answered.

Pulguksa Temple. This is where Sunae and Joe planned to meet.

Sunae did not show up on the agreed day. But, of course, Joe waited for her. He visited every nook and corner of the entire area, seeking to keep as busy as possible and not dwell on his anxiety. He never considered the notion that she would not eventually arrive. He was beginning to recognize some of the squirrels and chipmunks that followed him around hoping he would feed them.

He gave names to the more pesky ones. A thousand times each hour he glanced at the main gate hoping to see her entering through the huge wooden pillars, knowing he would recognize her even before he saw her face. And now he stood, once again, on the steps of the main temple and glanced, again and again and again, toward the gate.

No lilting walk. No Sunae.

The sun set and a cool, damp air settled down onto the temple grounds. Joe wandered out the main gate and into the village. He went to the inn where he was staying. After a quick meal that was served in his room he decided to go for a short walk into the village and then, perhaps, to bed early. He planned on rising before the sun and hiking up the mountain to the grotto to see if the sun would shine into the Buddha's eyes for him. He could be back down to the main temple before nine in the morning and continue his vigil for Sunae.

He strolled slowly through the village. Everywhere people were together. No one was alone but himself. A husband and wife. Children. Friends. But no one with him. It was almost too much to bear, so he headed back to his room and tried to sleep. The small sounds of the night deepened his loneliness. Even the insects had partners. Finally he fell into a restless sleep.

The temple bells woke him at three in the morning and the dank predawn air made their sound duller than usual. Blackness gave the sky a thick quality. Nothing moved. Stepping into the night air seemed like wading through a stream of heavy water. But soon he was on his way to Pulguksa. The monks didn't notice him as he walked past them on his way to the path that went up the mountain to Sokkuram. The path was covered with small pebbles crunching together as he walked over them. The noise they made in the darkness was louder than their daylight clamor would be, the heavy air amplifying their rumblings. In an attempt at silence for the sake of the praying monks Joe placed his feet down with a gingerly gait until he was away from the temple. And the monks heard nothing for they were at their meditations and themselves away from the temple and across the universe.

His walk up the mountain took over an hour. There was no one else on the trail. The way to Sokkuram was marked by white signs nailed to trees, with bold, black lettering in Korean script. And there also were arrows on each sign pointing the way to the grotto for the illiterate travelers. A faint light in the east. Not the sun just yet, but a prophet announcing his coming, an epiphany out of the Sea of Japan. The flashlight was unnecessary.

He had arrived at the entrance of the cave. The sun was getting stronger across the bottom of the eastern sky and in a moment the daystar would reach into the cave and to the Buddha's eyes, that is, if this day was one of those chosen.

Joe stepped quickly into the grotto. He was in the anteroom. The grayness expanded quickly and began replacing the blackness. As he looked about the room he saw the four Deva Kings, guardians of most Buddhist temples in Korea. Two stood silently on each side of the entrance to the inner chamber. He entered the main chamber. Its walls were decorated with relief figures of several saints, bodhisattvas and arhats as they are called by the Buddhists. A graceful figure with eleven heads caught his eye. This must be Kwanum, the symbol of compassion. But these were only guardians, retainers.

The round, domed chamber was dominated by the white, granite Buddha who sat on a lotus, cross-legged, with his right hand pointing downward. He dared the earth to believe the truth of his teaching.

Joe thought of the ancient Hebrew Temple and its Holy of Holies.

In a flash the sun entered the cave's entrance, passed through the anteroom, and into the main chamber. The Buddha's eyes became alive, vital, glowing. And in spite of being a non-believer Joe quickly made his wish.

And only a priest may enter the Holy of Holies.

A noise. Very quiet, then louder.

And blasphemy brings death.

How many ghosts were living in this place? Joe's arms were covered with goose bumps. But it was a human voice, human words. And as the sun's rays started to fade away from the Buddha's eyes the words became faster and faster in a race to finish the prayer before the magic was gone.

Joe was not alone in the Sokkuram grotto.

In a back corner of the chamber a man was sitting on the stone floor. He was very old and dressed in the gray clothing of someone mourning the death of a loved one. Joe stepped toward him and in a very quiet voice, almost a whisper, gave a greeting. A small, wizened old man looked up but gave no sign of rising. He wagged his hand at Joe. Then when he realized that Joe was a foreigner he gave a slight bow of his head and said his hellos in broken English. Joe answered in Korean.

The man must have been trained well, probably by his wife. The corner of the chamber where he sat had been neatly swept clean of the leaves and other mountain debris that had blown into the grotto from outside. The cleared off area was about six square feet and in the shape of an almost perfect square. Very neat work. A small straw broom of the type common all over China, Japan and Korea was propped against the stone wall.

Joe addressed him using honorific language. "Grandfather, I am sorry but I did not see you until you spoke. It is very dark in here and I thought I was alone." The room was becoming lighter. Outside the cave the sun was now higher over the horizon.

"American, you speak Korean very well," the man exaggerated. "What are you doing here? Did you come to make a wish or are you a tourist?"

"I am not a tourist. I am here to meet someone who has not arrived yet. But I did think about her when the sun hit Buddha's eyes." It was an honest answer as far as it went."Ah, you wait for a woman. I hope you are in love. Yes, that is best for a man. He needs a woman. He needs a woman to love."

"And why are you here, Grandfather? What did you ask for? What was your wish?" Joe decided to ask only once. He didn't want to impose on the man's privacy. The old man thought for several moments and, even in the pale light of the chamber, Joe read on his face something that had started many, many years ago, a personal story hidden in the lines and creases of his skin, a history that had brought him here to the cave, to an end or a beginning. Joe felt sad for the old man. He shouldn't have asked his question. His wish might be a private matter. Finally, the man spoke.

"I am here for a woman, too. I am waiting for a woman. My wife. She is gone and I want her back. Yes, I want her back. But the only way for me to get her back is for me to go to her. But I don't know how. That is my wish. To go to her. That is my wish."

Joe said farewell to the old man after being assured that he was fine and could get down the mountain by himself. A short way down the trail Joe cried. He thought of the old man and his love, his wife, his dead wife. Joe thought of Sunae and himself. He was afraid of being alone, to be alone, to die alone.

On the path that goes up the mountain from Pulguksa to the grotto there is a place where the trail goes over a narrow, very deep, gorge. Long ago the monks built a beautiful wooden bridge over the gorge. The bridge will always be on a postcard or calendar somewhere in the world. The bridge is old but quite substantial and perfectly safe to traverse, although scary. Only one or two people can cross at a time because of its narrow width. On the way back down the mountain the bridge can be seen from about a half mile away once a certain bend in the trail is passed.

Joe came to the bend. He saw the bridge. Beyond it the valley opened up all the way down to the main temple and then to the farmland on its far side. Korea was bragging to him about its name - The Land of the Morning Calm. Tendrils of steamy mist grabbed upwards at a slant while others napped in a horizontal position. They were alive with motion, a white flame of cool fire. But they knew they would soon die as the morning sun slowly drained them of their moisture. At the temple the monks were moving about but the distance precluded their noises from reaching Joe. Down in the valley, beyond the temple and the monks, farmers teased their rice plants to perfection. The rice had grown high enough to move like ocean waves whenever the wind changed its direction.

From the waving rice Joe's eyes swept back to the old wooden bridge. A lone figure was crossing over its wooden planks. Joe let his mind create the "clack, clack" of shoes on the old wood.

The figure on the bridge walked with a small lilt. He saw that at once. It spoke to him with a special whisper. He ran as fast as the downward trail permitted. He fell once but quickly jumped to his feet and started again, ignoring a red raspberry that formed on his left elbow. He ran faster. The figure on the bridge waved at him and happiness struck him so violently that he flinched. When he reached the bridge he grabbed Sunae with a roughness that made her shudder. But his touch quickly softened as he kissed her over and over as though afraid of losing her. He thought of the old grandfather up at the grotto who pined for his wife.

Standing there on the bridge, beauty above and beauty below, Joe told Sunae about the old man. He was worried about him and said that if he didn't come down by the next day it might be wise to tell the monks about him. What if he died up there all alone?

They walked down the trail hand in hand and by the time they reached the temple they decided to get married as soon as possible.

That night at dinner they made their plans. Sunae said that after their marriage there would be no problems with her family. Sister gave assurances of that. Koreans are that way, she had said, they follow their formal rules and prejudices until it becomes hopeless to resist, and then they accept what they cannot change. And in Sister's case, her marriage to the Cowman, there was a happy ending.

"That's good to hear because I want to be a part of your family. But I have a few more questions. Some things have been on my mind for quite a few years." Joe looked deep into Sunae's eyes.

She said, "Well, I'm not going to tell you all my secrets. No wife does that, and besides, we're not married yet." Joe knew a game was beginning that was thousands of years old. He wanted to play, but not now. Later would be fine. He did have questions.

"I have always wondered why you saved me that night in the village when the communist soldiers came. A small girl doesn't do such things. She usually runs after her own safety. Why did you do it?"

Sunae thought for a moment. The answer was not simple and she wasn't sure she understood it herself. But she wanted to answer him.

"I cannot give you an easy answer. I guess it all started back in Japan when I was a small child, during the war with America. An American pilot was shot down near our village and the soldiers marched him through the streets. He was bloody and dirty, but when he walked past me he looked down and smiled. He was very afraid, I could see that, and yet he smiled at me, and I felt sorry for him even though I was a small child. And later the war came here to Korea. Almost as though it had followed us. When the communists shot their big guns around our village I saw, once again, terror in the eyes of the people, this time my own village people. They were just like the American pilot in Japan. And even before that, I remember our desperation and terror at Pusan when Mother and Sister and I landed and lost everything in a few minutes. But the Cowman saved us. He didn't have to. He just did it! Maybe that's the way all people should act.

"And then I read in Captain Iwata's journal how a lady named Dolsun, an ancient ancestor of mine, saved him from death on a beach when he was bleeding to death all by himself."

Sunae paused for a moment, scratched her nose, rubbed her chin, and then continued. "Long ago when I was a child in Japan, maybe it was a dream and maybe not, I really don't know, and it makes no difference if it's true or not, a magic fox with a white scarf spoke to me and said that you must be beautiful inside. What can be more beautiful inside than loving and helping each other." Sunae paused for a moment and waved a hand at Joe.

"No, no, don't laugh. I don't know if the fox was real or a dream. But his message made good sense to me, and I will never forget it." She had finished her explaining and waited for a response from Joe.

He looked into her eyes and saw a clear pool of what he was not sure. But he knew it was simple and good, and innocent, yes, that most of all. Guile missing. Never there, never, ever there. He moved toward her and his body tingled.

There was something about her hair and skin, her eyes. There was something about her body that was much more than physical. Her features were an extension of her soul. Joe felt a small guilt because he was looking at her soul without permission. A violation of the confessional. He quickly looked away. She is very young and very old at the same time.

He loved her, but even though he was with her he felt

his loneliness return, just as it had when he left the old man up at the grotto. He wanted to cry. Then the feeling left him and he was happy again.

The next morning she asked him to walk with her up to the famous Sokkuram cave. A visit to Pulguksa without seeing the grotto would be such a waste. Early the next morning, but this time after the sun had risen, they climbed up the trail traveling at a slow steady pace. They were in no hurry. Two people in love walking up a beautiful mountain. The small bridge glistened in the sunshine as they trampled over it and they came to the bend in the trail where the valley below with its main temple and the rice paddies beyond disappeared behind them. The grotto lay ahead.

Sunae had never been to Sokkuram before and her first glimpse of the entrance to the cave was disappointing for it gave no hint of what was contained within. But as she entered the anteroom and saw the main chamber just beyond with its large graceful white Buddha her heart leaped. She did not believe in the religion of the one sitting on the lotus but the sheer beauty of the cave was overpowering. The cold granite god undulated with life. They walked into the main chamber and the old man was not there. Joe looked into the corner that a day ago had been swept so cleanly and neatly. A thick layer of leaves covered the area. Cobwebs and spider webs lay about as though undisturbed for years. There was even a moss, a parasite of some kind, growing on the stone floor of the cave at the exact spot where the old man had been sitting. And there was no broom propped against the wall. Joe worried about the old man. Had he seen and talked to him or not? Was he a phantom? A ghost?

When they got back to the main temple Joe told a monk about the old man. Was he still up there somewhere on the mountain? Did he need help? Should they look for him? Or had he just imagined the whole episode of the man, the neatly swept corner where he sat, the broom, the conversation?

The monk replied, "No, you are the only one who has been up to Sokkuram recently. The wooden bridge was closed for three weeks until yesterday. A government inspection of some sort. No, you were the only one."

"But couldn't he have gotten there some other way?" Joe asked.

"No, the trail from here is the only way. Especially for an old grandfather. He never could have gotten up to the grotto from the backside of the mountain. He would have had to be a trained climber, and a strong younger man. An ordinary climber could not have done it. And certainly not an old man. No, he could not have been there." The monk walked away, unconcerned, crazy foreigners.

The magic of Pulguksa seized them. The air was so clear that it tickled their lungs as they sucked it into their bodies, and the water from the temple spring left them as clean as the sky when they drank it and made their skin cool and fresh as they splashed it onto each other's faces. They walked around the temple compound and an enchantment separated them from the outside world. They decided to stay an extra day.

That night they go to the same small restaurant that had been so pleasant the evening before and as they sit on the floor alone in their private dining room waiting for their meal to arrive he lays his head down onto her lap and falls asleep and he dreams of her and the Japanese samurai and brightness and happiness and sadness and beauty and darkness and life and death and in the dream she comes to him and he takes her in his arms and they kiss and he tastes her and he feels her breath on his cheek and the swell of her breasts on his chest and back back back to Sokkuram and he remembers his wish in the grotto and the old man and both of them having the same prayer and the wooden bridge and falling down in his haste and the cycle is completed and he wakes up.

The noises and smells change back to the present. The voices and sounds of the restaurant come back. Korean voices, Korean sounds. A strong odor of garlic fills the room as the server, a young girl, a country girl, bows and places many foods of many kinds and many colors upon their table. Sunae takes Joe's empty dish and fills it with things he especially likes. And she arranges the food into small, neat piles that will look like a flower in bloom as the colors and textures mingle into a unity. For she has quickly considered the colors and decides what must sit next to what. Like a good cognac should be smelled before drinking, this feast is for looking at before eating. Joe considers his dream and Sunae and knows he will always love Korea no matter where he lives.

Sunae and Joe were married at Saint Marguerite Catholic parish in Seoul two weeks after they came back from Pulguksa. Several times during the Mass the altar candles flickered high, and then low, as three shades, phantoms, danced around the sides and back of the church. It was Dolsun and Iwata, and they were with the mudang.

And, just as Sister predicted, just as it had happened with the Cowman and her, Joe was loved and accepted by Sunae's family once they became husband and wife.

Twenty-six

Creator

From time to time the color purple rests upon the earth, not all of the earth but just a small part of it, and simple truth ties a bow around one or two conversations or thoughts or writings or music or art. The color is purple because that is the color of royalty and what is happening adds majesty to the universe. Truth, simple, rationed truth, can do that.

Saja was confused. Why was it all so important? It had nothing to do with food or shelter, the major concerns of birds. First it was Dolsun and Iwata and now it was Sunae and Joe. He had done what he was asked to do, at least in the latter case. But he didn't know why he was asked to do such things. As he sat on the mountainside next to the fox a very faint tint of purple hung around the boundary of white fur that made up the fox's white scarf. The fox looked down into the valley. He saw the humans doing ordinary things, living their human lives. He saw smoke from cooking fires, he heard temple bells and farmers singing in the paddies as they cultivated their crops. He heard husbands and wives and children talking to each other. He heard friends enjoying each others' company. He heard laughter and anger and the moans of passion.

"Saja, I can tell you part of the answer, but I think you have figured most of it out for yourself by now. You see, it is about love and freedom. Before the beginning of time, before even one atom existed, the Creator already was, that is, he always was and always is." The fox paused for a moment and rubbed his paw into the mountain earth as though to be sure that the atoms and molecules did indeed exist. Reassured, he continued. "Love is always the most important thing. This has always been true. But love without freedom is impossible. If love were to be ordered, or programmed, or given birth outside of the lover and then inserted, why it would not be love at all. Love must be chosen freely.

"The Creator yearns for love and so he creates creatures to love him. But they have to be free. They have to choose him. The Creator helps them, guides them, teaches them. but he never orders them to love him or each other. They have to be free if they are to do that. And even as they love each other they should love him more because he made them. He made everything.

"You and I, we are not human, but we are special. We also are free, but not as free as the humans. We are not as free as them because we know more about the Creator than they do and so our choices are easier. And the easier the choices the lesser the freedom. The Creator made it our duty, you and I and others like us, to help the humans. To help them love him and each other. But we can only go so far with our help. We must be careful. We must not destroy their freedom by helping them too much.

Perfect knowledge destroys freedom. And it is possible for us to fail in our mission because of our own limited freedom. That is what happened to you when you didn't warn Iwata of his great danger. You failed in your duty to the Creator and to Iwata. And so you were punished and made to stay and work here in the world longer than otherwise would have been the case. But now it is over. You are redeemed."

A question formed in Saja's mind. "How do we know how much we can help the humans without damaging their free will? How do we know when to stop helping them?"

The edges of the fox's white scarf became slightly, very slightly, even more purple. He answered, "The Creator watches everything. He stops us if we go too far. I have been stopped a few times. Sometimes we love the humans and we want to help them so much that we go too far. Then the Creator takes over. You see, freedom is fragile. Too much knowledge, or indeed, too much help, can destroy it. The humans have a prayer that some of them say to the Creator every day. Most of them don't understand what they're asking. They say, 'Thy Kingdom Come, Thy Will Be Done.' They are really asking for help when they say that. But they shouldn't want too much help for that might destroy their freedom, and they would end up as automatons."

Saja thought, *automatons*, me oh my, such a wonderful word!

The fox continued. "It is a delicate balance. You see, they don't have to accept our help. It is their election. Some are too proud. They do not want help. Some only want freedom and do not want love. They are unfortunate, the most pitiable of creatures. You see, love and freedom must go hand in hand. Separated they are nothing. That is why it is said that truth gives freedom. Untruth can only bind you. A simple reality, but quite an important one, that eludes so many creatures. But there is danger. Freedom brings danger, and possible harm. Evil can enter so easily. But what is existence without love? Even as evil stands in the doorway trying to enter, love must be given its chance to live."

Saja did indeed begin to understand. But he still wondered about Sunae and Joe. Why help them? The world is filled with people. Why them?

As quickly as questions were formed in Saja's mind they were known to the fox. Indeed, the fox read his thoughts and replied, "The Creator can choose whomever he may. No one can question his pickings and choosings. We should not even discuss the matter. He is the Creator. But let me say this about Sunae and Joe. Joe understood love, even though he didn't always acknowledge it or offer it or accept it. But he knew it. Many humans do not even get that far. As for Sunae, ah, what a wonderful child. Why so wonderful? Because she is without guile. But not perfect, a bit away from that, just ask her family, or Joe. But her sins are honest ones, sins of weakness and not guile, no, never of guile, not at all. And in this whole world there are no others for either of them to love. They need each other. It's as simple as that. And that is why the Creator used us as his agents to help them find each other.

"As for Dolsun and Iwata. That was simply the Creator's decision to help a new family get its start. And in spite of your stupid lapse it got started."

The fox immediately was sorry he used the word stupid. But it had been said, and that was that.

Saja asked, "But why do you call Iwata a poet? What is a poet?"

"Well," said the fox, "that is a difficult question to answer. There is more than one answer. But here is one of them. Poets create poetry and to know what a poet is you must first understand poetry." He paused, seemingly pleased with himself and his scholarly words. Then the lesson continued. "Poetry is a way of talking or thinking or writing that uses beauty, softness, harshness, similitude and rhythm to say something that may be important, or perhaps funny, or just beautiful. Or simply to describe something. Poetry can speak of anything and everything. The humans use poetry to look at their world, and each other, and beyond. It helps them understand the universe."

Saja shook his head. "I don't know anything about poetry."

"Oh? Yes you do. You have created it. Yes indeed, you were quite poetic when you talked to Sunae, and before that to the chungmae's wife. And before that to the mudang. And even before that. What your poetry did was emphasize your important messages to them. A rationing of words! So you see, my friend, you are a poet after all."

"No, I don't remember it that way. I just talked to them, that's all. I said what I had to say." He knew the fox would have more to say about that.

"But your words were exact and rationed. And words are important things and must be used very carefully. To often they are used carelessly. But there are other reasons for poetry. The humans resort to poetry so that they can travel in time and think and talk in any tense they desire. Because that is one of the things poetry can do, defeat time. And that is why it can be dangerous to read poetry unless this poetic time travel is understood, for there may be things behind and ahead than are obvious. And that can cause trouble. But also beauty and truth. And that is also what poetry is about.

"But beauty is not always beautiful."

Saja thought that a puzzling statement. The fox also thought about what he had just said. He too was somewhat confused. But he wouldn't tell Saja of his perplexity.

He continued. "Sometimes being a poet can be dangerous. It is very easy for the poet to reveal personal secrets in his poetry and he may not want to do that. In this respect the poet is a mysterious person. It's best not to attempt to understand him on a personal level but to think in universal terms. If he writes about anguish he may be seeing it but not anguished himself. If he writes of love he may be observing it but not in love Or he may be. But these questions should never disrupt enjoyment of his work."

Saja had a grammatical question. "If time is altered how should the humans write their poems? Should they write their poetry in the past, present or future? And will the reader know, or even care? And who is talking?"

"It's the poet's decision. And it's the reader's responsibility to understand his symbols and metaphors of time travel. He will know when the poet is moving forward and when he is moving backward, and who is speaking.

"Many of the humans are astonishing. They work it out somehow."

The fox rubbed a paw gently at the mountain earth, as he often did, and Saja thought this, too, must be poetry. Then Saja flapped his wings, a slight motion, and wondered if their feathery movement was poetry.

The purple feeling, a royal purple, left the earth just as dew evaporates in the morning sun. But, just like the dew, it had done its job. It had nourished the earth. Saja and the fox sat silently. They were closer to each other than ever before. The purple wave had tied them together. They looked up to the fleecy clouds and the silvery daytime moon, then down to the browns and greens of the mountain, and it was easy for them to see that the Creator himself was a poet. And Saja understood that freedom is indeed powerful enough to cause harm, even great harm. But that it is the only way if there is to be love.

The fox left Saja alone on the mountain after promising to return the next day.

Poor Saja was exhausted. So much talking, so much thinking. He closed his eyes and tried to sleep. He thought about Captain Iwata and how the Japanese samurai who became a Korean had complicated his life so many years ago. He thought about the wind that blew him to Japan so many years ago, to that land of round and gentle mountains and deep forests, and the fox with the white scarf. He pressed his body tightly against the side of the mountain and rested his head upon a soft patch of green, fresh moss that wasn't there a moment ago. Finally he fell into a deep sleep as the sun ducked into China to the west. It was pleasantly cool and dark. Time swept past Saja on quiet wings.

Then soft paws scraped the hard mountain rock, stirring him from his slumber.

"Hello, my friend." It was the fox. It was morning and he had returned as he promised.

Saja didn't answer at first. He just looked at the fox and, as it had happened more than once before, thoughts passed between the two. Saja and the fox. *We are happy to see each other. We are friends.* He felt at ease. "I feel peace and order as though you placed a robe of serenity around me while I slept. Did you?"

"No, Saja, you put it on yourself. You have done a wonderful thing. You have redeemed yourself and brought happiness to more beings than just Sunae and Joe. Now, at this moment, you have no idea of the breadth of your accomplishment, but you will, and not too far into the future. Are you ready?"

Saja had a tinge of sadness as he realized that a grand change was soon to take place. He was thinking of the magic land of Korea and the mountains and the pleasant coolness and silence high above the earth where he loved to soar, and his sadness lingered. He would miss it all. But then the thought of new adventure came to him. A new flight, a new country, a new beauty.

He wondered, where oh where are these thoughts coming from? But here they are, as clear as a temple bell in the early morning before the sun is awake. I must listen to them for they are telling me about reality, about life.

Saja answered the fox. "Yes, I am ready. But there is one thing that I want to do first. It may be silly, but I want to do it if I can. I want to visit my very first home. I want to visit the great eagle nest where I was born." He felt the fox's answer sweep over him like an act of love amongst equals, like equals, for he realized the fox was his brother.

Yes! Yes! Yes! Go and visit the Eagles. They are waiting for you.

Again, no spoken words, but there it was, and fox's answer was so delightful that it echoed down to the valley and up to the sky. Some of the villagers heard it and raised their eyes toward the upper peaks of the mountain. A small and gentle clap of thunder, that's what they thought.

Saja was no longer tired. He jumped into the air and headed up to the spot near the top of the mountain where so many years ago the mother and father eagles had built an aerie for their nest. Saja had never been back to the nest since, but he knew exactly where it was. In a matter of minutes his feet touched ground at the edge of the eagles' home. It was at the same spot as centuries earlier. In the nest sat a mother, a father and three small eaglets. Saja looked at the birds and bowed three times. Father Eagle said, "Saja, we have been waiting for you." As he spoke, Saja thought he heard the soft sound of fox paws on the ground. He looked around. But the fox was not there.

One of the babies, his eyes bulging because he had never seen a cuckoo bird, crept closer to his mother, snuggled under her wing, and said, "What is this strange creature? Are we in danger?"

"No, child, we are not in danger." Mother Eagle reassured the small bird and his eyes returned to normal size.

"This is a cuckoo bird and his name is Saja. I cannot explain it to you but you must believe me. Saja is your brother and he is here to say hello and good-bye. But one thing you must know. Life builds upon life. A long, long time ago Saja lived for a while in this very nest that we now call our home. Saja decided that we were his family and he refused to do what nature itself told him to do. By following his heart, and not his raw instinct, he gave us life. We would not exist if he had decided otherwise. Remember, one broken step, only one, and all future steps change. So here we are to shout to the world that Saja did not break the path of many steps that led here, today, to our very lives."

As Mother Eagle finished her story, the little eagles turned toward Saja. And he looked back at them, all five of them, one at a time, square in the eye, and then he stepped back and bowed three times. Then with a single bound he soared into the sky. Happy laughter followed him as he traveled up. It came from the nest. But as Saja listened more closely he realized some of the happy sounds were also coming from the earth below and the sky above.

Up,up, up. The wind was Saja's friend and helpmate, just as always. He hardly used his wings and yet traveled higher and higher. He had never been this high before, and the air, so cool and fresh.

And the sun. How could this be happening? The sun got brighter and brighter and yet Saja discovered that he could look directly at it with no harm to his eyes. The sun was more than a big ball of fire for it was sparkling and dancing. And it had a message for Saja.

Come to us, good friend. You have served well. You have done your duty and you have made the good choices. Yes, in the end you made the good choices. Now, come to us and we will give you happiness and peace and love. The struggle is over. The struggle is freedom. Without freedom no love.

The sun spun faster and faster. Saja flew higher and higher. The air became cool - clear - clean - sweet - fresh - pure. The family of eagles watched his flight into the heavens. And in one blink of an eagle eye Saja disappeared.

Twenty-seven

Epilogue

I remember two times when death came near, visiting, testing me. Each time it carried love along with its grief and, strange as it may seem, made life easier.

The cuckoo birds of Korea are one of my happiest discoveries. These grand, but small, creatures fly among the mountain peaks, but always on the other side of the valley, and never - it seems - where you are waiting and listening. I seldom saw one, but hearing was enough. One cuckoo shouts his "cooo, cooo," and another answers "cooo, cooo" from somewhere else, either up or down the valley, seeming far away and close by. The cuckoo has that magical quality. He is far away and near, and all at the same time. I cannot explain this phenomenon, but it's true. He might be far away, his musical notes in the distance, yet he sounds as if he is sitting on your shoulder. It is music and magic. He is a wizard.

His Korean name is "paeguki."

Silence on the mountain is thick. There is no better description for it. The cuckoo stirs the silence and the result is beauty and peace. Loneliness flees. And yet remains. What a remarkable bird! Yes, a wizard.

Sunae and I were on the mountain, about a quarter of the way up toward the summit. We had driven along a bumpy dirt road and then walked higher up the narrow trail when the road disappeared. It was a remarkable Sunday outing and she had packed us a wonderful lunch. In her exuberance Sunae had also brought two candles, two silver candleholders and embroidered table linen. We might as well have been sitting at an outdoor cafe in Paris. The mountain became our singular cafe, much cleaner, certainly much more beautiful than any other. And now, the cuckoo birds were serenading us. No violins needed here. The candles struggled against the mountain breeze as we ate.

We were alone and it was a beautiful summer day, balmy and warm. Soon the monsoon would start and bring its hot, humid days of rain, day after day, for four weeks. But for now the sky was high, clear and blue. There were clouds in the southern sky. They looked like buttermilk. It was a perfect day for a picnic with my wife. She was the love of my life and I didn't want this day ever to end.

And it never did. I still have it. Another paradox? Of course, but the cuckoos were explaining it to us, and we listened. They worked their enchantments. They taught us how to do it. All it takes is concentration. Anywhere, anytime, in my mind or in reality, a cuckoo sings and I am on that mountain with her.

We ate slowly. The candles flickered and slanted into diverse bearings, now high, now low, each time the breeze changed direction. But the candles always won, never dying, always springing back to full life, and the breeze finally gave up. After my meal I put my head down on the grassy earth and closed my eyes.

The world is phantom and mist, shadow and shade. I am inside my dream. I sense a battle. Suddenly, a cuckoo begins to sing, but I cannot see him. It is dark, but a change takes place. Murky figures come walking through my dream world. First comes a Japanese samurai in a white uniform with a black sash and long swords at his sides. A beautiful Korean lady in a blue dress is with him, holding his hand. They are followed closely by an older but quite attractive woman playing the small drums of a mudang that hang attached to a rope slung over her beautiful swan-like neck. Then follows a majestic fox wearing a white scarf. The fox's paws seem to float slightly above the ground. And flying above him, finally, is a cuckoo. The fox and the bird appear to be friends.

The figures pass by slowly and smile their dream smiles at me. And then they are gone. Even the echoing drumbeats fade away.

And then, as happens in dreams sometimes, I step back and I can see myself. I am climbing up a different trail but now Sunae is with me. We are holding hands. The cuckoo bird sings from somewhere else, offstage, across a dream valley.

Suddenly there is a bright flash. A beautiful light floods over us. I don't know where it comes from or what it is, but it is magnificent. I am blinded. When my eyes focus again, the light brings fear, its beauty frustrated. Sunae is gone. I am alone. The weight of loneliness comes on, falling, crushing, grinding into me.

"Joe! Wake up. Someone's coming up the trail. An old

man and an old woman."

I told her I was having the strangest dream.

She interrupted, "Look! Grandfather and Grandmother. They're dressed in death clothes and Grandfather is carrying a large cloth sack." They were not her family, but she referred to them with honor because of their ages as grandparents. Koreans do that, even for strangers.

The old man carried a sack flung over his shoulder, just as Sunae had said. Perhaps it contained food or other essentials. Maybe they lived further up the mountain, but that was unlikely. This mountain had no water. And in typical Korean fashion, the man walked ahead of the woman. But when he turned to talk to her there was softness and love in his eyes and voice. Korean husbands and wives seldom show their love publicly and the old man did not betray the custom, but his glance and voice did.

They approached us. As we exchanged greetings, a cuckoo on the other side of the valley chimed in. He was greeting them too. I wondered if he was the bird from my dream. The old man did indeed have on traditional mourning clothes, death clothes as Sunae called them, a high hat that resembled an occidental formal top hat, but made of a white-gray cloth, like cheesecloth, but more finely meshed, and a covering coat made of the same material, The old lady was dressed, head to foot, in a dress made to match her husband's clothes. (Later Sunae told me these outfits are worn not only to funerals and on the anniversaries of a close relative's death. The style, material and color made the distinction.)

I spoke to the man. "Grandfather! Grandmother! How are you? Please sit down and have a cold drink of soda. And food. We have plenty." I bowed as I finished speaking, and it fit well with the honorific verb endings I had used. My Korean language ability may not have been perfect, but it was quite polite. Sunae repeated my invitation. They accepted and their smiles revealed a scattering of gold teeth and twinkling eyes.

"Oh, you are an American. How can you speak to us in Korean? Sir, you must be very intelligent, and an educated man." He overreacted to my polite phrases, but I appreciated his comments. The old lady stood silent and continued her friendly grin. Then she chuckled, and I couldn't help thinking about the story of Hansel and Gretel, the old lady being the witch, but in appearance only, for her attention to the old man was tender. We had nothing to fear, she was no witch.

Korean old women often think I am a fine man. Perhaps it is my bald head. Maybe they think it makes me distinguished and powerful. That was Sunae's theory. Whatever the real reason might be, I always enjoyed their attention. Then I thought of Sunae and me. I hoped we could climb a mountain together when we were old, like this couple, and that Sunae would always like my missing hair, and think me distinguished and powerful. And, of course, quite handsome.

They sat with us and ate, picking at the food in small quantities, looking, smiling, nodding, chewing slowly, as though they were trying to please us rather than themselves.

"Grandfather, what brings you and Grandmother up this mountain? Where are you heading? There is nothing up this way but trees and rocks. I know this mountain. There isn't even any water. You have to carry it with you."

The old man looked at me. He was trying to decide if he wanted to tell me something or not. He looked at his wife and she nodded. He told his story -

"We have been married for fifty years. At first we didn't have any children, I don't know why because we really tried." He looked at his wife. She blushed and put her hand up to her mouth, embarrassed at his small joke of love. The old man turned back to me and her flash of embarrassment passed. Apparently she was used to the joke.

He continued, "Finally, we had a son. You can imagine how happy that made us. He was a fine boy, and good looking, too. Yes indeed. He made good marks at school and wanted to become an engineer. But then the war swept down from the north. The Chinese and our northern Korean brothers came at us. Our army took our son. Then we had to flee our village, which is just on the other side of this mountain. For two years we had no idea where our son was, and he might have thought we were dead or carried off to the north by the communists. The war ended and in all the confusion we had no knowledge of our son. Last year a stranger appeared in our village and asked for us. He told us he was a friend of our son, that they had served together in the army from start to finish. Their outfit was forced to retreat south when the Chinese entered the fighting and ended up near Taegu. That's where our army and the Americans decided to make their stand."

He started to cry. Then he paused and composed himself. He continued. "My dear son was killed by the enemy. Before he died, he asked his friend to visit us when the war was over and tell us that he loved us. But we already knew that. They buried him on a hill nearby where he fell and his friend offered to take us there and show us his grave."

The old man's eyes were moist. Again, he needed to collect himself.

"We could not leave our son near Taegu. Our home - his home - is here, this mountain, our village, and has been home for us and our ancestors for a thousand years. We are from Kyonghi Province, here, not Taegu, not the south. This is where my son should be. So we brought him here to rest in his own home soil forever. He loved this mountain and especially its singing cuckoo birds. Many times he climbed up here just to hear them sing. He told us they talked to him."

When the old man said this, I assumed that the Korean army had reburied the lad here in his home province and that the old couple were on their way to visit his grave. For the reburial of fallen soldiers in their home areas was a common practice after the war. I asked him, "And now you are coming up this mountain to visit his grave? Is that it?"

"Oh, no my friend. You do not understand. Our son is here with us now."

I thought the old man was speaking in a spiritual, poetic sense, meaning that his son was present in their thoughts and hearts. I questioned him no further, but he answered me anyway.

"Our son is here, he is in this bag. Take a look, we don't mind."

Before I said anything the old man reached for the large bag that he had never let get more than a few feet away. He unfastened its drawstring and swung the top of the bag in my direction. And inside I saw a pile of bones, human bones, with the skull sitting neatly on top. I swear the skull was smiling away at me.

A cuckoo bird was singing. The bird went on and on. It was a litany.

Grandfather continued his story. "Our son's friend took us to the spot where his comrades had buried him and we waited until everyone had left. Then, way past midnight, we dug up our son's bones and put them in this sack. It was not possible to get a bus or train. We were afraid the army would find out what we had done and come looking for us. Perhaps if our son's friend returned to the grave the next day, he would see it empty and report us. So we started to walk. And here we are."

Taegu is about two hundred miles from the mountain. This old couple, this old Korean grandfather and grandmother, had walked two hundred miles with their son's bones carried in a cloth sack on their backs. They probably took turns with the carrying.

"And today we are climbing to a spot near the top of this mountain." The old man waved his hand up toward the summit of the mountain. Then he continued, "Our son loved to go up there and listen to the paeguki. He loved them. He said they talked to him. But I guess I've already told you that. I didn't believe him then, but I believe him now. Just listen, they are talking to him right now. Listen! They are welcoming my son back to this mountain. This is where we will bury his bones!"

And sure enough, the cuckoo birds were chatting away at a tempo much louder and faster than I had ever heard them doing before. I now knew that the cuckoo birds had talked to others, not just to me. They also had a sense of humor. Their rising chatter sounded like happy laughter. They were anxious to receive their friend, the old couple's son.

The story was a sad one. Sunae and I were close to tears. I was glad that we had shared our food and drink with these simple country people. Then Grandfather and Grandmother said their good-byes and continued up the mountain. I watched them walking away. When they came to a curve in the trail, they paused, turned around, and waved a final farewell. The last thing I saw was the bag of bones disappearing around the bend.

It had been quite a day, one I will never forget. But it was time to go home. We packed up our belongings and hiked back to our car. That night, in bed next to Sunae, I thought about the mountain, the old couple, fresh loose earth resting on a new grave near the top of the mountain, and the cuckoos guarding it with great care and tenderness.

Many years later, in a land that had no paeguki, I discovered my wife had cancer. She was not expected to live more than six months. At first things went better than we expected. A cure seemed possible. But it was a false hope, a masking of our fears. Finally, our masks were ripped away and Sunae's condition worsened. I took her to the hospital. The doctors counseled no more treatment. They feared the chemotherapy and radiation were doing her more harm than good and suggested that she be made as comfortable and pain free as possible. It was hard for me to accept such a prognosis. But after many meetings the doctors convinced me they were right.

Early in the morning, a few days later, they told me

the end was near. So I moved into Sunae's room to be with her. What little sleep I got was on a cot placed there for me, right beside her own bed. Several more days went by. And then, early in the morning, perhaps at three, I was sitting there looking at her. She was in a coma.

This was not a mountain. No birds, no chirping insects, no wind. No paeguki. The air was not fresh and the sky not high. No buttermilk clouds rippling across golden sunbeams. I gently rubbed Sunae's foot. She always liked that.

I thought of the old man and the old woman, the old Korean grandfather and grandmother. Sunae and I were not going to match their long years together. Then I remembered something else. The paeguki! Where was the cuckoo bird? I wanted to hear his song.

Sunae's breathing was strong - a false hope - but the intervals between her breaths became longer and longer, pauses of stillness and terror, cruel and cold. The smells of medicine and antiseptic, decay and death, were everywhere. Small hospital sounds outside the room exaggerated my misery. Respecting my privacy, the nurses had shut the door to the room. I had not slept for two days. Everything was jumbled together.

I looked into Sunae's face. Her eyes were closed, her face pale and dim.

Then I saw it. Something was happening. At first I wasn't sure, but there it was. It started on her forehead. A tiny spot of very white light. Gradually it became larger. It was undulating at its edges like a candle's flame, alive with small motions, gyres, arrows, back and forth, back and forth. The light continued to grow, finally covering her entire face, but went no further. The whiteness had a shine to it, like cold enamel, but paler and softer than that. It continued its dancing, a quiet soft flame. I rubbed my eyes. Of course I must be dreaming, but I felt awake. I blinked several times and rubbed my eyes.

The light remained. I wanted to call someone into the room. Anyone. But, no, this was for me alone. So I left the room and walked down the hall. I wanted proof that I was not dreaming. I said "good morning" to the nurse on duty, thinking she could verify later that I had been there. Then I went back to Sunae.

The light was still there, covering Sunae's face.

I stood beside her, held her hand, just stood there, praying a prayer without words, simply looking at her. The light remained on her face for about ten minutes. It got neither stronger nor weaker. Then it became smaller and smaller, finally reaching the exact spot on her forehead where it had first appeared. The flames at its edges were moving faster, a final gasp. Then the light disappeared. I stood there dazed and silent for several minutes.

The paeguki were singing.

Sunae died that morning and I was with her. I held her hand as she took her very last breath. She was peaceful and, oh, so beautiful. Cuckoo Bird, please come and sing your song. I cannot wait any longer. Time is defeating me. I ache for your song. I ache for my wife.

Here lies Juliet and her beauty
makes this vault a feasting presence
full of light.

Perhaps the old man who made his wish and then disappeared from the Sokkuram Grotto many years ago has been found. Perhaps I am the old man.

Acknowledgement

As exciting as the process might be, creating a novel is a terrifying task. But the writing of "The Fox with the White Scarf" was bearable because of a wonderful editor who is also my dear friend, Linda McKain.

Thank you, Linda.

--- Joe Psarto

Printed in the United States
93136LV00001B/15/A